I0582448

Punch Down

**FROM WHIDBEY ISLAND TO WALLA WALLA
IT'S THE GRAPES, NOT THE ONIONS**

www.tedmulcahey.com

Copyright © 2023 Ted Mulcahey

All rights reserved. This book or any portion thereof may not be reproduced or used in any manner whatsoever without the express written permission of the publisher except for the use of brief quotations in a book review.

ISBN: 978-1-7354932-8-2

Contents

ONE

On the Road

The fog was socked in over the Saratoga Passage. For three days, the damn stuff had blanketed Puget Sound with temperatures in the mid-thirties. It was too cold to do anything outside, and we were tired of being cooped up inside, so we decided to take a road trip south. Being retired after selling our interior design firm allowed us the freedom to do things we'd never been able to do before. In this case, leaving our home on Whidbey Island at a moment's notice was one of them.

We're the O'Malleys. I'm Kevin, and my wonderful, beautiful, intelligent wife is Jenne (pronounced Jenny—she just liked how the "e" looked; don't ask). It's important I say that stuff about her—it's all true, by the way—because sometimes she sees what I write and, well, it's just better this way.

Anyway, we took the 6:30 ferry the next day, made it to Ashland, Oregon, home of the Shakespeare Festival, the first night, then soldiered on to the City by the Bay on night two. We already missed our German Shepherd, Emma, but she was in good hands. Our friends, Gail and Bob, also had a GSD, and the two dogs were great buddies. She'd be well taken care of until we returned.

While we gassed up on the outskirts of the city, I thought it made sense to have at least some idea of where we'd head the following day.

"Where to after this, kiddo?"

"I don't care; you pick."

"It's a big country. There's no place you'd like?" I knew I'd be in trouble if I picked somewhere and it was a bust. Not real trouble, just enough to give her ammunition to tease the shit out of me. *Nuh-uh, not gonna do it.* "How about you open up Google Maps, close your eyes, and pick someplace in the Western US?"

"Such a wuss. You're afraid to, huh?"

"Yup."

She saw that I meant business, so she cranked up her tablet.

"To be completely random about this, you have to put it on the console here and close your eyes. I'll turn it around, so you won't be able to memorize where you're taking us."

I pretended to move the tablet just in case she was longing for some fancy spa in Palm Desert. "Okay, put your finger on the spot, and that's where we'll go."

Jenne O'Malley had been my wife for over fifteen wonderful years and I still got chills whenever I saw her smile. It wasn't a timid grin; it was the kind of full-throated, ear-to-ear expression of glee usually reserved for toddlers on Christmas morning. I first experienced it on our second date when we met at a Starbucks for a mid-morning latte. She walked through the door, saw me, and *boom*, there it was.

If ever I was tempted to feel down about life, I simply pictured her walking over to me that day, which was enough to adjust my attitude. She was wearing that expression now as she circled her finger in the air and plopped it on the map.

"There! How'd I do?"

"Open your eyes; you can see for yourself."

"Shit, Kevin, you never moved it. I picked Walla Walla; it's back in Washington."

"Sorry, dear, I wanted it to be random, and I guess, unfortunately it was."

"We're here in San Francisco and now we gotta drive back north to Walla Walla?"

"Only if you want it to be an arbitrary destination."

"I was aiming for the desert."

"I thought so. It's why I pretended to move the tablet. We can still head there if you'd like."

"Nope. We agreed. Let's head to Walla Walla. But first let's spend tonight here in the city. We can find some fancy hotel, have a fabulous dinner, and then … we'll see."

'We'll see. Does that mean what I think it does?"

"We'll see …" *Damn, there's that grin again.*

Our one-night stay in San Francisco was superb. We managed to get slightly better than the rack rate at Hotel Vitale and had an exquisite meal at Boulevard, an old favorite dining establishment from previous visits. As former owners of an interior design firm, frequent visits to the San Francisco Design Center were necessary. Once we got back to the room, we eventually went to sleep.

"Are we going back the way we came, or should we take a more adventurous route?"

I wasn't sure I liked the sound of "adventurous," but I took a chance. "What did you have in mind?"

"I say we go through Reno, spend the night in Winnemucca, then make the next day a long one to Walla Walla."

"Winne— what?"

"Winnemucca. Says here it's the county seat of Humboldt County, Nevada. It's also almost five thousand feet in elevation, so they'll probably have snow."

"Oh, joy. I thought the plan was to get away from the crappy weather."

"According to the weather app, it'll be sunny the whole trip, just freaking cold. Any snow shouldn't be an issue. Think they're used to it there."

"Sounds exciting. Maybe see if you can find a hotel for us in beautiful downtown Winnemucca. Hopefully, they'll have one."

After an exhilarating six hours of playing I Spy, 20 Questions, and several others, we arrived at Winnemucca. At first glance, we should have chosen an alternative route, but Jenne seemed to enjoy the adventure, so I let it go.

"Right around the corner, Kev—Holiday Inn Express."

"Thanks. At least they've got one of those." In my experience, the requirements by the national affiliation for their franchisees were at least some insurance against terrible outcomes and terminal outbreaks of bedbugs.

"It says here that most of the industry in the area has to do with gold mining." Jenne was terrorizing Wikipedia.

"Maybe we'll find some lying around." The look I got was not her happy one. "Sorry, just kidding. What about dinner?"

"That might be a challenge. What would you say to pizza and a nice Oakville cab? We brought one with us, remember."

"I'd say, 'Welcome to my room, friends.' It sounds perfect, and maybe the pizza joint will have a salad too."

After checking in, we ate like we were starving, watched a stupid Hallmark movie, and hit the sack early. Tomorrow was going to be a long day.

We were up at six a.m. and enjoyed the self-serve breakfast buffet. While we were eating, Jenne looked at me, a curious expression on her face. "You know something?"

"I do, and I can guess what you're thinking. We decided on this adventure to escape the shitty weather, and now we're headed right back to it."

"Adventure?"

"Okay, road trip. Remember, it's your fault where we're headed." Never one to let a dig go by, Jenne responded with the almost imperceptible flash of a middle finger. Was she great or what?

From the look of the other guests, I suspected nearly all were engaged in the mining business. Most wore jeans and Carhartt gear; a few—most likely investment types—wore jeans too, but with open-collared shirts and designer outerwear. I guessed the Wall Street types did their best to stay on top of which direction gold was heading.

I presumed most of the hotel occupants were either new hires or looking for interviews with any or all of the three or four major mining groups headquartered here. Judging by the low vacancy rate, whoever owned this place was doing well.

We overheard several conversations discussing the shortage of available labor following the pandemic. It was a seller's market, and signing bonuses were the order of the day. The tables were nearly full, and the mood was upbeat. Even the Wall Street folks appeared to share in the optimism absent during the darkest days of Covid.

As we were leaving the two-story L-shaped motel, we managed to slide the loaded bellman's cart into the back of the new Tesla parked next to us.

"Nice one, Kev."

"I thought you were steering."

"Um, no. You told me not to, remember?"

Fortunately, the bumper had taken the brunt of the minor collision, and no damage was apparent. Unfortunately, the expensive automobile had only recently pulled in, and now the driver was emerging from its cockpit.

"Hey, did you guys just bump into me?"

"Yes, we did, and goddammit, we don't give a shit. Ain't that right, sweetcakes?"

Jenne, blocked from view by the trolley, looked over at me in shock. "Kevin, what the heck …?"

"Kevin? Is that you, Jenne? What are you guys doing here, especially in the middle of winter?"

Jenne finally moved around the cart and saw that our victim was a good friend and frequent golfing buddy from Seattle.

Butch Carlson was in his late fifties, in great shape, and a portfolio manager for a well-respected hedge fund from the Boston area. While a Harvard grad and very wealthy, he still found time to mix with us mortals. In reality, he was as charming and down-to-earth as could be.

"Hey, Butch, a better question is, why are *you* here? And sorry my husband smashed into your new rig."

After taking a glance at the location of the impact, he chuckled. "Looks fine, Jenne. Why do you let him drive, anyway?"

"Why do you think? It's Kevin; he's a master at everything, right?"

"You both know I'm standing right next to you, don't you? This conversation might have hurt a less confident person."

All I received was a "humph" from Butch and a deadpan expression from my wife.

"I drove all the way here because the powers that be back in Boston seem to think gold is going through the roof. A couple of the locals are talking about a merger, and if we can get a better feel for what might happen, we might be able to get a jump on most of the other funds."

"Is that legal?"

"Kevin, Kevin, c'mon. We're overly cautious when it comes to that stuff. Anything I learn here is public knowledge and is available to anyone. It's the secret shit that gets you in trouble. I'm sure some of the big boys will also have managers here. How about you? What brings you to this mecca of civilization?"

"Vacation, Butch. It's our goddamn vacation. Can you believe Jenne picked this place?"

He glanced at my wife just as her eyes finished shooting daggers in my direction. "It's a long story, and we're just passing through on our way to Walla Walla."

"Wouldn't it have been easier to head southeast from Seattle?"

Jenne took a deep breath and explained the saga in greater detail. She finished with, "So that's how we got here. Now, at least, we're going to the best wine region in Washington, where I intend to sample many, many glasses."

"I'd like to join you, but after I leave here, I'm going south to Scottsdale to play some warm-weather golf for a few days."

"Poor baby, we feel for you."

"Why don't you guys change your plans and come with me? There's room at my place." Butch owned homes in Scottsdale and Bellevue and a condo in Boston. I *said* he was stinking rich.

"As much as we'd like to, we've only got a week left. Anyway, we're committed to our plan. Right, hon?"

I could see the conflict on Jenne's face, but, ever the trooper, she agreed. "Thanks, Butch. We appreciate the offer. I need to follow my man here, however. He'd be lost without me."

"I know what you mean, Jenne. Listen, as long as you're going there, maybe you should stay at Uva Cellars."

"We know of them, but, as I recall, they're very private. I've heard that their wine club even has a five-year waiting list."

"Correct, Kev, they do. But they also have a cool guest house behind the winery for visiting restauranteurs and special guests."

"So?"

"So, I own the property. You can stay there as my guests. I'll have to make sure it's not booked, but it's not usually occupied this time of year."

"You *own* it?" Jenne looked as surprised as I was.

"I got a really big bonus one year and needed a place to put some money, so I bought the winery. I kept all the employees, including the winemaker; supposedly, he's the one who made them famous. With him in charge of the vineyards, plus Michelle, who runs everything else, I never really have to do anything. It's perfect."

"Um, a bonus? How big could it be?"

"I work for a hedge fund, remember? The bonuses can be huge when we have a good year—and that one was extra special."

"I'm guessing more than a few million?"

"You'd be right. It's not something I care to advertise, though, and you know I like to keep a low profile. Anyway, when you get there, ask for Michelle. I'll call ahead to make sure there's a room available. If you don't hear from me in the next couple of hours, she'll expect you."

"Geez, Butch, thank you very much. That's awfully nice of you."

"Hah—just don't spread the word. Remember, I have an image to uphold. Also I'll get fewer strokes on the golf course."

We said goodbye, loaded the car, and headed for Walla Walla. It was the last time we saw Butch alive.

Two

Walla Walla

The trip took us a little under eight hours. Not terrible, but still a little longer than ideal.

We hadn't heard anything from Butch, so we headed straight for Uva. While the sun was plummeting at only 4:30 p.m., the reflections off the snow-covered peaks of the Blue Mountains were spectacular. We managed to turn into the gravel drive just as the garden lights, highlighting a simple wooden sign with Uva carved into it, were illuminated.

The impressive two-story rustic structure was brightly lit from within. Its large factory windows showed several workers bustling about sizeable stainless steel vats. As we neared the building, we heard the clinking of wine bottles gently nudging others.

We parked next to a couple of old pickups, stiffly dismounted after the long drive, and walked through the open barn doors. Although the noise was significantly louder inside, it didn't stop an attractive thirty-something woman from glancing up from her work. She held up a hand, and one of her two helpers turned a valve while the other switched off the conveyor belt. It was suddenly quiet as she smiled and said, "You're the O'Malleys, right?"

"We are, yes."

"Welcome to Uva Cellars. I'm Michelle Browne. Butch said you were going to stay with us for a few nights. While waiting for you, we decided to bottle the rest of the new stuff we had in the barrels. Let's get you squared away while Oscar and Benny finish things up. We're on the last case anyway."

Jenne's eyes were bugging out at the captivating, though small, automated bottling equipment. "Geez, does it always smell this good in here?"

"Hah, I guess so. You get used to it after a while. I've been here for ten years, so I only notice the mixture of oak and fermenting grapes when I've been gone for a week or more. Butch said to take good care of you or you wouldn't give him any strokes on the golf course."

I had to laugh. Butch was a four handicap, and if anyone was going to get strokes, it was me. "Don't believe everything he tells you."

"Don't worry, I don't. After he bought the winery seven years ago, we were concerned there'd be big changes, but there weren't. The week after the deal closed, he got Evan and me—he's the winemaker—and the rest of the crew together for a meeting. He told us he had no intention of changing anything except to give us a raise. He left me in charge of the front end and Evan, the farming and production.

"He's a great boss and loves teasing everyone, so we know when he's trying to get one over on us. Truth is, we only see him a few times a year. He said he'd stop by on his way back from Scottsdale."

She led us through the tasting room, then outside to a lighted pathway as she spoke. "We haven't had guests here for a few weeks, so I had Benny spruce things up for you. There's a fire already built in the fireplace, and you should get it going right away. It'll be below freezing tonight. After Butch called, I had Perry make you something for dinner. After such a long drive, I figured going back into town wouldn't be any fun."

Even though it was getting dark, I was sure she could see the relief and thanks on my face. We arrived at what appeared to be a smaller building—a barn, actually—its similar factory windows tying in nicely with the main building. A warm glow spilled through them into the early evening dusk.

She opened the eight-foot pivot door and stepped aside to let us in. "Yikes, Michelle, this place is fabulous." Jenne was never one to hold back a compliment.

A large bluestone horizontal fireplace was centered on the wall to our right. The ceiling, at least twelve feet high over it, sloped to our left to eight feet over the bed wall. The seating group was transitional in front of the fireplace, with a nod to a more modern look. A beautifully made king-sized bed, complete with a down comforter and Pendleton throws, was nestled against the shorter wall. Two caramel-colored Bertoia Diamond chairs, flanking a small Saarinen dining table, were centered on French doors, which I assumed opened to the garden area. Strategically placed Tibetan area rugs only partially obscured the stained concrete floor.

"It was here when Butch took over, but it was a mess. He said I could do the remodel myself, so I did. Before I got into the wine industry, I was an interior designer, but I got sick of refereeing fights between husbands and wives over what color the doorknobs should be."

We looked at each other and smiled knowingly. "Did Butch tell you what we used to do?"

"No, don't tell me. You weren't interior designers …?"

"Um, yes, we were."

"Oh, shit, I'm sorry. I didn't mean anything by that. It was just my experience …"

I could see her blushing at the direction the conversation had taken, so a lifeline was in order. "No worries, Michelle. We completely understand how that can happen. Making many decisions when folks aren't used to doing it can create stress."

Jenne reached over, squeezed her shoulder, and said, "You did a terrific job. Butch is lucky to have you."

"Thanks. I appreciate that. The bathroom and closet area is through that hallway to the right of the nightstand. If you need something, make sure to call me. I'm going up to the main house, where I live, to see how Perry's getting along with dinner. I'll have him bring it down so you can relax after the long day. He's making a smoked salmon risotto with asparagus. What would you like for wine with that?"

This treatment was better than any we'd ever had, regardless of the hotel or resort's number of stars. "I don't know what to say, and this is way beyond what you should be doing."

"Here's the deal, Kevin. When Butch took over, he only had a few rules, but one he said was never to be broken. His exact words were, 'When guests stay with us, we treat them like family, only better. When it's a family member, you can tell them to piss off occasionally. That can't happen when we have guests; always do your best. If they end up being assholes, then I'll take care of it.'"

"That sorta sounds like Butch."

"In the five years since, I've never had to report anyone being an asshole—though I gotta say, one couple was close."

We both chuckled, and Jenne was curious. "So, how often do folks stay here?"

Michelle's dark ponytail swished as she turned her head, thinking. She looked about 5⊠6⊠, well-proportioned, and in great shape, I assumed from all the physical work around the winery. Her thoughtful brown eyes and easy smile had to be a perfect fit for her job.

"In the summer, we're booked all the time. This time of year, it's only when a restauranteur or magazine editor visits. When it's more than one or two people, we have a separate wing in the main house to accommodate them. Now, again, which wine do you prefer? The only caveat is it has to be from Uva."

Since everything they produced was sold out, even at over a hundred bucks a bottle, anything would be superb, but I let her make the choice. "How about you decide for us?"

"Okay, that's easy. We have a blend that's half cab and half sangiovese. It's new for us, and it's what we were bottling when you drove up. It's still a little young, but the grapes are from the 2018 vintage and have had three years in the barrel. It's my favorite wine we've ever made, and we haven't even shipped any out yet. We're rationing this first release."

We just nodded, confident that she knew what she was talking about.

"Good. Perry will be down in about forty minutes or so. That should give you time to freshen up and unpack. Oh, if you're interested, there's a nice chardonnay in the fridge by the bar area on the other side of the fireplace. See you in the morning, whenever you get up. I'll be in the tasting room doing some wine club mailings. Enjoy the evening."

"Thanks for everything." I knew my wife would kill me, but I just had to ask. "Um, Michelle, before you go?"

"Yes?"

"Is there a TV?" I could already feel Jenne's eyes drilling into me.

Our host smiled, almost as if she had expected the question. "Of course. Butch said you might want to check the scores on the Golf Channel."

"Um, where is it?"

"Oh, that bench at the foot of the bed?"

"Yes?"

"There's a remote on the nightstand. If you hit the correct button, the TV will rise from that slot. When I remodeled, I couldn't find anywhere to put it, so I hid it in there. It has a swivel, so you can sit anywhere to see it."

I felt like an idiot. We had provided similar contraptions for clients but had never used one. "Sheesh, of course, and I knew that."

Both women smirked at each other and nodded knowingly. "See ya, Kevin. Have a good evening," Michelle signed off, laughing, as she left our exquisite digs.

The bath area was equally as stunning as the loft-like main living area. It was as well-appointed as any spa we had ever visited, and Jenne was suitably impressed. "You know, Kev, I could stay here for a long time."

"What I guessed, hon. I suppose we owe Butch big time now."

"Even though he pretends to be a curmudgeon, he has a big heart and is generous to boot."

"Yeah, and now we know he owns a famous boutique winery, we can have him bring the wine to all our dinner parties."

Just as we settled down with a glass of Uva chardonnay, there was a knock on the door. I smelled the food even before I opened it.

"Kevin and Jenne, right?"

"Yessir, and you're Perry."

"Correct, and this is your dinner."

Perry appeared to be somewhere near forty, had a slight build, and expertly went about setting up our dinner. He was just as friendly as the rest of the staff, and he was wearing jeans, Doc Marten boots, a chef's jacket, and an apron.

"It smells wonderful. Do you work here full time?" Jenne asked.

"I don't. I own a restaurant in town. Whenever they have an event or someone staying here, I take care of them. It's much busier in the summer, so I frequently stay over."

"Huh?"

"The farmhouse, the original structure, has been remodeled several times. There's a wing for use by the guests, and the main house has three other en suite bedrooms. One is Michelle's, there's a spare for Butch if he's here when the barn is occupied, and I use the other."

"How can you do this and still run the restaurant?" I was eager to dig into the risotto, but I was curious.

"My brother owns it with me. When there's a catering job, I handle it and Chad runs Bottles—that's the name. Butch—well, mostly Michelle—is good about sending customers our way, and we've built up a great following. We even get to be the only place in town with a nice selection of Uva Cellars wines."

I was sure we would pay a visit to Perry's restaurant at some point and told him so as he turned to go.

The risotto was excellent and the wine superb. When we'd finished, we put the dishes outside the door as requested, checked the golf scores on the fancy hidden TV, and finally hit the sack after a long but exciting day.

I always considered Butch a close friend and still did. What surprised me was how well he'd kept this side hidden from us.

THREE

Walla Walla

Butch Carlson had been with Mathis Capital since his stint with the endowment fund for Brown University. He had been recruited heavily after Harvard Business School and suffered their angst upon signing on with a rival Ivy League college.

He had been with Mathis ever since leaving the Providence school—now going on twenty years. With almost ten billion in assets under his watch, he was afforded star status in the firm and was allowed to live anywhere he damn well pleased. Initially from the Seattle area and finding the climate far more desirable than that of New England, he opted to move to Bellevue, Washington. He had operated remotely from his home office for fifteen years, with only occasional visits to update the partners.

It was his choice to visit Winnemucca, but he felt better having others think it was someone else's. With so much of the firm's assets under his direction, he owed it to them to be diligent in his research.

The gold companies were always in the spotlight when global events were tenuous, as in the current climate. The challenges of the pandemic, climate change, and anarchists made the commodity a safe haven for investors. That two of the largest companies might form a merger was big news, and the firm that sussed out the eventual winner stood to profit handsomely.

He spent two days with the senior management of first GGC Limited and then Alpeza Inc. By the end of the day on Friday, he was more than happy to head south to Scottsdale. The only information he had gathered was that a merger was in the works, but it was too early to determine who would dictate the terms. A plus was his introduction to the negotiators for each firm; it might come in handy as things progressed.

In the comfort afforded by his new Tesla, the two-day drive went by quickly. After recharging in Tonopah, he made it to Las Vegas by the end of the first day. The second leg to Scottsdale was much faster without the need to plug in anywhere along the way. The drive gave him time to consider his life choices.

He had more money than any one person could spend. It allowed him great freedom and status, but so what? A couple of long-term relationships had stalled when the subject of marriage came up; he couldn't see the sense in it. His friends, his golf, and his job had always been enough. The winery had initially just been a place to stick some money, but now he enjoyed it. He vowed to make it more of a priority in his life—and he would, just as soon as he finished playing golf in Scottsdale.

Fresh from the sunshine and fairways of Arizona, Butch found himself in the accommodation recently vacated by the O'Malleys. He loved this place, and he loved what Michelle had done with it. He figured he'd check the books, review the wine club promotions, visit the team, and sample the new releases.

He usually met with Evan and Michelle separately and then with the team as a whole. He started with his rather famous winemaker.

"Are you happy with the new blend, Evan?"

"Both Michelle and I think it's gonna be a big hit. We haven't established a price yet, but it will be well received if we put it around $90."

"That high? For a sangio blend?"

"You haven't tasted it. The sangiovese is incredibly intense, and the cab we used is from the same lot we use in our single-vineyard juice."

He walked to the tasting counter, poured an inch into a tasting glass, and handed it to Butch, who swirled, sniffed, and took a sip. "Holy shit, Evan, this stuff is killer."

"Told you. I just wish we had more than a hundred cases of it."

"We'll need to ration it, right?"

"Yes. Club members first and then a few restaurants."

"What about the competitions?"

"We'll do the big ones in California and get the *Wine Spectator* folks out here. With the rest of our releases, that should be plenty."

"Everything else okay?"

"As usual, we'll be short-handed in the vineyards, but I can manage."

"If it's about wages …"

"It's not. It's just a shortage of knowledgeable hands. If we get someone without any experience, it wastes my time."

"Got it. It sounds like everything else is good?"

"No complaints."

"Great. Let's get with the rest of the gang."

FOUR

Bellevue

The drive from Walla Walla to the Seattle area, usually a four-hour event, took almost six. A low-pressure system that had invaded from Alaska had managed to clog the Snoqualmie Pass with several feet of snow. That stretch of I-90 was notorious for difficult driving conditions, and this time was no different.

Rather than continuing to Mukilteo to board the ferry to our home on Whidbey Island, we decided to spend the evening in Bellevue, allowing our good friends Bill and Shelly Owens to have us as their dinner guests.

I had met Bill while playing golf at Kelsey Creek. The local club was much more a golfing venue than a social platform for the elite to be seen and acknowledged. It was suggested that those seeking such admiration should look into membership elsewhere. Bill, the chief of detectives at Bellevue Police Department, was at times helpful, at others immensely perturbed by inexplicable complications resulting from our involvement in several high-profile cases involving murder and mayhem.

All business at work, he was famous on the course for his dry wit, cutting sarcasm, and being an all-around great guy to play with. He was also a notoriously lousy chipper of the ball, which produced endless joy for those playing against him, especially yours truly.

"Thanks for having us over, you two. We really appreciate it."

"You mean after you called us an hour ago and suggested you might be in town with nothing to do for the evening?"

"When you put it like that, it almost sounds like we might have imposed upon you."

Shelly and Jenne looked at each other, shaking their heads at the friendly sparring. "Bill, why don't you be quiet and open one of those bottles of wine that the O'Malleys were so kind as to bring?" Shelly tipped the scales at no more than a hundred pounds, but she was a master at getting her husband to obey. "How were you able to get something from Uva? I thought there was a waiting list."

"Guess who owns Uva?" Jenne looked like the cat who ate the canary.

Now Bill was interested as he turned the corkscrew. "Who?"

"Butch Carlson."

"Get out!"

"Not kidding. He said he wanted to keep it low profile, but I guess now it won't be. I think he's taking more of an interest in the winery these days."

"Oh boy, does that mean we can buy this stuff now?"

"I don't know, Shelly. He probably needs to make sure he takes care of all his club members first, but I'm sure we can cajole him into getting us some from time to time."

"Hey, maybe we can suggest he bring a few bottles to the gin game next week."

"I suppose we can try, but if you promise to lose, he'll be certain to do so." Bill was an especially poor loser.

"Good one. I'm afraid to ask, but are you mixed up in anything that's gonna piss me off? You know how you're usually knee-deep in shit and I have to bail you out."

I didn't quite remember our previous involvements in the same way but thought it best to play along. "Nope. We're taking time off from the seamier side of life."

"Let me say on behalf of the Bellevue Police Department and the Seattle office of the FBI, we appreciate it. Maybe we can concentrate on *our* caseloads for a while without you bothering us."

"Geez, Bill, it hurts when you put it like that." What I didn't say was that without Jenne and me, several high-profile cases would have gone unsolved. I secretly congratulated myself on my mature approach to the conversation and was certain Jenne would tell me later what a great person I was. Then Bill's phone buzzed.

"Just let it go, Bill. How important can it be?" Shelly, aware that her husband was always on call, still appreciated the infrequent uninterrupted evening.

He glanced at the screen, stood up, and said, "Let me get this, Shell. It's Julie; she knows not to bother me unless it's important."

Bill was referring to his young protégée, Julie Houser, a brilliant investigative mind wrapped in an annoying millennial package. I had had several interactions with her previously.

"What is it, Julie? If it's just a break-in, then ... really? Shit ... okay, I'll be there."

He turned to us, a concerned look on his face. "It's a break-in at the Bellevue Towers downtown. She called because she knew the owner is a friend. It's Butch's place."

"Carlson?" I was stunned by the coincidence.

"That's the one. The thing that concerns me is how anyone could manage it. That place is a high-security building. They have locked elevators, security cameras, and twenty-four-hour concierge service."

"When we ran into him last week, he said he was stopping at Uva on his way back. He said it was a long drive, but he wanted to try out his new Tesla on an extended trip."

"I'll get ahold of him after I've had a chance to look at the scene. You three enjoy the wine. I'll be back in a few hours."

I hated to stick my nose in, but I had to ask. "Can I come?"

"No!"

"Are you sure? Don't you want to think about it?"

"Yes, I'm sure, and no, I don't want to think about it."

"Really? Come on ..." *I* even hated the way *that* came out.

"Goodbye, Kevin." With that, he left and closed the door.

I looked at the two women, shook my head, and said, "Well, I guess he'll have to solve this by himself." They ignored me, looked at each other, shook *their* heads, and continued their conversation. I felt like the last kid chosen for the kickball team in grade school.

We spent the night at the posh Owens residence. Shelly had inherited a large sum of money after her husband, attempting to kill her, accidentally did himself in. But that was years ago in a gruesome attempt at mass murder by a band of white supremacists.

Bill didn't get in until late, so our first update on the break-in wasn't until breakfast. "Please fill us in, O wise one," I opened with.

After expecting and receiving a nasty look, our host addressed his remarks to my wife. "I'm speaking to you, Jenne, because your husband is being a smart-ass."

"Not a surprise, Bill. Please go ahead." It appeared I was on my own island this time.

"It was a bit odd. It was discovered only because another owner saw Butch's door was ajar. They reported it to the concierge, who investigated after receiving no answer from the intercom. That's when they called us. Not every room was tossed. A few drawers were pulled out here and there, especially in the office. Most of the shelves were in disarray, almost like they were looking for something in particular.

"I reached Butch on his cell after I saw the damage. He was upset. I asked him if he had anything of high value—cash, gold, guns, or something—that could be fenced. He told me there were expensive watches, maybe a few grand in cash, but that was it. He was concerned about his artwork, though."

I was familiar with Butch's collection of works by several Northwest Mystics, namely Guy Anderson and Mark Tobey. They were highly sought-after and worth tens of thousands of dollars. "Did they take them?"

"Strangely, no. After my call, I video-chatted and showed him the condo. He was relieved that none of the pieces had been taken, and one or two had fallen, but otherwise they were intact."

"Don't you find that odd?"

"Sure, but who said crooks were smart?"

"They were smart enough to get in and out without being seen." I was sure Bill knew this, and his quick retort was intended as a rebuke to get me to bug out.

"Yes, they were." Detective Owens was a clever sonofabitch, and he agreed in a way that brooked no further discussion. I, on the other hand, could not be silenced.

"Did they get the watches and cash?"

"You can't leave it alone, can you."

I thought the man knew me better than to ask, but Jenne put her two cents in before I could fire back with a snappy rejoinder. "I'll agree, Bill; Kevin can be a real pain in the ass at times. Maybe he's just concerned about his friend, though."

Women are amazing; at least my wife is. She always knows the right way to put things to sidestep any further conflict. If only the rich old white men would let them run the world.

Jenne's interruption had its intended effect. With a sigh worthy of Tom Selleck in Blue Bloods and a sip of coffee, Bill explained, "They took the cash but left the watches. We figure the theft was opportunistic, but the real reason for the break-in was that they were looking for something. They most likely didn't know the value of the art—that stuff's a little abstract for most folks. Even so, the fact they didn't take the watches shows that they can't be bothered trying to fence anything. No, we figure they had something specific in mind."

It was the longest answer I'd ever heard Bill give to an inquiry. Perhaps it *was* best to let my wife take the lead. She continued, "How is Butch doing?"

"He's upset, naturally, but he seemed to take it in stride. He's coming back from Walla Walla today to take a better inventory. I'll be supervising, but Julie's heading up the investigation. She'll let me know if they find anything else."

FIVE

Whidbey Island

We picked up Emma from her buddy's house—conveniently the home of our dog sitter—and managed to get back to our place by early afternoon. Not surprisingly, the weather still hadn't improved. Walla Walla may have been cold, but the sun shone considerably more there than in the Seattle area.

I thought briefly about reaching out to Butch but ultimately figured he'd have plenty on his plate once he got back to his condo. Jenne thought it best for me to spend the rest of the day helping her clean the house and fold the laundry, and I knew much better than to disagree with her sound reasoning. I suppose it made way more sense than watching golf on TV.

When the phone buzzed just after dinner, I was surprised to see that it was Bill Owens calling. Surely he only wanted to update me on the break-in.

"Hey, Bill, what's up?"

"There's been an accident."

"Huh? What do you mean, an accident?"

"Butch Carlson's car ran off the road this side of Snoqualmie Pass. There was quite a bit of snow and ice on the road, and the visibility was terrible. It was almost a twenty-foot drop off the side where he slammed into a big cedar. He's dead, Kev."

I was stunned and must have been quiet for a while, because the next thing I heard was Bill's voice again. "You there?"

"Yeah. Wow, tough to get my arms around this." When Jenne heard my side of the conversation, she looked over, sensing something terrible had happened.

"I know. I wanted you to hear it from me. Look, I have to go; there's still some stuff with the stateys. I'll call later when I know more."

I disconnected the call and looked at Jenne. "Butch is dead, honey. He crashed into a tree this side of the pass."

"Jesus, this is awful. We only just saw him."

"I know. Damn, it's just so sudden—so final."

"I know you two have been golf buddies for years, but I don't know much about his family. He was what—sixtyish?"

"Yeah, right around there. He and his wife divorced years ago, and his only contact with her was once in a while about the kids. I think she died a few years ago."

"They have two, right?" Jenne asked.

"Yes, two boys—Jason, the youngest, in Boulder, and John, whom I think is in Southern California somewhere."

"How will they find out about this?"

"I'm pretty sure the state patrol will handle that if they can reach them. Bill is tight with those folks, which is why *he* knows, I guess. He'll probably help with their names and locations too."

"Should we be doing something?"

"I don't know. Let's sleep on this if we can. Maybe things will be clearer in the morning."

Neither of us slept very well. We finally gave up trying and hit the Keurig machine just before six. "There's not much we can do, is there, Kevin?"

"I guess not. How about we go out and clean up the yard? At least we'll keep busy."

We worked hard, raking and pruning until there was no more left to do. My cell phone vibrated as I dumped last fall's dead leaves into the compost heap. It was Bill.

"Hey, how are things?"

"Not good. There have been some developments."

"Like what? Were they able to reach the kids?"

"They were. As you can imagine, they were crushed. Jason is the executor, and he and Butch, strangely enough, discussed his will the last time they were together. I spoke with him just a little while ago."

"Didn't the state troopers do the notification?"

"They did. It wasn't about that. A witness came forward this morning."

"How did that change things?" I was focused now.

"This witness told the troopers that a truck forced Butch's Tesla off the road."

"You mean on purpose?"

"That's what she says. Since Butch was a friend, they asked me to work on the case, and I'm scheduled to interview her in about an hour."

"How could she be certain, with the weather and all?"

"I don't know yet, but she seems to be."

"Well shit, this makes everything much worse. Did Jason say anything about the service? When and where?"

Bill took his time answering. He seemed overwhelmed. "He said his dad didn't want one. The only celebration he wanted was for Jason to pick a day next month to provide an open bar for all the golf club members. He wanted his pals to have one last drink on him."

"That sounds like Butch."

"It does. I'll miss him, and I know you will too. Kevin, you know how I have often given you shit for getting involved with cases in which you have no business?"

Usually I would have dished out a cutting, smart-ass response, but my heart wasn't in it. "I seem to remember a couple of occasions."

"Well, I'd prefer you leave this one alone too. I'd prefer it, but I know you won't, so here's what I'm going to do. I'll keep you in the loop on what transpires in the case. If it turns out that someone forced our friend to his death, then I will move heaven and earth to find out who and why. If that means feeding you information, then that's what I'll do. Do me one favor, though."

I was so shocked that I had difficulty forming words. "What?"

"Let me control the flow. I will let you know everything—or nearly everything—I know, and I expect the same from you. No more withholding. Do we have an understanding?"

This was a different Bill from my best friend, who was unceasing in his verbal abuse. He was rattled. "I promise if I find out anything, you'll be the first to know." And I meant it.

"I'll get back to you if this witness has any merit. Hug Jenne for me."

I signed off, thinking Detective Owens was in a place he had never been before. Hell, the fact that he'd said he would allow me access to the case guaranteed it.

Six

Whidbey Island

When I told Jenne the gist of my phone conversation, she was as surprised as I was. "They think it was intentional?"

"Someone does. We'll find out later, if Bill keeps his word about letting me know what's happening."

"Sort of unlike him, eh?"

"For sure. But he was close to Butch too. This has become personal."

With nothing left to do outside, we resorted to catching up on emails, starting the arduous task of income tax preparation, and general all-around computer stuff. Yeuch.

Finally, Bill called. "Hey."

"Just got out of my interview with the witness."

"And?"

"Her name is Cora Montgomery. When the accident happened, she was coming back from skiing up at Snoqualmie with a friend. Only she was adamant it wasn't an accident. According to her—and she said her friend would confirm this—a fairly new black GMC pickup shoved Butch's car off the road. She was in the left lane when it happened. She said the Tesla was in the right lane when this truck pulled slightly ahead, turned sharply into it, and forced it off the road. With the slippery conditions, there was no way for Butch to stop. She said she was afraid to pull over because the weather was so bad. She called it in as soon as she could."

"Could it have just been an accident? Maybe the Tesla was in his blind spot."

"According to Cora, it was intentional. She said whoever it was ran him off the road, and she thought the truck even hit him."

"Is there any way to confirm it?"

"I've got the forensic folks scouring the Tesla for scrapes or paint marks. It'll take them a day or two, but if it's there, they'll find it."

"I suppose it's too much to hope they could get a plate number."

"I asked, but no. The weather was so shitty that they probably couldn't have read it anyway."

"What can I do?"

Bill was quiet for a moment. "You know a lot of his friends. Maybe ask around some. If this was intentional, it was murder, and there has to be a motive. Maybe we'll get lucky and somebody will know something. I'll be doing what I can from my end."

It was a strange experience having him confide the details of a case to me. I wasn't sure what to say or do, so I just agreed and ended the call. Jenne sat there looking at me.

"From what I heard, the witness said it was intentional?"

"Seems like it."

"And Bill's letting you help?"

"Also seems like it. Strange, huh?"

"Very. He must be upset about this."

"Yeah. I promised not to keep anything from him, and I won't. Whoever did this is a murderer."

"I understand your resolve, Kevin, but I'd like you to remember something."

"What's that?"

"You're a 62-year-old retired interior designer who sometimes works out and frequently plays golf."

I knew these things; I did. "So?"

"So you're not a cop or a tough guy. I'll admit you—sometimes we—get involved with some ne'er-do-wells, but please don't do anything stupid."

"Ne'er-do-wells?"

She grinned as only she could. "Yes, I thought you'd like that. Promise me you'll behave, okay?"

I always find it best to agree with my wife, not just because she's much brighter than I am; she makes more sense too. "When you force me to deal with reality, it's depressing, but okay, I agree. I'll see if I can find anything and immediately turn it over to Bill."

"Atta boy. Knew you'd see it my way."

It was Tuesday morning before I spoke with Bill again. He had news. "The Tesla was seriously bashed up when they brought it in, but they did find a dent near the front left headlight with a smudge of black paint on it. When they checked it against their database, they found that GMC used it on their 2021 Denali pickups."

"So the witness was right. It wasn't an accident."

"Yes. We've got an APB out for a Denali with damage on the passenger side. All the body shops are in the loop, as well as all the dealers. It's a long shot, but maybe we'll get lucky."

"I guess that's something. I've talked to a few folks, but nothing's come up yet. Maybe his kids know something."

"Been there already. They don't know much about his work or private or social life. Seems like they've been off living their own lives and only talk to their dad every other week or so. At least Jason does—John maybe not as much."

"Where do you go next?"

"We have interviews set up with his employers, but I don't hold out much hope with them. Whatever it is, it has to do with the break-in at his condo. I'm gonna go back there later today."

I hesitated to ask, remembering the last time I brought it up. Then he surprised me.

"You want to take a look with me?"

"It's okay?"

"Yes, this time it's okay."

SEVEN

Bellevue

I met Bill at the Bellevue Towers at five o'clock. Getting off the elevator on the 25th floor, I noted that there was still yellow crime scene tape crisscrossed over the door. Only four residences were on this exclusive floor, each worth well over three million dollars. Bellevue had become a mecca for wealthy young techies, who sent the real estate prices upward in a seemingly never-ending spiral.

Even though the sun had just dropped below the Olympic Mountains, the reflected light from this unusually sunny day provided a breathtaking view of Lake Washington and the city of Seattle to the west.

Upon entering the foyer, I was startled to see how much of a mess the place had become. Because Butch was borderline OCD, I had fleeting thoughts of him rolling over in his grave. I thought to myself how crass the image was, but then again, it was Butch; if anyone could find humor in the situation, regardless of how dark, it was he.

"His son Jason—he flew in yesterday—said he'd come by on the weekend to go through things. That won't be easy for him. Even though he's the youngest, it seems he was closer to Butch than John was."

Because I was focused on how everything had been tossed about, Bill's words barely registered.

"Kevin?"

"Yeah, sorry—just trying to remember how neat the place was the last time I was here. It looks like they left the artwork alone, at least in the living room. Let me look at the rest of the rooms."

I wandered through the primary bedroom, the adjacent bathroom, and the guest suite. Whoever had tossed the home had been thorough, at least when it came to places where paperwork could be found. As I turned to join Bill in the kitchen, I noticed a naked picture hanger in the hallway just off the guest bedroom, and I stopped and tried to remember what had been hanging there.

"You got something, Kevin?"

"I don't know. At some point, something was hanging here, but I can't recall if Butch removed it and left the hook or if someone else removed it. Did you get this area when you did the FaceTime with Butch?"

"I don't remember. It was right when the break-in was discovered, and everything was sorta hectic. It's possible I missed it. Do you ever remember seeing anything there?"

"No, but Butch was always looking for unique artwork. He loved finding those hidden Tobey and Anderson works. It's possible something was taken. When I get home, I'll look through some pictures I took when we were here a few months ago. We were helping him with some lighting, and we took lots of shots to help us with the design."

"Not on your phone?"

"Nah, put 'em on a stick. When using them for work, we like to get them off the phone and save them to a flash drive. We got used to doing that when we had the business, and now, if we're helping friends, we do the same thing. It saves the memory on the phone, and we keep them with the other paperwork."

"You'll check first thing when you get back?"

"I will."

It was nine o'clock when I turned into our drive off Little Dirt Road. As I usually did, I had a lengthy phone conversation with Jenne while waiting in the ferry terminal lot and then during the twenty-minute crossing of the Saratoga Passage. The night was clear and cold, with a tiny sliver of a moon still providing plenty of light. I never got used to how quiet and dark the nighttime sky was on Whidbey. The stars were immeasurable.

I opened the door to the jumping and squealing Emma. Her effusive greeting was the same whether I was gone for two days or two minutes. People often commented that having a dog could limit travel and other social engagements, and they were right. It would be a cold day in hell, though, before we'd even consider life without our companion. She was a big part of our lives, and the hole left would be difficult to fill when her time came.

Although it was late, Jenne had produced a plate of cheeses and crackers, accompanied by a superb Russian River pinot noir. It was good to be home.

"Here's the flash drive from Butch's condo. I've already opened the files on my laptop."

"Geez, Jenne, you keep treating me like this and I may never leave the house again. Could you see any pictures of that hallway?"

"Yup, there was one of that very spot. You must have taken it to make sure the wall lighting covered the artwork. It's funny, Butch had all those collectible pieces and the burglars stole a wine award."

"Huh?"

"Yeah, the thing hanging in that spot was a framed wine award from *Decanter* magazine. I zoomed in and was able to read it. What's the big deal?"

"Let me look." I zoomed in on the picture; sure enough, it was a DWWA platinum award for a 2016 Uva cabernet sauvignon.

"Yikes, I had no idea they received this. The Decanter World Wine Awards are the most prestigious in the world. *Decanter* is a British magazine that started the awards back in 2004. Since then, it's been the gold standard against which all the other awards are measured. Platinum is huge; they have a best-in-show, but those are rarely given out. If a wine receives a platinum award from the DWWA, the winery can write its own ticket. This must have been the year after Butch bought the place. No wonder they've become so exclusive."

"How do *you* know this, and why would anyone take it?"

"I know this because I'm a well-read enophile. Also, I saw a blurb about it on Flipboard while waiting for the ferry. As to why anyone would take it, I don't know, and I can't imagine it has any value. The award is public knowledge."

"You going to tell Bill?"

"Damn, I forgot. I'll call him right now."

After I'd let the Bellevue detective know what had been taken, we chatted briefly and mentioned touching base the next day. Neither of us could see why the award would be stolen.

Eight

Walla Walla

The mood among the employees at Uva Cellars was, in a word, miserable. Michelle had received word of the owner's death from Jason Carlson the previous evening. She broke the news to Evan first and then to the entire staff.

Butch had been a terrific boss and friend to the team during his tenure—one in which the winery had become world famous, its wines synonymous with outstanding excellence and quality.

The depressing meeting was held in the tasting room with scones and muffins provided by Perry; understandably, they were left untouched.

Michelle, doing her best but not succeeding in holding back tears, relayed her conversation with Butch's son. "Jason told me to tell you there would be no changes here as far as he was concerned. He said what we all knew—that Butch loved this place and was proud of what we do and what we've accomplished. As you can imagine, he's a bit overwhelmed right now. He said to carry on and that he'd come by sometime soon to check on things. Butch left a substantial inheritance to his kids, and it seems his youngest son will be the one we report to."

After the staff had left the room, Evan approached Michelle. "I don't think I've ever met Jason. How old is he, and does he know anything about what we do?"

While distracted by the recent events, Michelle was sufficiently aware to recognize the concern in the winemaker's voice. "I think he's early thirties. I've only met him once, but during our call, I got the impression he was aware of what we do, and because of his dad, he followed our successes. Why?"

"It's just that the thought of reporting to some young neophyte who doesn't know shit doesn't excite me."

"It's a little early to form opinions. Let's give him time to get beyond this shock, get his legs under him, and then see how it shakes out. Besides, it's not like we have any alternative."

"Yeah. I guess we'll see what happens." He turned his back during his reply and left the tasting room.

Michelle knew that Evan was reserved and usually kept his feelings bottled up. She felt his communication with the vineyard workers was the bare minimum required to convey what needed to be done. She attributed his moodiness to the eccentricities most owners overlooked when it came to the stars of the industry—the winemakers.

Even so, his surliness of late, even before the death of their owner, was becoming tiring.

Evan Davis was recognized throughout the wine industry as the man who had brought a DWWA platinum award to the Walla Walla AVA. Still, it was obvious to the competition that Michelle was the glue that kept Uva ranked among the top wineries in the country. She routinely rejected offers of employment from winery owners both locally and nationally.

Even though Butch visited the location infrequently, he made it a point to video chat with Michelle at least every few weeks; he hadn't gotten incredibly wealthy without paying attention to details. After meticulous research and committing almost seven million dollars to acquiring Uva, he told Michelle that *she* was the reason he was confident in his investment. He found that their estate vineyards were sitting on some of the best dirt in the valley, and the enterprise was run by a former interior designer who knew her stuff.

Michelle's skills in project management and her ability to assume the role of peacemaker—both honed during her interior design days—served her well in managing the day-to-day activities at the winery. She left the chemistry and farming up to Davis, only stepping in when there were issues among the vineyard staff. She didn't know if he resented her intrusions and, frankly, didn't care. Butch had given her the freedom to run the operation however she saw fit, and she would continue to do so.

Jason Carlson had only visited Uva a couple of times, once with his dad and another with a female friend. Michelle thought the younger son was a chip off the old block and liked him; she had never met John. The difficult phone conversation she had had with the new owner after his father's death had given her no concern about the future of the winery. He had confirmed that things should proceed as they had in the past and to make sure to call him if she needed anything.

Nine

Boulder

After his parents divorced, shortly before his twentieth birthday, Jason Carlson was relieved. Attending the University of Washington was a two-edged sword. On the one hand, the highly regarded school was nearby, which meant he could still hang with his buddies. Conversely, it meant more frequent visits home than he would have liked. He loved his mother and father, but the atmosphere at home had become unbearable over the past several years.

Assuming his folks were hanging on until he graduated, he finally called for a family meeting. His older brother was in California with Google, so it was just the three of them. He started the conversation the only way he knew how—straight ahead. "I love both of you very much. However, it seems you two don't love each other at all."

Butch and Christie started to speak at this, but Jason held up his hands, stopping them. "Wait. I'm not here to argue or debate. I'm here to tell you how I feel and how it appears. I see how you talk or rather don't talk to each other. I see how much happier you are when you're not together. You guys can figure things out, I'm sure. My reason for having this meeting, intervention, or whatever is to tell you to pull the trigger if that's what you want. Please don't wait for me to be out of school. I'll still love both of you, and I'll still stay with you separately if that's what it takes. I'm leaving for class now, so you can let me know what you think later."

Jason never knew what the conversation was after his departure, but within weeks his parents had filed for divorce, and his father moved to an apartment in the city. He had been right. When he next visited his mom, she was in a better place and even smiled occasionally. His dad, too, seemed more upbeat when he offered to help move furniture into the new digs.

After moving to Boulder shortly after he graduated from the University of Washington, Jason became an avid outdoorsman. Whether skiing, hiking, climbing, or fishing, he attacked each activity with a zealot's passion. As the head of IT for a small software startup, he found ample free time to pursue all the offerings of the Rocky Mountain State.

Since his first days with the company, it had tripled in size and was now hailed as likely to follow in the footsteps of Microsoft, Apple, and Google. His stock options and conservative investments had made him wealthy, even without his father's money.

The network of friends and colleagues he had built over the years in Boulder was sympathetic and supportive after hearing the news of his father's death, which made taking temporary leave difficult. It was necessary, though, to handle the details of the estate as well as meet with Michelle at Uva Cellars. While his computer science degree had been the key to his initial employment, his keen sense of business made him indispensable at work. It also gave him the confidence to tackle the difficulties sure to arise in the upcoming weeks.

His efforts to contact his brother were futile. Five years his junior, he had never been close to John, and he had completely lost contact when his older brother had left for college. Reluctantly, he sent an email to his last-known contact info and a letter to his last-known address.

Ten

Bellevue

Whenever he returned to the Seattle area, his dad got him on the golf course; although he didn't play regularly, he was an excellent athlete and managed to sustain a ten handicap. As a frequent addition to the group, I never ceased to marvel at the distance Jason was able to hit the ball. His 6'3" frame and regular climbing excursions made him one of the longest hitters I'd ever seen, either professionally or otherwise.

Jason called a few days after the news broke and asked if we could get together for coffee. "I'll be in town on Thursday and wondered if I could discuss some things with you."

"Of course. Where should we meet?"

"I've got to discuss the arrangements my dad wanted at the golf club, so how about there?"

"See you then." I wondered if I would have handled things as well when I was that age.

When I got to the club, I saw Jason leaving the general manager's office. His face looked thinner than I remembered, but that was no surprise. Clean-shaven with a mop of curly red hair, he smiled hesitantly when he saw me.

"Hey, Kevin. Good to see you."

"Hi, Jason. I wish it was under different circumstances. How are you doing?"

"Okay. People have been wonderful. I knew Dad had lots of friends here; I didn't know how many liked him. A lot."

"Your dad treated everyone like a friend, regardless of how well he knew them. The entire staff here was upset by the news."

"I know. The GM said he'd open the bar up on the day I wanted without any questions. He even said the club would pay, but I insisted. Dad would be pissed if he thought he was getting something for nothing."

"Hah, you're right. Let's go grab a table."

We sat in the small dining room just off the lounge and were the only two in the room. After we were served coffee, Jason got right to it. "Dad had many friends, but he always loved the times you two had on the course. He said I should look you up if I ever needed anything and he wasn't around."

I was only a little surprised at this. Butch and I had played many rounds over the past twenty years and shared personal and business stories. He was the first to know about my divorce and subsequent marriage to Jenne, and I was the first to know of his. While he was one of the more gregarious fellows in the club, I could see why *truly* close friendships might have been arduous for him. The very nature of his profession suggested the need for discretion, and separating business from pleasure was not always easy. Hell, I'd only recently discovered he owned one of the most famous wineries in Washington.

"Your dad was a dear friend. We shared a lot of stories."

"Did you know he owned Uva Cellars?"

"Yes, but not until very recently. We bumped into him, literally, in a small town in Nevada. He found out we were headed to Walla Walla and spilled the beans. We stayed there at the guest house."

At this, he looked up and grinned. "Yeah, I took a date there the last time I visited. She loved the place; she was ready to marry me. Fortunately, I escaped her clutches."

"I can see how that might happen. So, what's next for Uva Cellars?"

"I don't know. Dad was diligent about keeping his will current, so everything is pretty clear. He had current valuations for all his holdings and split them evenly between John and me. He split the real estate holdings equally and left the winery to me. He left a healthy portion of the estate to the American Cancer Society, but even so, neither John nor I will ever want for anything."

"What can I do to help?"

"I can get all kinds of advice from winemakers and owners from around the country, and with my business background, I'm confident I can ensure the place is run properly. I need someone to tell me how my dad would have done things. He loved it there, and I'd like to continue running things like he would have."

"You've got Michelle. She seems to have a good head on her shoulders."

"From what I hear, you're correct."

"And you've got that Evan guy, the winemaker …"

"Yeah, he's got a great reputation, at least; I haven't spent any time with him."

"Okay, Jason, what would you like me to do?"

"You and Jenne are retired, right?"

I still wasn't sure where this was going. "Yup."

"Would it be too much for me to ask you to spend some time there? I want to get your take on things before I do anything. My dad spoke highly of you—even said you knew a little about wine." He said this with a raised eyebrow.

"I can picture him saying that. We used to talk about different wines all the time. Of course, this was *before* I knew he owned Uva. He was playing me … oh, sorry, Jason. Didn't mean anything by that."

"Don't worry. I know how you two zinged each other. I'm just sorry he's not here to see your face right now."

It was easy to see that the apple hadn't fallen too far from the tree.

"If you and Jenne could stay there for a few days and see how they do things, what goes on in the vineyards, how the employees get along, that sort of stuff, I'd appreciate it. I'd be happy to pay you too, of course." He said the last quietly, unsure if it was an insult or the proper thing to do.

"Whatever we can do to help, we'll do. Your dad was important to us. We appreciate the offer." He looked crushed, almost as if the weight of his situation was becoming too much.

"We would be happy to help on three conditions. First, we'll need to bring Emma, our German Shepherd, with us. Second, there's no way we're taking a dime from you, and third, we might need a bottle or two of your vino while we're there."

The look of relief on his face was unmistakable. "My dad was right about you. Thanks. No problem with Emma, and you can drink whatever you want while you're there. I won't pay you, but you must let Perry provide your meals. Call it a way for me to show my appreciation."

"Geez, if you put it like that, I don't see how we can refuse. When should we go?"

"Whatever works for you two—um, three."

"We'll have to get a few things in order, but I think we can be there the day after tomorrow. Will that be okay?"

"Of course. I'll let Michelle know what we're doing, and you can break the news to Jenne. I don't think anyone is scheduled for the guest quarters, but if they are, I'll have them stay in the farmhouse. The barn is yours for as long as you're there."

"I can't wait. She'll flip when she hears where we're spending the week."

Eleven

Walla Walla

Jason Carlson called Michelle Browne immediately after he met with Kevin and informed her of his plans. "I want you to know I have complete confidence in how you're managing the winery. My dad was fond of you and never failed to tell me what a great job you were doing when I spoke with him. Kevin was one of his best friends, and if anyone can look at things with a similar eye to his, it will be him."

"Thanks, Jason. Your dad was one of a kind, and I'll miss him. What can I do for Kevin and Jenne while they're here?"

"Make sure they're comfortable and give them access to anything they want—the books, the projections, everything. I don't expect much will come of this, but it will be the closest assessment to my dad's that I can get. I appreciate your putting up with me on this."

"Jason, you are the owner and boss. My job is to do the best I can at running this winery *for you*. You're the person I report to, so if it helps to have the O'Malleys here to look at us, I welcome them."

"That means a lot, thanks. I'll spend a little time talking to them when they're done, and then I'll come by for a visit."

"What about your job in Boulder?"

"They've given me as much time as I need to handle matters. I told them about Uva, and they said, 'No worries, do what you need to do.' I'm grateful for their support. I'll stay at my dad's place and tie up some loose ends. Being the executor of the will, at least this one, is becoming a full-time project."

"I'll do what I can to help. I'm looking forward to having Kevin and Jenne back. They seem really nice."

"They are. I'll talk to you next week or sooner if you need me."

When Michelle ended her call, Evan walked into the tasting room. From his appearance, she assumed he'd been out in the vineyards checking out the last of the late winter pruning. His muddy boots left clods of dirt on the concrete floor of the rustic tasting room.

"Hey, Evan, how about scraping the mud off *before* you come in? Now I'll have to clean your mess up."

If he even heard her, he offered no acknowledgment. "When is our new owner deigning to pay us a visit?"

Michelle rolled her eyes, tired of Davis's lack of respect for Jason. "It seems as though he wants some friends of Butch's to spend a little time with us before he comes by."

"What friends?"

"The O'Malleys. They were here a couple of weeks ago."

"That retired couple that stayed in the guest barn?"

"Yep."

"What the fuck are they coming for?"

"Easy. They were close friends with Butch, so Jason wants their opinion of our operation."

His weather-beaten face suggested he was much older than his forty-six years. His reddish cheeks turned scarlet when he got angry, which was more frequent lately. "We're supposed to take orders from some old farts who don't know grapes from gerbils?"

"I'm pretty sure Jason only wants an additional pair of eyes looking at us. He feels that because they knew Butch, they might be able to see what he saw in us—what we should aim for going forward."

"I don't get it. Just after Carlson bought us, I delivered a platinum award from *Decanter*, which put us on the map. Sure, he gave me a big raise, but Uva gets all the press, and my name is left out of it."

"That's not fair. *Decanter* gave you a big spread in their award issue."

"Maybe, but I don't get anywhere near the recognition the big names in Napa do."

Michelle felt that Davis was mistaken but knew better than to say anything. She also thought that the quality of the wine produced by

Uva had been improving every year since the original owners invested in the property. She was convinced that the soil Uva Cellars sat on was among the best in the world and that even a less talented winemaker would still have produced great wine.

"It's what Jason wants, so let's make our guests' stay as comfortable as possible." She knew Davis would stew over this perceived slight, but she no longer cared.

While Michelle cleaned up the mess the winemaker had left in the tasting room, he strode purposefully toward his three-year-old F150 pickup, the only vehicle left in the gravel lot. He climbed into the cold cab, waited for the engine to warm up, then turned the heater on full.

Spending the day in eastern Washington's vineyards during winter's waning days meant frozen toes and fingers. Oscar and Benny were adequate as far as vineyard workers went, but it seemed he still needed to supervise their work personally. He was a perfectionist and couldn't care less about how others felt.

He had begun his career immediately after obtaining his degree from the Department of Viticulture and Enology at UC Davis, one of the most respected programs in the country. After apprenticing for the Mondavi family for several years, he managed to land a position as the head winemaker at a small Russian River winery just north of Healdsburg.

The owners, a husband-and-wife team—both doctors—knew nothing about winemaking. As such, they left it up to Evan to run the entire operation. It proved a grievous error, since his skills, while agronomically and technologically superior, were sorely lacking when it came to interacting with people. Financially speaking, he was also inept. It was a short time before the doctors realized his shortcomings and set about rectifying the situation.

Davis was incensed when they hired a general manager to supervise the entire operation, including their winemaker. He became surly to his superior, downright abusive to the vineyard workers, and worst of all, disrespectful to the owners. In two short years, the doctors cut him loose.

He bounced around Napa and Sonoma Valleys in supporting roles for a dozen years before finally landing a head winemaking position in the Santa Ynez Valley. Again, it was for an inexperienced owner. This time, Davis had finally managed to curtail his less attractive attributes. The owner, a former code writer for Microsoft, loved wine and was relatively knowledgeable about quality and value. He asserted up front that he would be managing the business side of things while his winemaker would be in charge of the producing and growing facets of the enterprise.

SBV was located eighteen miles north of Santa Barbara and produced pinot noir and chardonnay varietals. Before Ivan Medved purchased the hundred-acre property, it was treated as a cash cow by an elderly couple more interested in selling quantity than quality. Their viticultural practices were deplorable, and their winemaker was less enthusiastic about making respectable wines than he was about drinking them.

Medved had searched for a talented winemaker for a year before he found Davis. In his conversations with previous employers, they were complimentary about Davis's specialized talents; he had been relieved of his duties because of his people skills.

As sometimes happens with young, successful, technologically savvy professionals, Medved was confident in his ability to resuscitate dormant brilliance. So he took a chance on Evan Davis, and for five years, his was regarded as a steadily rising winery in the highly competitive Santa Ynez Valley.

Eventually, though, the nastier side of Davis reared its ugly head. The breaking point was an expletive-laden outburst in the tasting room with a dozen customers present. Apparently, one of the women tasting the new pinot noir vintage had the temerity to suggest the wine could have compared better with a competitor down the street. No amount of urging by Medved could dampen his winemaker's rage. Eventually, the customers left, embarrassed, and Evan Davis was handed his walking papers.

It was another half-dozen years before the widowed owner of a boutique winery in Walla Walla would give the winemaker another opportunity. Because of the recent death of her husband, who had handled the chores of the wine production himself, she was pressed to make a quick hiring decision. She found a sparkling résumé for a winemaker from Santa Barbara on Indeed. Had she been in a less urgent state, she might have investigated why such a well-regarded professional was looking for work—in Washington, no less.

Michelle Browne, her former interior designer, was a natural in the tasting room and even more talented at running the business side of things. Helen Hurly was confident her new hire would fit in nicely with the current staff. It was another two years before she was sure she had made a mistake, but then she sold the winery. Rather than throw a wrench into the sale, she just ignored her assessment.

Butch was new to the game when he purchased Uva, so leaving the staff in place made sense. The winery was profitable and well regarded, and the second year after he took over the reins, they won the platinum award. Any negative feelings he harbored about his winemaker were put on the back burner. Davis's penchant for boorish behavior might have been less tolerated if Butch had spent more time on site.

Michelle seemed to tolerate him as long as he spent most of his time in the vineyards and the production areas. When a winery received a platinum from *Decanter*, the winemaker received most of the credit, regardless of their level of contribution or the likeability of their personality. It appeared Davis was the beneficiary of more good fortune than he deserved.

Always afraid that the less attractive side of his personality might be revealed when objectively observed, Davis was justifiably concerned about the prospect of two more pairs of eyes passing judgment.

TWELVE

Walla Walla

Before heading southeast to Walla Walla, I checked in with my good buddy Bill Owens. I had nothing new to report from my side, and I figured it was the same for the cops.

"Hey, Kevin, what's up?" He sounded all business but slightly more upbeat than our last conversation.

"Jenne and I are going back to Uva Cellars for a week or so. Jason asked us to stay there for a few days and give him our thoughts on the operation. Any news on the Carlson crash?"

"Nothing. We've got all the body shops in the state keeping their eyes open for a damaged Denali pickup, but so far, no luck. We'll keep at it, in any case. Why you two?"

"We're renaissance types who know good wine and food."

"Let me ask again, why you two?" It didn't sound as though Bill was buying my explanation.

"I think Jason wants another appraisal of the situation. He knows I was close with Butch, so he thinks we can see things through his dad's eyes."

"I guess that makes sense. If you happen to stumble on any motives or people that might have had a hard-on for Butch, you'll let me know. Right?"

"Stumble? That almost sounds like you don't appreciate my investigative skills. Yes, I'll be sure to fill you in. I'll call when we get back, if not before."

"Let me guess—that was Bill." My wife was either clairvoyant or maybe just used to the back and forth between me and Bellevue's finest. "It didn't sound like they're making much progress."

"You're correct; they're not. All they've got to go on is a fairly new Denali pickup with a dent in the rear passenger side. It's a stretch to think they'll find the person through the vehicle. Maybe they'll have more luck trying to come up with whoever broke into his condo. It has to be connected."

"I agree, but I still can't see what anyone gains by Butch's death. Everyone loved him."

"Maybe something will turn up while we're out of town." I wasn't sure if my reply was for Jenne or me. At best, it was a prayer.

We left Whidbey Island on the 9:30 ferry the following day. March was just around the corner, and the weather—well, the weather still sucked. Forty-three degrees with a constant drizzle was the poster child for the climate we chose to live in. At least once we got over the Cascades, we could expect some sunshine.

With the anticipation of a week-long holiday at a place where we'd be paying for nothing and with the best wine *and* food available, the five-hour trip passed quickly. Even Emma was relatively calm on the drive, and Michelle appeared genuinely happy when she greeted us upon our arrival. If she harbored any concerns about our presence, she was adept at hiding them.

"Kevin, Jenne, good to see you again, and so soon. This must be Emma. Jason said you were bringing a dog, but I had no idea she was such a specimen."

I laughed at this. Usually, her barking took away from her classic GSD looks, but now, for some reason, she was well-behaved. "Don't let her hear you say that. It'll go to her head."

"Somehow I doubt that. I'm just sorry your visit had to be under these circumstances. Jason said to take good care of you and to give you free rein of the place. Let me know what I can do to assist you, and don't hesitate to ask me anything."

Jenne smiled the smile that said "thanks, we appreciate it, and we sympathize with your situation" as she clasped both hands around Michelle's. It always amazed me that women were capable of such feats when for some reason, possibly genetics, men were nowhere near as emotionally evolved.

Feeling like a wallflower, if only for an instant, I offered a verbal attempt at commiseration. "Butch was a close friend, and we'll miss him. For now, though, I think the best thing we can do for him is to give Jason whatever help we can. I only know him from the times we played golf, but if that's any indication, he's honest, empathetic, and intelligent."

"Thanks, Kevin. I'm glad to hear that. I met him just once when he visited, and I've spoken with him recently on the phone. The little I know so far reminds me of his father. We'll be in good hands if he's anything like him. You two know the way to the barn, so I'll let you get to it. Need any help with your things?"

"We're good, thanks. Say, Michelle, what are you doing for dinner this evening?" Once again, Jenne reminded me of why she was such a terrific business partner. She rarely lost sight of the mission.

Our host appeared confused by the question. "Um, well, nothing. I was gonna catch up on some wine club stuff, then hit the sack early."

"Please join us. Is Perry cooking tonight?" This was Jenne taking over.

"Yes. I'm not sure what he has on the menu, but if I let him know, I'm sure he can make whatever it is for three."

"Great. Kevin will have Emma fed and walked by six—right, dear?"

It was comforting to have my wife plan my future; zero thinking was needed on my part. "Yes, I'm sure I can accomplish all that by then. Um, what will you be doing?"

"What do you think? Cleaning up, washing, and drying my hair. It's a lot of work keeping up this youthful appearance, you know."

This was where my following words would dictate any hope of carnal activity for the foreseeable future. "Geez, Jenne, with your looks and body, you could go four, maybe five days without a makeover." It wasn't my best comeback, but I hadn't prepared well. The look I got wasn't terrible, but I had my doubts about any indoor sports being on the horizon.

Michelle seemed to enjoy our repartee and thankfully offered some assistance. "I think he's saying that you're beautiful, and regardless of your efforts, that's not gonna change anything."

I was beginning to like this woman a lot. Now even Jenne was grinning. "I think you're probably right, Michelle. The man has a golden tongue, right?"

With a full-throated guffaw, she headed for the door. "I'll see you two in a little while. It seems as though I need a little primping myself."

Since fresh seafood was in short supply at this time of year, Perry suggested his special burgers, whatever those were. We were guests, sort of, and anything we'd ever eaten from him was delicious, so we agreed.

Michelle arrived shortly after six. The side table near the fireplace was a drop-leaf and opened up nicely into a 40-inch round, perfect for three or four diners. While we waited for the food to arrive, we got to know our host better while sipping the previous year's chardonnay.

The fire crackled, the lighting was warm and subdued, and a napping Emma was in her bed in the corner. Michelle was fifteen minutes into giving us a primer on the day-to-day activities of the winery when there was a deafening alert from the formerly sleeping Shepherd, immediately followed by a knock on the door.

"Wow, does she always do that, and how does she know?"

Jenne went to the door to let Perry in while I grabbed Emma on her way to see who the interloper was. "She can smell someone approaching and hear them before a human can. I gotta admit, her bark can be startling at times, but she never seems to be wrong."

Once I showed Emma that Perry was one of the good guys, she quieted down. Of course, it might have been the smell of the sizzling burgers with a spicy shallot barbecue glaze that did it.

Jenne was the first to comment. "Geez, Perry, does that ever smell good."

"Thanks. The ground chuck comes from a local ranch, and the buns we bake ourselves at the restaurant. I've also got some smoked salmon pâté in case you need a seafood fix. Normally I'd have selected the wine, but I think Michelle better handles that chore."

While he set up things on the table, Michelle reached into the basket she had placed on one of the shelves to the right of the fireplace. "I thought you'd enjoy a bottle of the cabernet that won the *Decanter* award with dinner. We still have a couple of cases left, but it's only for special events like this."

I didn't know what to say, so I chose stupidity. "With hamburgers?"

Michelle looked at me, then Perry, and then settled on Jenne. She shook her head slowly, rolled her eyes, and said, "Rookie. Jenne, how do you put up with him?"

"I'll admit it's not easy, although he has some redeeming qualities. You should explain it to him so he won't have to go through life so uninformed."

As Perry quietly left the premises, both women turned to me with opaque expressions.

"What? Was it that stupid?"

They burst out laughing simultaneously. There must be some non-verbal language among women that I don't understand.

"Nah, it wasn't *that* stupid. Right, Michelle?"

"We're just jerking your chain. Burgers may seem too ordinary to have a fine wine with, but not necessarily. I've had these before from Perry, and the shallot sauce gives them a deep earthy flavor that pairs wonderfully with a big cabernet. This one is huge. Trust me, you'll like it."

I felt a little better. Then I tasted the wine after a bite of the burger and felt a lot better. "This is unbelievable."

"Told ya. The weather was perfect that year through harvest. If there's any left, this stuff will be good for another fifteen or twenty years."

"I can see why you got a platinum for this."

"The dirt here is among the finest in the country, not just this AVA. Evan's a good winemaker and his efforts played a role, but I think even a less talented person could have produced an award-worthy wine that year."

It was the first I'd heard anything other than praise from Michelle regarding Evan Davis. After a glance from my wife, I let it slide. I've learned that it's never wise to ignore a glance from Jenne.

We continued to enjoy the meal, the wine, and each other's company. It was clear that Michelle had an excellent grasp of the winery, and even though it was early days, she seemed to be as dedicated to Jason as she had been to Butch. It spoke volumes about her security within the industry.

We asked if any issues might become more worrisome. Still, aside from the usual concerns about vineyard labor and tasting room staff during the summer, she saw nothing on the horizon. It was only when the subject of the winemaker's responsibilities came up that Michelle appeared to be less than forthright.

Jenne, appearing to notice as well, attempted to discover if there was a question mark over Evan Davis. "Whenever we ask about Evan, it seems you're not enthusiastic about his contributions, Michelle, or am I mistaken?"

Taking some time before answering, she appeared to choose her words carefully. "It's just that he's difficult to be around. Sure, he *is* a brilliant winemaker, but that's not a small club. Emma here could make good wine if the grapes were really good. What we have growing here on the property are some of the best grapes in the world. Most talented professionals would be thrilled to be here, but not Evan. He's just pissed that he doesn't get more recognition."

Once she got warmed up on the subject, it seemed her real feelings were revealed. I wanted to hear more. "Was Butch aware?"

"I think so. It was hard not to notice, especially when he visited. Evan would kiss up and try to ingratiate himself with him, but I'm fairly sure Butch saw through it. After we got the award, I think Butch just tolerated him. Those of us that are here all the time are the ones having to deal with his antics. We'll put up with him for now, but I think he's part of why we're having difficulty getting vineyard workers."

I noticed a "let's turn the page" look from Jenne, so I moved on to greener pastures. "What does the coming year look like?"

Michelle looked as though she too was happy to move on. "Our wine club is maxed out, as you know, and we have a waiting list over five years long. We'll still have tastings, because creating demand for our brand is always good. We acquired another twenty acres after the 2016 harvest and planted it the following year with cab, sangiovese, and merlot. The terroir is very similar to what we already have, so we're hopeful that will help to bolster our production."

Jenne sensed a possible shift in Michelle's focus. "Was that something Butch was trying to do? Increase production?"

"I think his approach to life was to keep improving and continuing to grow in many different ways. I gathered from our talks that he thought it a wise investment to plant the additional acreage as long as we could maintain quality. This will be the first harvest we'll use the grapes for wine, and we should get a little over two tons per acre on that parcel to increase production by another twenty-five hundred cases or so."

That seemed like a lot of wine to me, and I said, "Wow, that's a big increase. How many cases a year do you produce now?"

"We're doing about four thousand a year. We're still considered a 'boutique' winery. It would be a major step up for us. If the quality is even close to what we already make, we could easily sell it to the club waitlist and probably take on additional restaurants."

"Would you have to add to the production equipment?" Jenne was hooked on the possibilities; I suspected it was because she liked the smell of the fermenting grapes.

"Mostly we need to increase our barrel commitment substantially, and we'll need to dig out a section of the cave."

"Cave? What cave?" I had started to drift from the conversation, but now I was right back into it.

"You know that hill behind this barn?"

"Yup."

"On the other side, you'll see two huge sliding barn doors. The original owners dug out and reinforced the hillside to use for barrel aging. It's where we keep the stuff. We've already started construction there. We need to make room for another seventy-five or eighty barrels."

All this talk of grapes and wine had made me thirsty. "I don't know about you two, but I might need to find another bottle of something, you know, so we can keep talking about wine." I stood up.

I wasn't sure if the look from Jenne was one of disapproval or something else. I sat back down.

"I'm right there with you, Kevin. I think you'll find a bottle of our 2018 syrah over in the basket."

"Why, what a great idea." I glanced over at my wife with a smirk.

She ignored me and turned back to our host. "You *do* know that if you keep humoring his every wish, he'll stay here forever?"

"Hah, no worries, Jenne. Butch warned me about him when he called to tell me you were coming the last time. He was very fond of the both of you." Her tone turned suddenly serious. "I'll miss him. He was a good friend and a great boss. I sure hope his son works out."

I had just poured the syrah into three glasses when the conversation turned. "We're on the same page. I think Jason will follow in his father's footsteps, if it's any consolation. Even from my limited exposure to him, he seems solid."

I handed both women a glass and raised mine. "Here's to Butch. Let's do everything we can to keep his dream alive."

Thirteen

Bellevue

Detective Bill Owens was a busy man. As head of detectives at the City of Bellevue Police Department, there were more than enough crimes to investigate. Even though the rate of serious crime per capita was relatively low in the city, that left plenty of robberies and thefts to be explored.

There was the occasional bodily harm event, but the murder rate was meager for a city its size. The wealthy youngsters working for Microsoft, Facebook, and Amazon, who comprised a healthy percentage of the population, were disinclined to roam aimlessly, committing murder and mayhem.

While poring over a few of the many reports on his desk, he mused that most of the recent serious crimes, at least for the past several years, always seemed to involve his good buddy and frequent golf partner Kevin O'Malley. Intelligent enough to comprehend that his friend's involvement certainly wasn't by design, he secretly wondered how a retired interior designer could attract such a menagerie of murderers, drug kingpins, embezzlers, and downright bizarre individuals.

And now his friend was in the middle of the Carlson investigation. Yes, he had asked for Kevin's help, and yes, Butch was his friend, but now he and his wife were staying at a winery in Walla Walla and getting into God knows how much trouble. Maybe Jenne would keep him on the straight and narrow, but wasn't she just as much of a magnet? She was the one, after all, who was the catalyst behind that whole Waffle battery thing.

He pushed those thoughts aside while considering what he knew about the Carlson case. The break-in at Bellevue Towers was strange, and it would have been a mystery even if something had been taken besides the wine award. Just the ability of the perpetrator to get past the security at the front desk, then avoid the security cameras was perplexing. Then the I-90 crash—it was intentional, of that he had no doubt—so soon afterwards. Was the guilty party the same one who had broken into the condo? How had the person known that Butch would be on the road at that time?

As he contemplated these thoughts, Detective Julie Houser knocked on his door. He had tasked her with investigating the security lapses at Bellevue Towers.

"Hey, boss, I found out why there was no CCTV of the break-in at Carlson's place."

"And now you're gonna tell me, right?" His impatience was on full display these days.

She delivered her report with a swish of her purple ponytailed hair and a distinctly forced sigh. "All four cameras on that floor had been disabled. There was no record of who did it, and no one could say how it was done without some recording of it. Security says they're up and running now, BFD. I went through every second of their cloud storage and could find nothing."

"Shit. Julie, I need you to stay on this. Interview everyone on staff at the Bellevue Towers—and I mean *everyone*. This doesn't happen without somebody seeing something. At least on some level, the break-in must have something to do with Carlson's death. I'll follow up on the murder end as best I can, but this is your baby in the meantime. Find something!"

With a sober nod and no trace of her usual indifference to authority, she turned her diminutive frame and retreated to get back to work. She was a pain in the ass on occasion, but if anyone could get a handle on this, Owens was confident it would be Detective Houser.

FOURTEEN

San Francisco

After receiving his acceptance letter from Stanford, John Carlson wanted nothing more to do with living at home. A successful father and a loving mother would typically have provided the perfect foundation on which to build one's life, but John's was the exception.

The five-year difference in age between him and his brother, Jason, was just enough to ensure they were never close friends. In middle school, Jason was just in the first grade and way too young to be seen with. By the time John got to high school, he was too cool to associate with a snotty-nosed kid that had yet to get to the sixth grade.

No amount of encouragement, cajoling, and ultimately threats were sufficient to coax him into shouldering any caretaking responsibilities for his kid brother. His parents' constant urgings finally planted the seeds of a smoldering rebellion within the psyche of the young high schooler, which resulted in an even greater dislike for his younger sibling.

Possessing significantly above-average intelligence allowed John to skate through school with excellent grades requiring minimal studying. While a reasonably good athlete, he eschewed any organized school teams, preferring to "hang out" with a few less intelligent members of the species. The indoor malls in the winter months and the Bellevue city park were regularly visited venues. Even at the Carlson home in one of the wealthier sections of the eastside city, he paid little attention to his brother.

His choice of acquaintances left little room for sensible conversation but did suffice for the standard high school experimentation with booze and weed, neither of which he considered indispensable. Because his grades were excellent, his parents had little to complain about save for his rudeness to Jason, but that appeared to be an end without means for the Carlsons. When he was finally accepted into Stanford and he suggested he move to San Francisco upon graduation, Butch and Christie were glad to see him go. The extra cost for his Bay Area apartment was a small price to pay for a home with less hostility.

His early college days were filled with required classes, new surroundings, and exposure to a broad range of young people, most of whom were overachievers. Once again, he found that what was required by his teachers to excel in class came comparatively easy to him; he was blessed with an intellect that very few of his peers could match. Born into relative wealth in a comfortable white privileged society, he found it difficult to understand why most students were so driven to excel.

As he walked across the main quad one chilly Friday afternoon in early November, he cut across a trampled, muddy lawn to avoid a crowd of young women ahead of him. He was looking forward to returning to his apartment to get an early start on an alcohol-infused weekend.

John wasn't quite as tall as his brother but still was a pinch over six feet and on the slender side. With longish brown hair and his mother's Irish-Italian features, most of the opposite sex found him attractive. On this day, he was wearing a Stanford sweatshirt under a cream vest and light denim stonewashed jeans.

Cutting off the walkway, he jogged for a moment to pass the gaggle of girls. As he turned back to the sidewalk, he shifted his weight to his right foot, the sudden change of direction causing the soggy mixture of mud and grass beneath to slide away along with 180 pounds of John Carlson. He was sitting on his butt in less than a second, wet mud and multiple grass stains now decorating his stonewashed Polo jeans. His cream vest displayed evidence of the tumble as well.

The five or six female students were stunned, then concerned, but when they saw no injuries, their hands went to their mouths to stifle embarrassed chuckles.

"Dude, nice work there. I've been trying to get their attention since class got out. Looks like I was trying too subtle an approach." A short muscular-looking fellow with scraggly facial hair extended a Popeye-like forearm to help him up. As the cluster of onlookers moved along, John grasped the tendered assistance and pulled himself out of the muck. His rescuer displayed a broad grin showing what had to be the product of extensive orthodontic success at an earlier age. His teeth were perfect.

"I'm Aedan Boyle. Nice move on the hotties."

"Thanks for the rescue. I feel like a douchebag, and I look even worse."

"Look at it this way. You've given those girls something to talk about for the next few days. You're a popular guy now."

"Thanks, Aedan." John had regained his composure and was now curious about his new acquaintance. "How come you helped me?"

"It looked like you needed it. Besides, I've been trying to get that one chick's attention for two weeks now. Maybe she'll remember me."

The deflection brought a smile to John's face. "Well, thanks anyway. Feel like a beer?"

"Silly question. Where?"

"Come to my place. It's just a mile or so off campus." He gave his new friend the address and said he'd see him shortly.

Boyle turned out to be a trust fund kid from Montecito. The affluent suburb of Santa Barbara was home to movie stars, sports icons, and plain old filthy rich inheritors.

With an investment banker dad and a social butterfly mother, the only child had been burdened by a life of country club golf, European vacations, and expensive sports cars. When he showed up at John's apartment, he did so in a Porsche 911 Targa.

"Nice ride. That the new model?"

"Yeah. The folks think I'll love them dearly if they spend inordinate sums of money on me. Don't get me wrong, I do like them; they've just never been around long enough for me to get to know them."

"Sounds like you've led a rough life. At least you didn't have a kid brother following you around expecting you to hang out together."

"Nope. Just me. Sometimes I think having a brother or sister would have been nice, though."

"Not if your folks ignored you and made you feel guilty about not being with the little fucker all the time."

It appeared that Aedan suspected these were issues better left to the professionals, and he moved on to other topics. "Nice place you've got here. Not interested in campus housing?"

"Hell, no. Wouldn't be caught dead there. My folks were kind enough to spring for this. I think they were just happy to get me out of the house."

As they traded back stories and scholastic preferences, they polished off their first Lagunitas and moved on to beer number two. The two new friends discovered they were both in business school, and neither knew what they wanted to do upon graduation.

"I didn't know what to say when my dad wanted me to come to Stanford, so I just came. My grades were good, and whatever friends I had in Santa Barbara couldn't get in here, so I came by myself." Aedan seemed as unprepared for the future as John did.

As their trite introductory patter wound down, they looked more at the sweating IPA letters on the label than at each other. Finally, Aedan said, "Why don't we start something."

"Huh? Start what?"

"A fraternal group; a small select one."

"Not sure where you're headed with this. What about the other fraternities?"

"They're all too big, and most think their shit doesn't stink. Here's what I'm thinking. Both of us are here at a school with mostly over-achievers, geniuses, and geeks. We're just here passing time, glad to be away from home—me from my rich parents, you from your little brother. Maybe we'll run into others in the same boat who want nothing to do with the mainstream frats."

"So what you're saying is that anyone with rich parents and who doesn't give a shit about their position in the graduation class is a candidate?"

"Sort of. They have to be smart too."

"We're at Stanford; they have to be smart just to get in here."

Aedan thought for a moment before he explained. "I don't mean book smart, I mean clever. If we're gonna spend time with other folks, at least they should be interesting—agree?"

"Works for me. Are you thinking we actively recruit?"

"Nah, I'm thinking we keep our eyes open for guys like us. If we suspect someone is a possibility, we talk about it and either agree or not. We both have to agree, though, right?"

Both young men seemed energized at the prospect of putting their own club together, and as they shook hands on the deal, John confirmed the approval process. "Absolutely. If we both don't agree, then no deal. Perfect."

And so was born the Stanford Society for Independent Thinkers—the SSIT for short. John thought it should have been just *Independents* but gave in to Aedan's preference for *Thinkers*. Besides, if the two s's were pronounced shh, then *shit* was the perfect handle for their little club. Since it was just the two of them, they saw no need for formal meetings or bylaws; that could wait.

The two freshmen spent a great deal of time together over the next several weeks. Because they were in the same curriculum, they discovered they shared many of the required essential business introductory classes. One would often attend while the other either goofed off or slept and then shared notes. Although both John and Aedan were of superior intelligence, neither was motivated by high grades. This proved to be a highly efficient method of managing a B at the minimum.

One Saturday afternoon in November, they found themselves at a local watering hole not frequented by their college classmates. Both had the requisite fake IDs, and since this was their third visit to the place, the bartender didn't bother to card them. Stanford was playing UDub, and most of the tavern was glued to the three large TVs positioned strategically in the bar. Even though the only two members of the SSIT did their best to avoid looking like proud attendees at the highly regarded institution, they couldn't help but quietly root for the

Cardinal when they were playing. Stanford was up by two touchdowns, which was especially gratifying for John, as they took it to his younger brother's hopeful college.

"You really don't like your brother?"

John took a deep breath and a long pull on his long neck before answering. "I don't think I *hate* hate him; it's more that it pisses me off that he's the one who gets all the attention. Then when I was told I either had to babysit him or watch out for him at school, it made things worse."

"Is that why you're glad we're kicking your hometown school's ass?"

John grinned at the thought of his brother constantly idolizing the Huskies. With pennants and purple jerseys adorning the walls in his room, his dream for college was to attend the highly regarded university on the shores of Lake Washington. The kid would be crushed after this defeat. "Yeah, I guess that's why."

As the game wrapped up and the afternoon patrons transformed into evening ones, Aedan and John negotiated the narrow alleyway leading to the parking area at the rear of the single-story brick building that housed Frank Tomlin's Bar. It was often suggested that the proprietor lacked imagination in naming the place, but there was little doubt about who owned the establishment.

It was dusk, the cool fall temperature hovering around the mid-fifties as they approached Boyle's tomato-red sports car. He'd left the top down because the weather was clear, and his security alarm was among the best. A skinny, shortish fellow, a joint hanging from his lower lip, was leaning over the Porsche, seemingly performing a close inspection of the vehicle's interior.

"Dude, help you with something?" Aedan, now only a dozen feet away, startled the little guy, his long greasy hair only partially hidden by a Stanford ball cap, who was leaning over his ride. Both he and John had now stopped, arms crossed, eyes glaring, and lips thin and tight as they did their best to suggest a threat.

Startled, the trespasser turned to look at them. His face displayed a poor excuse for a mustache that did little to disguise more than a few recent acne scars. "Shit. Sorry, man. Wasn't gonna do anything. I just never saw the inside of one of these. Pretty sweet, I bet, huh?"

John pegged the fellow to be a year or two younger than him and Aedan. Even though the temperature was cool, the kid was wearing only a dirty gray T-shirt, generously stained with various food-like substances.

They approached him with any perception of danger dismissed as he backed away. "I mean it. I was just looking." The furtive look in his eyes exposed his discomfort.

John asked, "Who are you, and how come you're hanging out back here?"

Taking a deep hit from what looked like a spliff, he seemed to relax, if only a little. "My name's Billy Tomlin. I came back for a few hits, saw your ride, and thought I'd take a look."

"Your name sounds familiar." John knew he'd heard it before.

"It should—you've been drinking at my old man's bar all afternoon."

"Frank's your dad?"

"Yeah. He's got me working in the back, and I'm supposed to keep things clean here in the parking lot too."

Aedan now walked directly up to him. Although they were about the same height, the weight difference had to be at least forty pounds. Billy took another step back.

"I'm Aedan, and this is John. We're students. Got time for a spin?"

Billy's eyes looked longingly at the expensive car, then back at Aedan. "Man, I'd love to, but my old man'd kill me. He's footing the bill for Stanford, so I work here whenever I can."

"You go *there?*" John was shocked at the possibility.

"Yeah. I guess I don't look like much, but I've got one of those eidetic memories. Nobody knows where it came from. My dad owns this bar, and Mom died when I was just a kid; go figure."

John looked at Aedan for assistance, who, on cue, asked, "You've got a photographic memory?"

"Eidetic. They're sorta different. Also, mostly it's in younger people before their minds get cluttered with language skills and accumulated memories. There isn't much on record of older people maintaining one. I guess I'm a freak."

Looking over at John, it was clear Aedan was curious about this Billy character. "Tell you what, Billy, we'll come back when you've got a few minutes and take my car for a ride. Maybe you can even drive it. What's tomorrow look like?"

"Well, it's Sunday, and we don't open until one, so any time before then is good."

"We'll be by around eleven. Does that work?"

Judging by the grin on Billy's face, John was sure it did.

"He's a different dude, eh?" John glanced over at Aedan as they drove back to his apartment.

"Yeah, but he seems harmless. It'll be interesting to see what he's like."

"I didn't think there was anyone with a true photographic memory. Thought it was just tricks and scams."

Aedan thought for a moment before answering. "That's what they say, but look at him. He sure as hell doesn't come across as someone with any brains."

"I suppose, but he *is* attending Stanford."

"So he says, but don't you think he's a little young for college?"

John considered this before answering. "I can't imagine why he'd lie about it. What's there to gain?"

"I guess we'll see tomorrow. Pick you up at ten-thirty?"

John shouted "Later" with a thumbs-up as he hopped out and headed for his 55-inch Samsung TV and more beers. There *had* to be another game on tonight.

The following day, John and Aedan found Billy Tomlin pacing back and forth in the now-empty rear parking lot behind Frank Tomlin's Bar. He appeared surprised when they pulled up. "I wasn't sure you were coming."

"We told you we would," Aedan answered.

"I know. It's just that lots of times people say stuff and don't mean it."

"Not us. Why don't you climb into the back? They're small seats, but you're not very big. We'll drive up through Skywood and then you can drive us back." The look on Tomlin's face was that of a kid with his first bike.

The three made small talk about the weather while meandering up Woodside Road to the upscale Skywood neighborhood. There were glimpses of the coast, the Stanford campus, and the entire peninsula from several viewpoints along the way. The temperature was in the low sixties and the sky a cloudless robin's-egg blue. Even though they were three first-year males, always prone to silliness and the potential for encounters with the opposite sex, they found that the confluence of nature's most attractive elements was worthy of quiet contemplation.

Eventually, Aedan pulled into a brick-paved turnaround to the side of an iron-gated drive lined with colossal laurel bushes. "Okay, Billy, your turn. The paddles on the side of the steering wheel are shifters; you'll get the feel of it."

Looking nervous and uncertain, the diminutive member of the trio unfolded himself from the back jump seat. "You're sure this is okay?"

"Yup. I'll get in the back. John, you're a little too long to fit in there. Just pull your seat up some."

At first, Billy was tentative, trying to get the feel of the sensitive shift paddles. The incredible power of the sports car made for numerous fits and starts, but eventually he got the hang of it and seemed to enjoy taking the twists and turns coming down the mountain. Traffic was light, but the switchbacks in the road limited his speed, which was okay with John, and Aedan seemed to agree.

They returned to Frank's with Billy still at the wheel, an ear-to-ear grin on his face. While he dismounted, Aedan unfolded himself from the back jump seat, and John immediately powered the seat back and stretched his legs.

"This has been the most fun I've had in a long time. Thanks for letting me drive."

"My pleasure, Billy. We've got to get going, but we'll be in touch." Aedan sat behind the wheel and chirped some rubber as he left the lot.

As they sped through the center of Menlo Park, John glanced at his friend behind the wheel. "He's a little quirky but seems okay in a sort of childish way."

"I guess we'd be a little fucked up too if we were saddled with a photographic memory while growing up."

"Eidetic."

"Whatever. You wanna invite him in?"

John looked surprised. "To the SSIT?"

"Yeah. It's not like we're busting at the seams."

"I thought we wanted people sorta like us. You know, from money and slightly annoying," John offered with a grin.

"I know what we said, but how about this? He appears to remember everything, whatever you call his gift, curse, or genius. Think about how he could help us by going to class while we screw off. We could even use him to help with assignments and shit."

"I see where you're going with this. I like it. I vote yes."

"It's unanimous, then. We can head back to Frank's for beers and a burger later and tell Billy."

When they returned to Frank's later that day, Billy was busy bussing and taking orders from the occupied half-dozen tables. Sunday evenings were light, necessitating only a cook, Frank behind the bar, a dishwasher, and Billy handling the chores up front.

"Can you sit for a minute?" John asked Billy as he approached to take their order.

With a hurried glance to ensure he wouldn't be missed immediately, he pulled out a chair and sat. "Hey, you guys, what's up? And thanks again for this morning."

"You're welcome. We wondered if you'd like to join our small fraternity. It's just the two of us right now." Aedan took the lead.

Billy looked shocked and didn't speak.

"You okay? If you don't want to, it's fine. We just thought, you know, we all get along, and we could hang together." John was beginning to have second thoughts.

"I'm good … I don't know what to say. Nobody has ever asked me to join anything or be their friend. And you two are the nicest people I've met since I started at Stanford."

"So is that a yes?"

"Hell, yes. Do I have to do anything?"

John turned his head at the question. "What do you mean, *do* anything?"

"You know, initiation, secret shit, stuff like that."

Both older men laughed at the same time. Billy looked embarrassed, and Aedan picked up on it. "Sorry. We only laughed because we don't do any of that. It's one of the reasons we dislike that whole Greek system scene. We want to hang out, have fun and not bother with secret handshakes and ass-paddles."

Billy looked relieved. "Whew, good. And yes, I would love to—"

"Billy." A shout came from behind the bar.

"Sorry guys, gotta get back to work. I'll give you my cell number, and you can let me know what's going on." He hurried to the kitchen to pick up an order.

As they watched their new addition hustle back to work, John seemed to speak for the two of them. "Well, the next few years should prove interesting—very interesting."

FIFTEEN

Walla Walla

We hadn't planned on finishing the entire bottle of syrah the previous evening. Still, the conversation was easy, and the warmth from the fireplace was a perfect companion to the silky-smooth potion produced by the award-winning Walla Walla winery.

Michelle left us a little after eleven, and we left our glasses where they were, brushed our teeth, and hit the sack. Based on previous encounters with the fruit of the vine, I expected to feel a bit fuzzy or at least a little headachy in the morning, but that was not the case. Maybe the stuff was so perfectly crafted that it avoided any possibility of a hangover; either that or, as I suspected, I was just lucky this time.

Per our host's suggestion, we met in the tasting room around nine a.m. to outline the activities for the day and the balance of our time at the winery. Michelle seemed to have nothing to hide and enthusiastically supported our efforts to understand the operation from the ground up.

"I've asked Evan to give you a tour of the vineyards. This time of year, there's not much happening, but at least you'll get a feel for the size of the property and the extent of our production capabilities. Don't be concerned if he's a little off-putting; you'll remember our conversation from last night."

Just as the words left her mouth, a blast of frigid air blew in as the eight-foot door to the tasting room was shoved open. At 5'6" and slightly built, the winemaker exuded confidence. A battered ball cap displaying the winery's "UC" logo did little to hide his weathered complexion, which could only have been earned through years in the vineyards. Piercing green eyes and a prominent nose grabbed my attention; his salt-and-pepper three-day-old growth did little to distract from the overall presentation. Although he was probably in his late forties, he could easily have been mistaken for someone a decade older.

Unlike the description given last night by Michelle, this person greeted us with a warm handshake and a welcoming smile. "You must be the O'Malleys. I'm Evan Davis. Michelle says you were friends with Butch. I'm sorry for what's happened. He was a great boss. I understand his son is taking over, and you two are here to get a feel for the operation. Do I have that right?"

If this guy was unhappy and sullen, he was doing a terrific job hiding it. "That about sums it up. Michelle said you'd be giving us a tour of the property." I glanced at my wife, who also had a questioning look.

"Well, let's get to it. It's still in the twenties outside, so I've left the truck running. We can cover most of the vineyards without freezing our asses off. Sorry, Jenne, vineyard talk." This last was offered with a self-deprecating smile.

"No worries, Evan. I've followed Kevin's bullshit long enough to become comfortable with most colloquialisms."

"Hey, you do know I'm standing here, right?"

All four of us laughed—Evan's maybe a bit too forced—as we left for our tour. As the last one out, I closed the door looking at the face of a perplexed Michelle Browne.

The day was clear and crisp; the high temperature was expected to be in the low forties. The crew cab of the Ford pickup was surprisingly tidy with no lingering nasty smells save for what could have been Mennen Skin Bracer. I sat in the back, allowing Jenne the comfort of the twelve-way adjustable seat, standard on this, the Lariat version of the F-150. My position also allowed me to study the winemaker's face and actions.

We left the parking area and proceeded up a gentle slope on a rutted two-track that served as the eastern border for most of the land owned by Uva Cellars. At only five miles per hour, the ruts were plentiful enough to jostle the three of us as we gazed upon endless rows of the dormant, skeletonized vines, the promise of clusters of ripe, juicy fruit still months and months away.

"This slope is home to the fruit for most of our finest estate wines. The first section is cabernet, the second is merlot, and the one coming up on our left is syrah."

"What about the rest of the acreage if this is where the best grapes come from?" Jenne's eyes widened at the military precision of row after row of the leafless vines, each spaced precisely six feet apart.

Evan, perhaps revealing a hint of arrogance, replied as if instructing a small child. "This is the best soil in the valley. The balance of our acreage is also planted in the same varietals, but those we use for blending and in our less expensive releases." The tiniest of smirks that only I could see reinforced his condescending attitude.

"What about the sangiovese you use in the cab/sangio blend? I thought that was the good stuff too." I noticed a few rapid blinks as if he was becoming aware that we weren't in first-grade reading class.

"Oh yeah, that's from the new acreage. The dirt there is very similar to this side of the property."

"Michelle said it could be as good as what you have here." I was curious how Evan would respond when Michelle's name came up.

"Jury's still out on that. Even if the soil is close, it's still an entirely different microclimate—different light exposure, breezes, small temperature fluctuations, and many variables to consider. Michelle spends most of her time inside, so she's less informed."

Jenne and I let the explanation hang there with no follow-up questions. After a minute or two of silence, our tour guide turned left to begin the loop back to the central cluster of buildings and continued his discourse. "The balance of the vineyards are duplicates of this section, only with slightly different soils, sun exposure, and the rest. I hear you'll be on site for a while, so if you need any other info or want to chat, look me up; I'll make myself available. I hope you enjoy the rest of your stay."

As Jenne and I exited the pickup and took the short cold walk to the tasting room, my wife spoke the words on the tip of my tongue.

"Geez, Kevin, he seemed to cut things short there, and am I ever glad he deigned to make himself available for us."

"Maybe he's an acquired taste, hon—either that or an eccentric perfectionist."

"Or … he's an asshole."

She had a way of cutting through the bullshit, one of her most endearing qualities.

"Yes, or that."

When we entered the tasting room, Michelle was behind the counter, concentrating on something on her laptop, and she looked up as we closed the door.

"Hey, you two, that didn't take long. How was the tour?"

I decided to say exactly what we thought. "It was, um, short. It appears that Evan is only friendly when he's directing the conversation. We asked him a few things; that was all it took for him to clam up. When we suggested that you thought highly of the vineyards on the newly acquired property, he seemed to lose interest in showing us anything."

With a grimace, she explained. "When the previous owner first hired him, Evan was friendly and much easier to be around. I think it was because she let him do whatever he wanted, and he didn't need to answer to anyone. He ignored me, and I was fine with it. Things stayed the same when Butch bought the winery until we won the platinum award. After that, he became insufferable. I talked to Butch about it, and he met with Evan to smooth things over. Since then, he's kept to himself mostly. I think Butch was going to let him go as soon as he could find a replacement for him."

Jenne looked at Michelle with sympathetic eyes. "It couldn't have been much fun working with him."

"Butch gave me free rein of the operations. He told him I was in charge and that he should keep out of my way if he wanted to stay. I'm certain Evan resented me for it, but he kept to the vineyards, and we had somewhat of an understanding. Now that Jason is the new owner, I expect he'll try to reassert himself."

"If it's any consolation, I think Jason is of much the same mind as his father." I would be sure to mention our impressions of the winemaker when we reported to Butch's son upon our return to the Seattle area.

"Did Evan take you into the cave?"

"Nope. He seemed to have other things to do." Jenne was still miffed at our abbreviated tour.

"Well, let's go take a look. I'm tired of updating our mailing list. It can wait."

We went back into the cold, clear late morning and took the tumbled concrete paver walkway several hundred yards around the hillside to two enormous barn doors that rose at least a dozen feet above us.

"The original owners cut away this side of the hill and reinforced what was left with concrete and rebar. The soils are not structurally sound enough, so the entire interior was also reinforced."

She entered a code in the keypad on the huge right-hand door and I immediately heard a barely audible click. "Help me push this, Kevin. I told Benny to lubricate those rollers, but he hasn't gotten to it yet."

We shoved the door aside just enough to allow the three of us to enter. The freezing outside temperature immediately gave way to a slightly humid mid-fifties—far more comfortable.

Michelle flicked on the light switch, revealing multiple racks of oak barrels lying on their sides. Most of them showed red wine stains at the site of the bunghole, and I assumed this was the result of topping off as well as barrel tastings and sampling to discern optimum aging time. There was a twelve-foot farmhouse table off to the left with several decanters and rows of Riedel wine glasses alongside.

"When we host guests or restauranteurs, we always bring them in for barrel tastings. I'm never sure how much anyone but a seasoned enologist can tell at such an early stage, but they seem to enjoy it."

Behind the racks of barrels was a newish-looking plywood wall with a curtained doorway off to the side.

"What's behind that plywood?" Jenne was interested.

"On the other side, we're working on enlarging the cave. We put up a temporary wall to keep the dust out during construction. It's tedious work because we need to dig a little and then shore up the roof and sides as we move ahead. Would you like to take a look?"

We nodded as we followed her through the plastic flaps separating the rooms. The lighting, nothing more than caged bulbs strung throughout, revealed a room almost the same size as the one we had vacated.

"It looks like you've made great progress. How much is left for you to do?"

"Evan started supervising the project, but midway through, he said he was too busy to continue, so I've been overseeing the construction. All the digging is complete; now we have to finish the concrete work on the last section. After that, we'll install the permanent lighting, bring the racks in, and then we should be ready when we need the space."

"This has to have cost a bundle."

"It has. We're a small community, and contractors are usually swamped. We were lucky to get the outfit that worked here ten years ago. A few bids were slightly lower, but Butch said to go with the person who did the original construction. I'm glad we did, too; George Hargreaves, the owner, talked us into opening up the hill's south side. This way, we can use the new opening to remove all the dirt without messing with the existing storage area. Once the new doors are built, we'll have another entrance to the cave."

"Won't that affect the temperature in here?" Jenne was always a step ahead.

"Very little. The new doors will only be eight-footers and well insulated. We'll still be able to maintain a constant fifty-five degrees."

If I hadn't been aware of Michelle's grasp of everything going on here at Uva, I certainly was now. Jason was fortunate indeed to have this woman running things at the winery.

We spent the next two days wandering the vineyards, observing additional bottlings, barrel-tasting several vintages, and acting like tourists. Michelle made herself available whenever we had questions, and

Evan made himself scarce. Now that we were pals with Michelle, he did his best to avoid us.

Since we planned to return home the following morning, Michelle agreed to join us for a farewell dinner. Perry prepared another feast, and we sampled more of Uva's best vintages.

Michelle looked introspective momentarily, then asked, "What will you tell Jason, if you don't mind me asking?"

I appreciated her directness and answered her honestly. "I'll tell him he's lucky to have you running this place. You appear to have a handle on everything, and, except for the conflict with Evan, he shouldn't worry about anything. From our short exposure, though, I think you'll be better off in the long run with a different winemaker. I *will* tell him that."

She looked relieved and then concerned. "Thank you, Kevin. I appreciate it, but I'm worried about Evan's reaction if and when we let him go. He has a bit of a mean streak that's popped up occasionally."

"I'll talk to Jason about it. I'm sure he'll handle it when the time comes. He seems to be a very capable individual. It's probably best to go about business as usual until Jason wants to make a move."

Sixteen

Stanford University

The SSIT never got beyond three members. Aedan and John were independent sorts, although Billy less so, and their personalities did not lend themselves to seeking out other potential candidates for their little fraternity.

John was content to let Billy attend the classes they had in common, which were most of them. He'd debrief Billy on the weekends—the kid remembered everything in minute detail—and then show up to take the exams. Aedan leaned more toward the investment side of things, real estate and the like, and shared fewer classes than his two fellow club members.

As bright as John was, he was also a tad on the lazy side. He drank more than his buddies and was totally dependent on Billy for his grades. When Google made Billy Tomlin an offer for employment after his second year, he couldn't pass it up. It started at $200K annually and included a $25K signing bonus. People with Billy's talent rarely came along, and Google recruited aggressively.

With his source for easy marks gone and Aedan increasingly wrapped up in his studies, John lost all interest in school. His contact with his parents was only enough to ensure the sustained funding of his education. Still, his lack of enthusiasm for continuing his studies was finally reflected in his grades, resulting in an unannounced visit from his father.

It was just shy of eleven a.m. when he heard a firm knock on his apartment door. He was still hung over from an evening of uninspired sex, copious amounts of alcohol, and several high-potency spliffs, and his place reeked of stale pizza and cheap perfume mixed with the penetrating, organic vegetative fragrance of marijuana. His hired sex worker from the previous evening had escaped just after midnight, the thought of spending the night too disgusting even for someone in her profession.

"*What?* If it's you, Aedan, I'm tired. Leave me alone."

"It's not Aedan; it's your father."

"*Shit.* Just a minute, Dad." He hurriedly threw some clothes on, attempted to hide the residue of the previous evening's indulgence, and finally opened the door.

Rather than enter his domicile, his father just stood there surveying the clutter and filth his son had managed to accumulate while pretending to attend the prestigious institution of higher learning.

"So this is what going to Stanford looks like."

"I can explain, Dad. We just had a little party last night." John's whiny effort sounded insufficient even to him.

"Do you know why I'm here?"

"If it's because of my grades, I can explain …"

"Not necessary, John. I got a call last week from a friend in the dean's office. We are one of the firms that manage the college's endowment fund, so I know these folks. Frankly, it's the main reason you ever got into this place.

"I'm done paying for you to piss away this opportunity. As of this moment, you're on your own. You've been suspended from Stanford because of your performance, so you'll either have to get a job or, if you'd like, you can live with me until you get back on your feet. In any case, you're done here. Let me know what you decide, and don't worry, your cell phone bills are still being paid." And with that, Butch Carlson turned and left.

Sitting on the edge of his tousled bed, still nursing a stage four hangover, John stared unfocused at the mess. He was fucked.

Later that afternoon, he reached Aedan on the phone and relayed the morning's events.

"Geez, dude, really bummed to hear about your situation, but I tried to tell you not to rely solely on Billy. What are you gonna do?"

"I've got another week here before the rent is due, so I guess I'll use the time to come up with something. What have you got going?"

"I'm spending the week at my dad's firm, and he's letting me intern there to learn the ropes. Lately we've spoken more than ever, and I'm getting to know him better. The business seems interesting, and I think I have a knack for it."

John felt a fleeting sense of resentment, but it passed. It looked like his fellow club members were deserting him. *Screw them*, he thought; he'd manage by himself. His elevated lifestyle was coming to an abrupt end, and while he had no idea what fortune held next for him, his misplaced sense of entitlement allowed little room for doubt.

When his lease was up, he piled his belongings into his three-year-old Ford Explorer and began looking for someplace to sleep. The ride wasn't as sexy as Aedan's Porsche, but at least he owned it, a gift from his parents when he departed for college.

He still had close to a thousand bucks after closing out the balance of his checking account, but he was well aware that it would soon be gone. He'd tried to reach Billy several times without success and was pleasantly surprised to see his name on his vibrating cell phone.

"Billy, what's the haps over at Google?"

"I know you called a few times, John, but things have been crazy here during the new product launch. Also, Aedan gave me a call and told me about your situation. Sorry to hear it."

Although he was surprised that Billy had spoken to Aedan first, at least he wouldn't have to suffer the indignity of retracing the circumstances resulting from his current predicament. "Well then, I guess you know I'm in a bind. The last place I want to go is back to Seattle to live with my dad. I was wondering if I could crash with you until I figure something out."

After an uncomfortable pause, Billy finally tossed him a lifeline. "My place isn't very big, and I'm busy most of the time, but you can bunk here until you know what you're gonna do."

Acknowledging the reluctance in Billy's voice, John nonetheless took the proffered assistance. His future was a blank page at this time, but at least he'd have a place to stay. He turned his vehicle around and started the short six-mile journey to Mountain View, the home of Google Headquarters.

A week went by, then two more. Billy had been right when he'd said he was busy. John had the small apartment to himself most of the time and spent days watching TV or surfing on his laptop.

John may have been lazy and sometimes insensitive, but he wasn't stupid. He had a knack for making friends but was surprised when those friends were disinclined to help him after it became apparent they were being used to get what he wanted. When Billy was home, he wasn't as friendly as John remembered.

After rising from another night on Billy's sofa, he decided to get some fresh air. He strolled to the nearest Starbucks, which meant the next corner in Mountain View, ordered a latte, and sat at an empty table.

He had had the foresight to bring his laptop and promptly opened it to his default browser. He skimmed a few articles and gradually noticed the place's hustle and bustle. Because of the proximity to Google Headquarters, everyone seemed to be his age or younger. They dressed similarly to his former Stanford classmates, but unlike his student associates, they moved with purpose. It was as if they had someplace to be and things to accomplish.

Looking through the window, he observed many youngsters arriving in expensive sports cars while brandishing the hottest new phones and smartwatches. If there was this much money to be made at Google, he might figure out some way to get his share. The thing was, he had no fucking idea about programming or anything remotely connected to the sciences.

He walked back to the apartment, considering then immediately discarding his options. He spent the rest of the day learning all he could about the company whose name had become a common verb. When Billy walked in the door at eight p.m., he was ready with questions.

"Billy, why did Google hire you when you didn't have a degree in computer science?" It was the first time John had asked his roommate anything that wasn't self-serving, and it seemed to take a few seconds before he responded.

"You remember that I have an eidetic memory, right?"

"Yeah, but that doesn't mean you know anything about computers."

"I don't—that is, I didn't. They have me going to various team meetings to observe and listen to all the presentations. After I've spent time with all the teams working on a specific product or algorithm, I sit down with the project managers and report what is happening. It seems easier for them that way."

"Do you understand what you're talking about?"

"Mostly. After a while, the stuff makes sense, especially if you remember everything you see and hear."

"I don't have a mind like yours, but everyone at Google can't be a computer wizard, right?"

"You're correct. Just most of them."

John's research led him to ask, "What is an account representative?"

"They interface between the product teams and the companies that use our products and services. They're basically salespeople."

"Do they know much about computer stuff?"

Billy smiled at this. "*Everyone* knows *something* about computer science, but most of them are business majors, and they pick up the knowledge as they become exposed to it."

"Is it something I could do?"

"I suppose so. I don't have much to do with those folks, since I'm on the development side."

"Do you know anyone there I might be able to talk to?"

Billy's mouth always scrunched up to the side when he was thinking. "Let me ask around tomorrow. I have some meetings with some higher-ups. Maybe they'll know who you should talk to."

"Thanks a million, Billy. I appreciate it." As he walked to his room, Billy appeared slightly more upbeat than he had been before. John hated to admit it, but the prospect of having his place to himself was most likely the reason. *Like I give a shit. Maybe he'll be motivated to find me a job.*

Inspired by having his own place again, Billy sought out the HR person in charge of hiring the account reps the following day. Because of his unique talent, he'd become somewhat of a celebrity around the campus, and all but the newest hires were in awe of him. Getting an appointment was easy, at least for him, and getting his friend hired was even easier. Doing a favor for one of the more celebrated associates could never hurt.

John's interview was a mere formality; by the next week, he was going through the new hire indoctrination. It was less than two weeks before he had his own place. When a landlord heard someone worked for Google, credit checks were unnecessary.

Even though his scholastic trajectory at Stanford was less than admirable, judging John Carlson by that chapter in his life would be a mistake. With money as his prime incentive, he managed to charm the pants off anyone and everyone. From his superiors to his customers, they all loved him. By tucking away his resentment for his father and pushing the petty jealousy aimed at his brother into the far recesses of his mind, he could concentrate his talents on rapid success.

He was promoted twice in a matter of months, and by the end of his first year, he had become a team leader. Unlike many of the younger associates at Google, John eschewed the latest sports cars and preferred to drive his Ford SUV while fortifying his bank account with every cent he earned. Even his generous bonuses went directly into his savings. In moments of surprising clarity, he mused that some of his father's talent for finance must have somehow found a way into his psyche. By the end of year five, he'd amassed over a million dollars, which was the first step in his strategy.

Such was his focus on acquiring wealth, he rarely dated, and even then, it was never the same woman twice. He was still friendly with Billy when they crossed paths on campus, but they hadn't gotten together since he'd moved into his own place. He made a point of staying in touch with Aedan, who, after graduation, had gone to work in his father's firm. John's only break from work was to visit Aedan in Santa Barbara after his friend's graduation and subsequent decision to work for his father. It was then that John's aspirations began to take form.

SEVENTEEN

Whidbey Island

We live on a 200-foot-high bluff on Whidbey Island. Overlooking the Saratoga Passage with the Cascade Mountains in the distance, it's a peaceful place that we've chosen for our retirement residence. Our property includes the beach, which we can only access by driving down a steep switchback of a road reminiscent of the famous Lombard Street in San Francisco; we do it frequently in the summer, only sporadically in the winter, when the weather permits—which is rarely, in the environs of Puget Sound.

Today was iffy; still raining, but only a drizzle. The tide was out, providing sufficient beach for us to take Emma for a stroll. Beneath the high bluff, the recent late-November storm had deposited all manner of driftwood in every possible size and shape.

Down here, with no homes in sight and only the gentle lapping of the Salish Sea to invade our auditory senses, it was as if we were wearing noise-canceling headphones. Jenne and I were content to experience the quietude as we allowed Emma to run and splash through the shallow tidal areas before galloping up the beach to smell dead crabs, decaying seaweed, and many other tidbits too numerous or disgusting to name.

We had returned from our Walla Walla journey the previous week and still needed to give our full report to Jason. As executor of his father's will, he spent all day with attorneys, bankers, and representatives from Butch's firm. After a brief phone call, we agreed to meet this upcoming Wednesday. His newly acquired real estate portfolio and investments were forcing him to spend more time in Washington than initially planned.

For a moment or two, both of us were lost in our memories stirred by the salty breeze of the sea, and we forgot about our canine companion. Then we heard her barking—the kind of bark that says she's either afraid or anxious or pissed off. I'm never sure what the subtle differences are, but the sound always gets my attention.

"Where is she, Kevin?"

"She must be ahead. We would have seen her if she'd gone the other way." We were about a half-mile from the road that had taken us to the beach, right where there was a small inlet beneath the bluff where we lived. The portion of the beach belonging to our property was coming into sight as we jogged up to the small cove.

"What the fu—?"

"I can see it, Kevin. It's a boat washed up against the driftwood piles."

"Emma, hey, Emma, come here." She finally stopped barking and trotted over to us. Now that her pack was together again, she relaxed.

"Yeah, I guess. Let's take a look."

As Emma sat, keeping a watchful eye on the proceedings, Jenne and I circled the small cabin cruiser. It was three minutes before my wife offered her opinion of the craft.

"Man, what a piece of shit."

Did I tell you that, while usually easygoing and non-judgmental, she occasionally reverts to her previously demanding executive experience and delivers a succinct and immediate assessment?

"Um … I'm inclined to agree with you, hon. Let's see if we can look inside."

"You can do that if you want. I'm staying with Emma. No telling what might be in there."

"Really? You mean to tell me you're gonna let your husband, he of sixty years on this planet, climb up on this ratty old boat by himself?"

"If my idiot husband wants to risk his health by venturing onto a crappy old derelict boat, he deserves what happens to him."

"Did you say idiot husband?"

"Uh-huh. If he climbs on that boat, he is."

When she says shit like this, it makes me think twice about what I'm doing. Still, I thought information could be gained, so I continued the climb. "I'm going up there to see if I can find out who owns this thing."

"Judging by the looks of it, the owners are better off without it. It's a junker, and you're still an idiot."

Ignoring my wife's slanderous insults, I got a foot on the back platform, then hoisted myself up to the aft railing. When I could finally see the rear salon and peer into the cuddy cabin, I had to admit her instincts were on the money. I climbed over the railing, stepped on a dozen empty beer cans, and peered into the small cabin below.

The temperature was probably forty-five degrees, and the light was beginning to recede at four in the afternoon in late November. Still, I could make out several items scattered about the dirty, malodorous lower level. Along with the aromas of beer, seawater, and rotting food, I could make out numerous bottles, old clothes, garbage, and a Converse high-top sneaker. A nastier smell made its way into my olfactory nerve—one I'd only experienced in the vicinity of roadkill or the occasional dead rat.

Still hoping for something to tell me the vessel's origin, I asked my bride if she could pass me up one of the hundreds of bleached sticks piled amongst the driftwood.

"I'll do it if you promise to hurry up. It's getting dark and cold, and Emma's hungry. Me too."

I was starting to get the feeling Jenne would rather I wasn't investigating. "I promise. Just hand me something I can reach in the cabin with and I'll be done."

I was handed either a six-foot gnarled root or a white petrified snake and used it to shove around the items on the floor of the lower deck. There was nothing to provide any helpful information, and with a final flick of the wrist, I whacked the sneaker aside.

It didn't move, and its weight caused the skinny stick to crack. I thought it odd, so I carefully hooked a small knot on the end of the root on the top of the shoe and was able to flip it up so I could look inside. Dozens of tiny crabs scurried out of the opening. In their absence, a shiny white bone protruded. I could only imagine what filled the rest of the sneaker.

"Kevin! You okay?"

I thought it odd that she would ask me precisely at this time if I was okay. "Yeah, why?"

"Because you yelled something like you were startled."

"I did?"

"Cut the shit, Kevin. What's going on?"

Instead of answering her, I hopped down onto the sand, grabbed her by the elbow, and led her and Emma away from the sad-looking Chris Craft. I turned for one last look and noticed the name on the transom. It said *Island Hunter*.

Eighteen

Whidbey Island

"What did Roger say when you told him about the boat?" Jenne was still disturbed since learning of my finding a foot. Me too.

I'd called Deputy Roger Wilkie of the Island County Sheriff's Department when we'd got home. We knew him from a previous encounter with some sketchy characters. It had taken him an hour or so to get back to us, and I'd just hung up from our conversation.

"He said a few derelict boats a year get reported washing up on shore, but they're usually small tenders or skiffs."

"Do many of them have body parts scattered around?"

"He asked if I could have been mistaken—you know, because the light wasn't great and I didn't get that close to it. Maybe he thinks I just saw something that *looked* like a foot."

"What's he going to do?"

"He said he couldn't get there tonight because of the high tide and the darkness, but he'd be out first thing tomorrow. The tide will be out then too, and we can walk to the boat."

Jenne's hazel eyes rolled up to the ceiling, seemingly trying to see the situation from the deputy's point of view but obviously failing. "You'd think if someone saw a human foot lying about, it might suggest a greater sense of urgency."

"Yes, but remember, Whidbey is an island, and the deputies are scattered everywhere. Plus, as you know, there are some quirky folks, and I imagine the cops get more than their share of crank calls." I thought I would have done the same thing if I were Wilkie. Because of the tide, he'd have had to get a police launch over to the site in the pitch-black night. The prospects seemed mighty risky with a limited upside. The *Island Hunter* would still be there in the morning.

Rather than share my thoughts, I opted for a safer response. "How about a nice glass of chardonnay, some smoked salmon, and that Irish cheddar you like? Ya think that will take your mind off things?"

"You always know how to treat a lady, Kev."

"Does that mean later on we'll get to do other things to take our mind off this nasty business?"

She showed that dazzling smile that I loved, leading me to think she knew what I was thinking.

The following morning, amid discussions that alternated between Uva Cellars and our new yacht, Deputy Wilkie knocked on the door just before sunrise. In this neck of the woods, in late November, that meant a little after seven.

"Hey, Kevin, good to see you again, even if it is under unusual circumstances. Let's get down there early while the tide is still out."

"Good idea. I'll grab a coat."

We took the curvy road down the bluff and parked opposite the community boat ramp. The walk to the boat was about as long as a healthy par five, and we arrived in fifteen minutes or so. The effects of the tidal action had turned the boat almost forty-five degrees but nowhere near enough to dislodge it from the sandy shore.

We both stopped when we were about ten feet from the *Island Hunter*. The sound of the gentle lapping of the waters of the Saratoga Passage was frequently pierced by a pair of nesting eagles high above, repairing their home in the boughs of a 200-year-old Doug fir nearly halfway up the cliff.

"If you don't mind, Roger, I'll let you do the honors. One look at that thing was enough for me." With a resigned sigh, the deputy hoisted his well-toned six-foot thirty-something physique up and over the transom in seconds. "When I was up there yesterday, the thing was at the bottom of the stairs, a little to the left. The lower level was so messy that I didn't want to go down there. Now I'm *really* glad I didn't."

While talking, I could hear Wilkie descending the five steps leading to the small cabin. "What a shitshow this is down here. Smells too."

"I tried to tell you."

"Where did you say it was? I can't see any— *whoa!*"

"I'm guessing you found something other than a beer can."

"Yup, you got that right. I'll be right out. We'll need to get this thing cordoned off. It's now a crime scene."

He reappeared on deck, looking noticeably paler, even in the early morning light, and quickly hopped down onto the sand. "Can't say as I've come across anything like that before and would rather not again. We'll need to get the state cops involved. They've got way more resources when it comes to crime scene techs and investigators. Would you do me a favor and stay here for a few minutes? Radio reception is nonexistent down here, and I need to put the word out. I'll be back as soon as I contact the powers that be."

He obviously saw the angst on my Irish face, because he continued, "Don't worry, I won't be very long, and this time of year, I'd be surprised if you see anyone. That foot isn't gonna hurt you either." This last was delivered with a mischievous grin.

"Geez, thanks, Roger. Your reassurance is calming." Ignoring me, he turned and jogged off down the beach back to his cruiser.

The sky was overcast, so although the level of daylight was improving, the only colors were shades of gray—medium gray sky, dark gray water, and light gray beach. I sat on one of the huge bleached logs that served as the foundational buffer for these bluffs fronting the sea. As the dampness seeped in, I tightened my Carhartt jacket and waited.

The beach was deserted here at the base of the bluffs and towards the north, where fifty or sixty summer homes were a stone's throw from the water. Even the chattering of the eagles had quieted, and now only the muted slosh of the Salish Sea could be heard.

While pondering the provenance of the derelict boat in front of me and the portion of its occupant that remained, I noticed a small eruption of sand several feet before me. Then another a foot closer, followed by another even closer. I couldn't imagine what insect or animal could cause that, but the sharp crack of the log on which I was sitting instantly convinced me that this was no act of nature … someone was shooting at me!

As fast as my rusty reflexes could react, I hurried closer to the high bank where more logs and driftwood stumps had piled up. I got as low as possible, and my thumping heart began to settle a bit. Since I hadn't heard even a whisper of a rifle, I assumed the shooting was from somewhere high above, where, if a rifle were silenced, no sound would carry to the beach. I was mildly pissed off that Wilkie had left me here, but the feeling took a back seat to my fear.

The stump I had chosen for cover was ginormous. During its lifetime, it must have seen the passing of hundreds of years—possibly a thousand. Some of these northwest giants had lived centuries before the Europeans invaded the place and stood silently while various cultures engaged in numerous conflicts in the name of morals, money, and religion. At least now, as it rested in petrification on the shores of the Salish Sea, it served as my salvation.

My ruminations on history and life must have taken more time than I realized, because I now heard the faint sound of Roger Wilkie yelling my name.

"Over here."

"The state boys will be here shortly to take over. What the hell are you doing hiding behind that old stump?"

"Someone started shooting at me, and I took cover."

"*What?*"

"I was sitting on that log"—I nodded toward my earlier position—"when someone began shooting at me. It must have come from above, since I never heard the shots."

Wilkie looked at me with what appeared to be patronizing concern. "Are you sure, Kevin? How did you know someone was shooting if you couldn't hear anything?"

"I saw where the bullets were hitting the sand. They made little *phtt* sounds when they hit."

"You do know that there's all kinds of insect life down here? Maybe you were mistaken."

Never famous for my patience, especially when I felt I was being treated like a doddering old fool, I let him have it. "Listen, Roger, I'm well aware of the little, teeny beings that exist on the beach, and I damn sure know what a fucking bullet strike looks like after spending several years in the army. Maybe look at the log where I was sitting and see if that gash sways your thinking."

Now, appearing slightly contrite, he ambled over, took a look, then turned back to me. "Geez, Kev, looks like someone was shooting at you."

"Told ya."

NINETEEN

Whidbey Island

The rest of the morning was a blur. The state police took over, and Wilkie returned to taking care of less pressing issues on the island. Detective Tom Wenzal of the Washington State Police, wearing jeans and a leather bomber jacket, arrived on the scene, relieving Deputy Wilkie.

"Roger tells me someone was taking potshots at you." Without preamble, he addressed me. Wenzal appeared to be in his mid-forties, of shortish stature, about five-nine. His closely cut hair, at least what I could see, was graying at the sides, and whatever was on top was concealed by a Mariners ball cap. He had a weathered face, deeply tanned. His milky blue eyes were the only exception to his remaining facial features, which were average in every way.

I know cops are just doing their job, and most have overwhelming workloads, but, dammit, that's no excuse for less-than-acceptable social discourse. "Hi. My name is Kevin O'Malley. Nice to make your acquaintance."

I wasn't sure what to expect after my blunt response to his direct assault, but it wasn't what I got.

He removed his cap and ran his fingers through spiky brown hair cut very short. "I'm sorry, Mr. O'Malley. Please excuse me. I've been up all night, and then just when I was headed home, I was told to get my ass on the next ferry to Whidbey Island. Let me start over.

"Hi, Mr. O'Malley. I'm Tom Wenzal from the Washington State Patrol. I'm sorry you had to experience this trauma, but we're taking over here, and I have some questions for you. There, that better?" This was asked with a forced grin and itty-bitty smile lines crinkling the corners of those blue eyes.

"You know, Detective, if I didn't know any better, I might think that was an attempt at sarcasm."

"No sir, no sir … that *was* sarcasm, not just an attempt. Now, will we do this dance all day or can we sit and talk? Besides, we've only got another two hours before the tide is in too far to stay here."

He was beginning to grow on me a little. "Call me Kevin. What do you want to know?"

"Can you tell me what happened from when you discovered the boat until now?"

I rehashed everything that had happened since the previous afternoon and concluded by showing him the bullet damage to the log I'd been sitting on.

"You'd never seen the boat before?"

"Nope."

"And no idea why someone would be trying to kill you?"

"Kill me? What?"

"You do understand, Kevin, when bullets are fired at you, they are intended to end your life."

I had just reacted to getting shot at and not even considered that someone wanted me dead. "Could they have just been trying to scare me away?"

"Possibly, but why use a silenced rifle if you're saying is true? It seems like a big noise would help to do the scaring."

I thought about this for a moment and then developed an overwhelming need to return home to my wife and dog. "You're right, of course, Detective. Are we finished here?"

"We are. It wasn't my intention to rattle you, but it's something to consider. We'll do as much as we can here before the tide is in, and then we'll see if we can tow the boat back to Everett to do more forensic work. With it gone, maybe whoever shot at you will disappear. I'll get back to you if we have any more questions, but just to be safe, stay alert."

"Thanks, Detective."

"It's Tom, and Kevin …?"

"Yeah?"

"Don't worry too much. Whoever took those shots at you was probably too far away to know who you are, and they probably *were* trying to scare you. Still, it's a puzzler. Anyway, I'll let you know when we find out something."

"Thanks, Tom."

Since my ride was gone, I trudged up the hill back to our home at the top of the bluff. I was certain Jenne would be anxious over the several hours I'd been down at the beach; cell service at the bottom of the bluff was virtually nonexistent.

"So, let's see if I've got this straight. You and Roger went down to the boat, and he saw the foot. Then he left you, a civilian, in charge of things while he left to get the state cops. Then, while you were waiting, you, a civilian, get shot at and have to hide out till the posse arrives. Then you have to walk back here while maybe, just maybe, someone wants you dead. Does that sound about right?"

After I'd relayed the morning's activities to Jenne, my wife seemed to be looking at things slightly differently than me. "When you put it like that, I feel like a victim."

"That's because you are."

"What's with all this 'civilian' thing?"

"Roger shouldn't have left you alone. You could have been killed."

I could see she was a little shaken by my near-death experience. "It didn't seem like a big deal. The place was deserted—except for the foot, of course—and Wilkie had no way of knowing that someone would shoot at me. Besides, that Wenzal cop from the state police said they were probably trying to frighten me away."

"Still, Kevin, it scares *me*."

As she said this, the waterworks commenced, and I rushed to hug her. "Hey, c'mon, hon. I promise never to discover any more feet."

That was the thing about our relationship; there was never anything so serious that it couldn't be made fun of. Of course, there were always consequences. "Shut up, asshole, and don't ever do that again or I'll kill you."

I knew better than to point out her faulty reasoning, so I just stood there hugging her for a few seconds longer. Emma, sitting quietly taking all this in, trotted over and attempted to get in the middle for a group hug.

"Promise me you won't go anywhere without Emma for a while."

Even though she was getting on in years, the ninety-pound Shepherd was still a serious deterrent. "You have my word."

Twenty

Bellevue

The following day was Wednesday, and I agreed to meet Jason for lunch at Bis on Main, conveniently located on Main Street in Bellevue. The small but elegant eatery was a favorite of the locals, and there were rarely any empty tables. Although happy to join us, Jenne seemed to think meeting up with Shelly Owens for some Nordstrom therapy was the better option.

I had yet to let Bill know the details of the shooting from the day before, but I was planning to stop by his office after lunch. I was certain Jenne would share the happenings with Shelly, and I thought it prudent to let him know what had happened, or he'd kill me.

Sitting at a table by the window, Jason seemed pensive and started a bit when I pulled out the chair.

"Sorry, Jason. Didn't mean to surprise you."

"Hey, Kevin, no worries. Just thinking about my dad and how I didn't know him as well as I would have liked. I guess many folks feel that way when a parent dies."

"Probably more do than don't. I remember when my father died, I was out of town on a project. There was a message with the job super to call home as soon as I could. Jenne told me over the phone, and the entire plane ride back to the East Coast, I thought the same thoughts you are now."

"Has time given you any perspective?" Jason seemed genuinely interested in my opinion.

"I think so. I was so wrapped up in the business that I had little time for other thoughts. I wasn't one of the lucky sons who lived near

"

his dad and got to go to ball games and fishing together as adults. When he died, I felt sad for having missed what most perceive as the perfect father-son relationship.

"I've got more than a few brothers and sisters, so my folks had their hands full with them after I moved away. I understood that he was doing his best as a provider and father, and we were both living our lives as best *we* could without giving it much conscious thought. That doesn't mean I don't still think about those images, but I've realized we both loved each other, I can't change the past, and I'll cherish the good times we had when I was a youngster. That's all I've got, and whenever I think of my dad, I go back to my younger days and revisit them. That seems to work for me."

Jason was quiet for a few seconds, then looked up. "Thanks, Kevin. I can see why my dad liked you. I'll get through this, and when I come out the other side, I'll think about how you handled things. Hopefully it'll work for me too.

"Now, tell me about your trip to Uva."

"We had a great time. First the good news. Michelle is a peach. She's smart, a good manager, and great with the employees and customers. Jenne also loved her. If we still owned a business, we would be thrilled to have her running things. Everything seems to be operating smoothly. The new addition to the barrel storage area is almost finished, and the vineyards are ready for the new growing season."

"Did you say first the *good* news?" Jason didn't miss a beat.

"I did."

"So there's bad news?"

"Not terrible news, but both of us—and I think Michelle too—have concerns about your winemaker, Evan."

"Isn't he the one who produced the platinum cab?"

"He was there at the time, but we think serendipity played a role in that. It was a fabulous harvest, and you have some of the best soil in the country. Yes, he's talented, but he's a poor manager and terrible with customers. If you could keep him isolated in a cave, maybe he'd be okay. But he needs to be able to direct the vineyard workers and meet with customers and publishers. He's awful at it."

"And Michelle thinks so too?" Jason's boyish face showed a hint of concern.

"Yes. Jenne and I think you could lose Michelle if you keep him on much longer. That would be a real problem."

"Do you think he'd be difficult to replace?"

"I don't know much about the people in the industry, but from where I sit, I think Uva's reputation alone would be more than enough to attract winemakers with exceptional talent. You'd have to let Evan go first, I would think, before you could solicit candidates."

"That makes sense. And you're sure about Michelle?"

"She's gold. I bet she could even vet candidates for you. You're very lucky to have her."

What had been a look of concern slowly changed to one of relief. "I can't thank you enough. As soon as I square some of these legal things, I'll get down to Uva and begin to smooth things out there. I'll call Michelle and let her know we've chatted."

"Make sure to say we gave her a glowing report."

With the first genuine smile of the day, he replied, "No worries. I'm all over that."

"What!"

I had just filled in my buddy—Bill Owens, chief of detectives for Bellevue—on the previous day's events. He was equally furious with me, for some reason, and happy that I was still alive … I think.

"Why the fuck didn't you call me yesterday?"

"Well, mostly because that state guy, Wenzal, was handling things, and I know how pissy you get if I don't go through the proper channels." I was sure I had him here, since he always gave me shit about appropriateness.

At times like this, his soulful eyes, in a face produced by a Native American mother and an African American father, seemed to perform a mind-meld with whoever he was speaking to. It was why he was forever underestimated and interrogations always seemed to tilt in his favor. Even as his closest friend, he gave me the willies when he looked at me like that.

"Okay, okay, yes, I should've called you. Sorry."

With a deep sigh, he calmed down a bit. "Kevin, I'm your friend *and* a cop, and I want to know when the shit hits the fan, especially where you or Jenne are concerned. Who else is gonna bail you out when you get in over your head? Which you most certainly will." The last was delivered more with a smile than a frown. "I know Tom Wenzal. He's a good cop. I'll get in touch with him and see what I can find out. Meanwhile, take your wife's advice and don't take stupid chances. Keep Emma with you—and Kevin, if you don't tell me about stuff like this from now on, I'll kick your ass back to Whidbey Island."

Twenty-One

Santa Barbara

John Carlson spent the next six years at Google. If not well-liked by his peers, he was tolerated, and often well-respected by his superiors. He managed to salt away a small fortune, at least if judged by the dwindling middle class in America.

During this period, his brother, Jason, attended and graduated from the University of Washington while his father continued to make large sums of money doing whatever he did at his hedge fund. Of course, John was only subliminally aware of these events because he either saw them on Facebook or gleaned them from notes written in the greeting cards he received from his family on his birthday and at Christmas. At no time did he consider attempting to communicate with them, even at the urging of his mother, who had become somewhat of a recluse since her divorce.

He hadn't forgiven his father for cutting off his funds while at Stanford, and for no logical reason, his envy of his brother continued to flourish. Although not precisely defined, a plan for retribution had begun to emerge from the darker recesses of his mind. A well-adjusted individual might have moved on with his life, content to let the whims of fate and karma rule the day, but not John. Perhaps a flawed conscience or maybe just an additional dose of nastiness, whatever the cause, produced an emotional yet calculated response to his father's and brother's perceived slight for the egregious act of being firstborn.

Upon the completion of his fifth year at Google, he resigned. He had maintained a relationship with Aedan, who was now fully ensconced in his father's Santa Barbara firm and had taken to investments like a duck to water. During his final six months in Mountain View, John's corre-spondence with his college friend had seen an intentional uptick. With luck and Aedan's investment savvy, his small fortune could become much larger. And it did.

After a dozen or so years with nothing to do but hang out at the Santa Barbara beaches and bars, John's nest egg had grown from a measly million dollars to almost five million. There were sketchy invest-ments that failed, of course, but Aedan knew what he was doing on balance, and John trusted him enough not to doubt his advice.

With time on his hands and money in his pocket, the potential for coming to grips with his irrational animosity toward his brother and father was always within reach. Alas, John chose a darker path rather than finding a way to a civil relationship with his family. During this time his brother had moved to Denver, his mom had passed away, and his father had continued his inexorable march to becoming one of the one-percenters. Even the passing of his mother couldn't compel him to reach out to his remaining family. Instead, he blamed them for his loneliness while his resentment towards them multiplied.

Both Jason and his father had attempted to reach out to mend fences with zero success and finally given up. The last contact either had had with him was shortly after his mother died, but that was years ago.

One late Wednesday evening, John sat by himself, nursing an IPA from one of the local Santa Barbara breweries. His rented bungalow on the west side of Alameda Padre Serra was within walking distance of the El Encanto Hotel. Its small but tastefully elegant bar had become a frequent stop before he turned in for the night.

His expanding fortune gave him the freedom to do anything at any time, but he was growing weary of this tedious way of life. Midweek at the hotel was quiet, and John looked up as a slender, outdoorsy-looking fellow took up a seat four stools away. Being the only two patrons, a nod towards each other seemed appropriate, and both men complied.

After the bartender had supplied the glass of house cabernet requested by the new arrival, she stepped into the back area momentarily.

John was used to solitude, but some conflicted vibe emanating from the new arrival triggered an awkward atmosphere.

Although somewhat out of character, John broke the silence, "This your first time here?" Peering out from under a Santa Ynez Valley ball cap, the newcomer's green eyes initially startled him.

"Been here a few times and always liked the place. Right now, though, it's a bit depressing."

John regretted striking up a conversation with the fellow, but he couldn't help himself. He waited a few seconds longer before asking, "I don't know. It was a beautiful day today, and we're sitting in this lovely hotel. What's depressing about it?" As soon as the words left his lips, he regretted it.

"What's depressing is that I just met with my boss. He canned me."

Just then, the bartender came around the corner. Her smile did little to dispel the pall in the air, but John was thankful for the distraction.

"Another one?" she asked with a pleasant smile.

Before John could answer, Green Eyes said, "Put his on my tab and bring me another as well."

"That's not necessary." John was slightly uneasy about the stranger's offering, but his curiosity won the day.

"I know it's not, but it seems I've dampened the mood, and I'd like to make up for it."

While the bartender delivered their drinks, the stranger moved closer to John's perch. He reached a hand across the open stool, "Name's Evan—Evan Davis. Sorry about disturbing your solitude."

Over the last half-dozen years, John had made it a point not to form bonds with anyone. Other than Aedan, he spent all his time alone. There were the occasional dalliances with members of the opposite sex, of course, but when a woman showed interest in more than a one- or two-night stand, he flatly rejected the idea. Although his plans for retribution for the spurious slights imposed upon him by his remaining family members were still unclear, he was driven to accomplish *something* to salve his fragile ego.

He hesitated to engage with the stranger, but it was impossible to refuse the proffered hand. "I'm John Carlson. Thanks for the drink, but I should be buying yours. Didn't you say you just got fired?"

"I did, but that doesn't mean I'm broke. In my line of work, you tend to stash away money to take you through the next time you're terminated. I guess it's a fickle profession."

John's curiosity piqued, he asked, "Okay, I'll bite. What do you do that makes it seem likely that you'll eventually be fired?"

"I make wine."

John had consumed copious amounts of wine but never thought much about how it was made. "Huh?"

"I'm a winemaker, and I've worked for a few of the more famous places up in Napa and Sonoma and then moved to SBV a few years ago. I finally whipped that place into shape, and the owner thanked me by canning me."

"I've heard of them. Don't they make some pretty expensive pinot noir?"

"They do, and they've got me to thank for it."

"Then how come they shot you?"

"Some bitch in the tasting room was complaining that our stuff wasn't nearly as good as Sanford, one of the neighboring wineries, and I guess I lost my shit. Told her if she didn't like it, she could get the fuck out of *my* tasting room."

John thought that the winery owner had a point when he fired Evan. He suggested, "Um, not to pick sides here, but it kinda seems like an overreaction on your part, doesn't it?"

His new acquaintance, nose flaring and eyes glaring, stared at him for an awkwardly long time. Then he sighed, and his face seemed to deflate. "Yeah, I guess. It's just that the wine is personal to me. When somebody shits on it, it pisses me off, and I can't control it. It's probably why I've bounced around some."

Surprised at the fellow's honesty, John attempted a play at empathy. "I can see how you could take it personally. What are the employment prospects in the area?"

"This time of year, it's not great. We're into the crush, so anyone looking for a winemaker already has one. The good news is that I can find a lower-level job anywhere to tide me over. I'll be fine."

At this, John finished the last of his beer, stood up, and slapped Evan on the back. "It was nice meeting you, and thanks for the beer. I hope you find something quickly." He walked purposefully to the door, thinking he'd seen the last of Evan Davis.

Twenty-Two

Whidbey Island

The open house at the golf club had been held the previous week, and, as expected, the turnout was immense.

The search for the black Denali pickup had provided no tangible leads. In the four weeks since Butch's death, over five hundred vehicles within a hundred-mile range had been inspected. Every truck dealer and body shop had been alerted to be on the lookout for such a truck, with no success.

I was sitting on the sofa, with my wife at the opposite end, relating my just-finished phone call with Bill Owens. "There was even a suggestion that the witness might have been mistaken and it *was* just an accident—that maybe the truck didn't know what happened."

"What do you think?"

"Geez, I don't know. The pass can be treacherous there, especially during a snowstorm. Still, Bill says the Montgomery woman was certain the pickup intentionally ran into the Tesla."

"What happens next? And what about that person shooting at you?"

"As far as I know, they'll keep looking for the truck. Bill talked to Wenzal—he knows him, by the way—but he didn't have much to offer. He said they checked the bluff but didn't know if they'd found anything. They confirmed the marks on the stump were from bullets, so at least they know I wasn't making stuff up."

"And the foot thingy?"

"Bupkes. Yes, it was a foot, but it's been there so long and it's so degraded that they're having trouble dating the thing. They've taken DNA from it, so at least they have something."

"You'd think they could figure it out if they saw someone hopping around on one leg."

I knew better than to goad her when sarcasm was her tool of choice, so I let that one slide. "Also, Detective Houser has figured out how whoever broke into Butch's place managed to turn off the CCTV cameras."

"And you're going to tell me?"

"Um, yes, dear, I was about to. They found a way to log into the building's wireless LAN, which controls the cameras, and shut them down."

"So a past employee, then?"

"They figure it had to be. Thing is, a facility the size of Bellevue Towers has a fairly high turnover rate, so there's a significant number of folks to check out. To compound matters, they haven't changed the password on the thing since the day they set it up. May as well have published it in the *Seattle Times*."

"Let me see if I've got this straight—no progress on the Carlson crash, too many people to check out on the break-in, no idea on the foot in the boat, and no fucking idea who was shooting at you. Have I missed anything?"

I thought something could have fallen through the cracks, but I also knew better than to do anything but agree with my lovely, although at this point slightly riled-up, wife. "I think you've nailed it, Jenne. How about those M's?" It seemed to me this was an excellent time to use the lamentation of all the wanting Mariner fans in the northwest.

"Kev-*in*?"

I could have been mistaken about using the M's line. "Um, yes, hon?"

"Aren't you just a little pissed off about the progress on some of these things?"

I was, but I also knew Bill was doing his best on his end, and whoever this Wenzal was was also solid, according to Bill. "I'm frustrated too, but you know how seriously Bill takes his job. He's busting his ass on this because it's personal to him. I'm certain he'll figure it out. We need to cut him some slack. As for the foot, I got nothing. I'm gonna do a little research of my own on that. He did say they traced the boat back to a couple of brothers up on Vancouver Island, and they're checking them out."

My explanation must have made sense to my wife, because she seemed to settle down. "I'm sorry. I know that about Bill. He's aces. I'm just still nervous about you getting shot at."

"If it's any consolation, nothing has happened since, and it's not like I've been in seclusion. Maybe it was just some asshole playing games."

She didn't look like she bought this, but she seemed to choose to accept it. "I still want you to be careful."

This was the time for a hug, and I willingly complied using the famous quote from "The Great One"—that's Jackie Gleason for the youngsters out there. "Baby, you're the greatest." I meant it too.

After a suitable snuggling period, Jenne got serious again. "So, what's next? How can we help Bill with this?"

I should have said that Bill would rather we *didn't* help. What I *said* was, "Why don't we spend a few days off island? We can check in with some of Butch's buddies at the golf club and see if anything turns up. I'd also like to follow up with Jason and see how he's making out on his trip to Uva."

"I'll pack some things. You call Gail and Bob to see if we can drop Emma off there. If we're going to be gone a few days, she'll be better off staying with her buddy." Now that we had something of a plan, Jenne was in her comfort zone—the one where she gave orders and expected them to be obeyed. Things were once again right with the world.

Twenty-Three

Walla Walla

As he looked around his quarters, Jason Carlson couldn't help but be impressed with the quality of the furnishings and the overall comfort level.

After a week of meeting with lawyers, making arrangements with the funeral director for the cremation, and then the celebration at the club, it felt good to be alone. The four-hour drive from Bellevue to Walla Walla had helped him organize his thoughts and formulate a plan for the immediate future.

Much of his dad's wealth was in land and property, and management companies were handling these efficiently. Uva Cellars was the only ongoing business entity that Butch had owned, so Jason thought it best to see what needed to be done, at least in the short term. Kevin O'Malley had been a vital help in bringing him up to speed on the day-to-day activities at the winery, and it seemed Michelle Browne had things under control.

After numerous calls to his brother went unanswered, he finally gave up. He hadn't spoken with John in years, but he was still his brother. It seemed insensitive to leave a message that their father had died and left him a substantial inheritance; however, he had no choice but to do so. Still, there was no response. He had the lawyers prepare a package that, at the very least, needed to be acknowledged by his brother and directed them to send it to his last-known address.

It was an hour since his arrival, and the realization that he'd spent it lying on the bed, his mind cluttered with things that had to be done, dawned on him. Throughout his life, in sports, school, and business,

Jason had always been a man of action. Not to say he didn't think things through; he did. When there was a choice to be made, though, he made one and acted upon it rather than getting bogged down in the endless pros and cons of a decision. He always assumed a decision could be made with ninety percent of the information rather than waiting indefinitely for another three or four percent to trickle in.

When he arrived at the winery, he was met by Bonnie, who notified him that she was a new hire whose duties were to help out in the tasting room and do whatever Michelle told her. She said this with a smile, nervous about meeting the new owner without her boss to help. Jason had shown up unannounced on purpose.

Bonnie showed him to the barn and ensured he had everything he needed. "Michelle had to go into town to pick up some supplies, but she should be back soon."

He figured he might as well start looking at things from an owner's viewpoint rather than that of a visitor, and now was as good a time as any. Although there was still a month or so before bud break—it was still early March—he took the opportunity to use the remaining hours of daylight to stroll through the closest rows of vines. With the late afternoon temperature hovering close to forty, he zipped up his fleece vest and tugged his knit cap over his ears.

Spending all his adult life in offices, in team meetings, and in front of computer screens was in stark contrast to the quiet solitude he now experienced. While foreign to him, he found the experience soothing, and, for a moment, he caught a glimpse of what had drawn his father to the industry.

The alternate freezing and thawing of the rows made for ankle-twisting walking, and he was glad he'd worn his Brunt Perkins boots; street shoes or sneakers would have been doomed.

"Help you?" The intrusive voice startled him. He was amazed that someone could have walked up behind him so quietly. He turned to see a thin-lipped, weathered face that wore a suspicious squint.

"Oh, sure—hi. My name is Jason Carlson, and I was getting a feel for the place." The stranger shook his hand with a leather-gloved one of his own. His expression changed instantly to a forced smile, more patronizing than genuine.

"Hi, Jason. I'm Evan Davis. I'm the winemaker here. Sorry about your father."

Jason hesitated a beat, thinking there was more to be said. When the moment stretched to discomfort, he took the lead. "Nice to meet you, Evan. You have an excellent reputation, and I'm here to look things over now that I'm responsible for the winery." Even though he was the *owner*, the title seemed more deserving of his dad.

"That's what Michelle told me. If you'd like to talk about the winery or need anything, please let me know. Michelle's mostly inside, and I'm in charge of the grapes and the wine. Here's a card with my cell on it. I'd better get going before it's too dark."

Before Jason could respond, Davis turned and purposefully walked back the way he'd come.

So that's Evan Davis, he mused. *I can see why he's not the most well-liked member of the team.* He spent another hour just wandering about the property, trying to come to grips with his newly inherited, hugely complex, yet somehow rewarding—at least to his father—enological enterprise.

By the time he returned to the barn, it was dark, and a note was pinned to the door. *Welcome, Jason. Bonnie said you were here, and I'm sorry I missed your arrival. The chef's not here tonight, but if you're up for it, we can go into town and eat at Bottles. I can go over the operation here at Uva then, if you'd like. Just text me to let me know. Michelle.*

Jason was starving, and everything Kevin had reported about Michelle was admirable. He texted as requested and received a reply that she would pick him up at six. He took the opportunity to shower and change and was ready when there was a knock at the door promptly at six.

On his previous visits to Uva Cellars, Jason had been on holiday and had taken little notice of the winery's personnel or operations. When he thought about Michelle, he only remembered a woman in a ball cap and a wine-stained sweatshirt ordering people here and there.

When he opened the door, the woman he saw was attractive, with full lips, a warm, welcoming smile, and smoldering dark brown eyes, which he was reluctant to look at for fear he wouldn't be able to look away.

"Um, you're Michelle …"

"I am, and you're Jason. Welcome to Uva Cellars. Let's get going, and we can chat on the way."

Michelle's ride was a Honda Ridgeline, and she drove the back roads like she owned them. The twenty-minute drive into town passed in a blink. She expressed sincere sympathy for Butch's death and told Jason how much she enjoyed Kevin and Jenne's company. "You're lucky to have such good friends. I liked them very much."

Jason, stealing a glance whenever he thought she wasn't looking, was thankful she carried most of the conversation. It allowed him to remind himself why he was there and which areas of the operation needed addressing the most. He just hadn't been prepared for this woman to have this effect on him.

The bistro was located in the charming old town section of Walla Walla, and even though it was off-season, the place was hopping. They parked on the street and were greeted by Perry at the door. "Michelle, great to see you, and this is Jason, right?"

He offered a welcoming handshake and led the pair to a table near the front window. Subdued lighting and lighted Glassybabies on the tables made for a friendly atmosphere, and once again, Jason felt the need to remind himself that he was here on business.

"I take it you know Perry well."

"Yes. I thought you knew, but how could you? Perry does the catering for us at Uva. Whenever we have an outside group or visitors, he cooks. He and his brother, Chad, own Bottles. Butch liked them a lot, and he's the best chef in town."

"I remember my dad saying something once, but I probably wasn't paying much attention. I spoke with Kevin about his impressions of the winery, which were mostly favorable. He wasn't too sure about you, though."

The smile instantly disappeared from Michelle's face, and her neck turned scarlet. "Huh? Really? I thought we got along great."

Jason immediately felt awful about the tease and hurriedly made up for it. "No, no, Michelle, they loved you. I'm sorry. I always remember that line about you'd never waste time teasing someone you didn't like, and sometimes I take it too far. My dad thought the world of you, and so did Jenne and Kevin."

Her color had normalized, but now her eyes had more of a twinkle. "Is that so? Because Jenne told me a few things about you that concern me."

It was Jason's turn to show worry. "C'mon, that's not possible … I hardly …"

Now her face broke into a broad grin.

"You know, Michelle, that now that I'm your boss, you can't try that shit with me."

"Sure, sure, what's good for the goose …"

"Okay, okay, truce, point made. I give up."

They both had a hearty laugh, and the dinner continued with Uva Cellars as the main topic of conversation. The food was excellent, the ambiance exemplary, and, as far as their table was concerned, the company superb.

As if both had been avoiding the elephant in the room, the subject of the winemaker came up as they were having coffee. "The one negative Kevin mentioned was Evan Davis, and he said you have some issues, too, regarding him."

With a deep sigh, Michelle attempted to summarize her worries. "He *is* very good at viticulture and making wine. The problem is his lack of empathy for others and his unwillingness to address the issue. I suppose he might be able to manage people, but he pisses them off so soon that there's no chance. I've brought this up numerous times, even suggesting some courses or online presentations that might help, but he won't hear it. I'm afraid he's become toxic to the rest of our team, and it's having a destructive effect."

"So you're saying we should fire him?"

She waited for a beat before nodding, then capitulating. "I hate to say it, but I think he has to go for the sake of the rest of the employees. Finding a replacement will probably be a pain in the ass, but it is what it is. We need to do this."

Jason appreciated her directness and her willingness to make difficult decisions. He began to understand why his father and the O'Malleys were so high on this woman. "If that's how you feel, then I'm with you a hundred percent. How about this? I'll meet him in the morning and tell him I've decided to go in another direction. Since I'm the new owner, I'll tell him I'm bringing in my own team. We'll give him a couple of months' severance to smooth things out somewhat."

Michelle's serious expression made him wonder what was bothering her. "I think that's generous of you to be the one to fire him, but maybe I should handle this."

"I understand how you feel, but let's do this my way. You're too important for you to be the fall guy. From the little I've seen of Davis, he appears to be the kind to hold a grudge, and I'd rather he's pissed at me than you. I'm sure he'll still harbor some ill will toward you, but that can't be helped. No, I'll do it."

A look of relief flashed across Michelle's face. "Thanks. I guess that makes sense. What can I do to help?"

"What time does the tasting room open tomorrow?"

"This time of year, we open at noon. Traffic is usually pretty light except for the holidays."

"Okay. Text Davis to meet me in the tasting room at ten. Tell him we're meeting to review the upcoming visitors or something. I'll take it from there. Does he own his truck, or is it ours?"

"We give him an allowance, so the truck's his."

"How about notes, formulas, and documentation for the wines?"

"We keep all those in the lab. That's the closed door behind the restrooms."

"Let's make sure we get that locked up so we retain possession. It's always a little iffy what the reaction is when someone's termination surprises them."

"It sounds as though you have experience of doing this."

"A little. It's never easy, but I've learned the hard way to prepare for the worst. Even when folks expect to be fired, it isn't easy, and they can do things totally out of character. In Davis's case, he's surly to begin with, so I don't want to take any chances."

With the dining experience ending on this solemn note, the couple returned to Uva Cellars, with Michelle dropping Jason at the barn before she headed to the farmhouse.

Exiting the pickup, he turned to her and said, "Thanks for a lovely evening, Michelle. I know we had to address some serious stuff, but I enjoyed the company immensely. I'm fortunate to have you running things here, and I hope we can smooth out this rough patch and produce vintages that would make my dad proud."

She appeared to be entertaining more thoughts than she could process but produced a thousand-watt smile. "Thanks, Jason. Aside from the sobering items, it's been more fun than I've had in ages. I'll text Evan and see you after you've met with him. Good night."

Jason arrived at the tasting room at nine-thirty. He had received a text from Michelle confirming that Davis would meet him there at ten sharp, and he wanted the time to prepare for the distasteful upcoming task. She had warmed the room and thoughtfully provided a pot of coffee and a tray of warm scones. *Damn. I'd better not do anything to cause her to quit. She's remarkable.*

A blast of thirty-degree air blew into the room as Evan Davis arrived at the top of the hour. *At least he was punctual.*

"Hey, Jason. Michelle said you wanted to review a few things."

"Thanks for meeting me, Evan. I'm sorry, but there's no easy way to do this. I've decided to terminate your employment here at Uva. I'm going to go with a different winemaker."

Davis had just begun to unzip his down parka when he stopped halfway. He looked stunned and took several seconds before speaking. When he did, it was almost a shout. "*What?* You're firing me?"

"Yes. As of today, you are no longer employed here. We'll provide you with two months' severance and continue your vehicle allowance for the same period. If there are any personal belongings here or in the lab, we'll send them to you."

With a shocked, morphing to angry, look on Evan's face, he delivered this next in a quieter, almost threatening manner. "I brought a fucking platinum award to this shithole of a winery for your goddamn old man and this is the thanks I get. Why are you doing this? Did that bitch Michelle put you up to this? Did she make shit up about me? Motherfucker …"

Jason had expected some reaction, but this was a bit over the top. He was happy he had insisted on doing the honors and not risking Michelle handling the brunt of the storm. He also knew better than to get into any discussion or answer any gripes, since to do so would ultimately end up in disagreement without any change in the outcome.

"I'm sorry it has to end this way, Evan. If you leave a forwarding address, I'll ensure you get your final check and anything left behind."

Jason's dismissal of Davis quieted him down and left him standing there with gritted teeth and flaring nostrils. "I need my notes from the lab."

"No, they are the property of Uva Cellars. We paid you for your work, and now it's ours. I'm going to ask you to leave now." He wasn't sure whether his superior height, weight, and physical strength were a factor, but if they were, that was fine. Davis zipped up his coat, walked out of the tasting room entrance, and slammed the door, almost breaking the window glass.

Jason breathed a deep sigh of relief, refilled his coffee, and sat on one of the stools pulled up to the tasting bar. In his current position in Denver, he'd had to fire at least half a dozen people, which was never easy. He usually felt terrible for them, but he was thrilled to be rid of the man this time. *What an asshole.*

He texted Michelle to see if she was available, and she came through the lab door in seconds.

"You were in the lab?"

"I was. I wanted to be sure we had all the notes on the current vintage in the barrels. I heard him yell something, so I'm guessing he didn't take it well."

"Let's say he left Uva Cellars an unhappy man. I'm more certain than ever that we made the right call on this. Anyone who reacts like that is someone we don't want as an employee. I don't care how good he is. By the way, nice call on the coffee and scones. I was starving."

She chuckled pleasantly, and he was reminded how much he enjoyed her company. "I figured you could use fortifying, since you had to be the big bad guy. And, seriously, thanks for doing this. I'm not sure how well I would have done if it was as unpleasant as it sounded."

"From what I've seen, I don't think anything is coming your way that you can't handle. Let's talk about where we go from here."

Twenty-Four

Medina/Bellevue

We checked into the Archer Hotel in Redmond just after dropping Emma off at her buddy's place. Whenever we spend a few days away from our home on Whidbey, we stay at this boutique hotel. It's centrally located, very understated, and quiet, and the staff take great care of us. They're also incredibly dog friendly—perfect for the times we have Emma with us.

There are no secrets between Shelly Owens and Jenne, so when she heard we would be in the neighborhood, she insisted on having us for dinner again. She owned her home in the wealthy suburb of Medina before her marriage to Bill, which occasionally causes him embarrassment. That the local head of detectives lives in a multi-million-dollar home in the same community as Bill Gates and other titans of commerce never escapes the scrutiny of his contemporaries. Had they known the full story of how he foiled the mass murder plans at the local golf club and ultimately married the wife of one of the major players, perhaps their judgment would be less harsh. On the whole, though, Bill deals with the issue just fine.

"You know, Kevin, Bill's terribly upset that you and Jenne aren't staying with us this trip." We had just sat down to eat when Shelly said this.

She had made it clear that there was room for us in their guest quarters whenever we wanted. It was perfect for a night or two, but it was no substitute for having our own space, allowing us to come and go as we pleased. Plus I was positive Bill was *not* upset, especially after he commented, "What Shelly *means* is that we're happy to have Jenne here whenever she's in town; you, not so much."

To the casual observer, his comment might have seemed somewhat offensive. To me, it was simply an invitation to counter with an equally sharp rebuke. "We were planning on staying here, but when we heard you would be home for the week, we heard the hotel beckoning."

This caused our wives to exchange glances much the same as young mothers did while sitting on park benches as their two- and three-year-olds fought ceaselessly over a toy truck. Their looks weren't missed by the two of us either, and we took it as an invitation to raise our efforts at sarcastic insults to a higher bar.

"Okay, okay, enough! If you adolescents don't knock this shit off, Shelly and I are going into the family room." Jenne, it appeared, was through with our childish antics.

Finally getting the response we were looking for, Bill and I laughed and offered each other a fist bump. "It took them a little longer this time, eh, buddy?" I congratulated my pal.

"Shelly, know any good divorce attorneys?"

"I'm certain there are one or two in the neighborhood. I can start looking in the morning."

The balance of the evening was spent in the comfort only genuine friends can provide. The four of us knew well each other's strengths and weaknesses, and that knowledge only strengthened our bond. It was rare to find a couple as simpatico as the Owenses; we were thankful for our good fortune and never once took it for granted.

We played amateur detective during the following two days, doing what we could to try and get a lead on the Carlson case. Since Bill had allowed me access to the investigation, I paid a visit to Bellevue Towers while Jenne stopped at the golf club to check on the scuttlebutt from Butch's buddies.

"Can you give me a list of employees with knowledge of the wireless password who have either been fired or resigned during the last twelve months?" I was meeting with the HR manager at Bellevue Towers. At first, she was reluctant to provide the information, but with a quick call to the Bellevue Police Department's Detective Houser, my bona fides were verified.

"This is the list I gave the detective, but I'll tell you what I told her. Many were in entry-level positions like maintenance and front desk personnel. It's quite possible that they could have passed the network password on to other people as well." The forty-something woman reminded me of Jane Leeves, who played Daphne Moon in *Frasier*, and her English accent lent a professorial air to whatever came out of her mouth.

"Might you hazard a guess as to how many people we're talking about?" I wasn't sure why, but I felt the need to be a little proper myself.

"The list only has a few dozen people on it, but if they told someone and then *those* people told someone, the number could be very large indeed."

"Yes, indeed … indeed." I couldn't help myself, although her look suggested I had perhaps infringed on politeness, so I reined things in a little. "Were any people more likely than others to share this information?"

"I really can't answer that. My position is primarily administrative. If you want more information, you should talk to the facility manager or the desk manager. They have the last word on hiring and firing." She turned back to the credenza to do whatever she was doing on her computer.

"Where can I find them?" I asked the back of her head.

"You'll have to go to the second floor. That's where their offices are."

Feeling as dismissed as when Cheryl Rocco rebuffed me when I asked her to the ninth-grade dance, I headed off to the elevators.

I thought it made sense to start with maintenance for no other reason than I'd have better luck talking to someone of the same sex. I was wrong—not that my luck was about to change, just about the head of facilities. *She* was short, youthful, and wired like the Energizer bunny. The name on the door said Penny Kirkland, and she bolted upright as soon as I knocked.

"Help you?"

I introduced myself, told her my reason for being there, and asked if any of the past year's employees might have passed on the wireless password to someone with nefarious intentions.

"What we do here is keep this place running. Heating, cooling, fire suppression, security—everything is my responsibility. The folks that work for me are mechanics, electricians, and a few even have engineering degrees. Sure, we have a few people that do the grunt work, but most are professionals who would never do anything remotely sketchy."

"Even so, do you think you could maybe review the ones who quit or you had to let them go for some reason—see if anything jumps out at you?"

"That lady cop already asked me, and I told her nobody did."

I let out an exasperated sigh and gave it another try. "Look, this break-in happened to a guy who was a close friend. Now he's dead. He was run off the road by a hit-and-run driver. I'd appreciate it if you could look again. It would mean a lot to his family and friends."

She pursed her lips, picked up a paper from her desk, and looked at it. "Tell you what, I'll take this home and look a little closer, but there are no promises. I'll call you if I come up with anything."

I thanked Penny again and headed off to meet my wife.

Her only success was setting up dinner the following evening with a group of Butch's close friends from the club. I told her about my meeting with the facilities lady and said there wasn't much hope of getting anything from her. We hadn't expected to accomplish much, but we felt deflated at the slow progress on all fronts.

One bright spot was a call from Jason, who was back in Bellevue for more lawyerly activities. When he heard we were in town, he agreed to meet us at the Archer for an early dinner and an update on the state of Uva Cellars.

Twenty-Five

Redmond

We were meeting in the loft-like lobby bar of the Archer, and Jenne and I arrived a little early. We decided to whet our appetites with one of the local IPAs and settled into the comfy booth while we awaited its arrival. Jason and our ales arrived simultaneously.

"I'll have one of those too, please," he told the server as he pulled up a chair. "Great to see both of you. That drive can be a little rugged through the pass." As the words tumbled from his mouth, the three of us instantly recalled the circumstances of Butch's death.

The table was quiet for a few seconds before Jason finally spoke. "Ahh, shit. That hit a little too close to home. Sorry."

"No worries. I'm sure those reminders will pop up from time to time. Hopefully we'll get beyond it. Tell us about your visit to the winery. How did your impressions compare to what we reported?" I figured moving on was the best approach.

"It's a wonderful property. I can see why my dad loved it there. It's beautiful and peaceful, and Michelle Browne is a star. I don't think any challenge is beyond her. She runs the place like it was her own."

I stole a glance at my wife, whose ever-so-slightly tilted head indicated that she believed there was slightly more than just professional admiration going on here.

She, of course, said, "So you liked her?"

Jason's complexion reddened a shade, and he hurriedly responded, "Well … she's professional, brilliant, and extremely capable. I'm lucky to have her … as an employee."

"I thought she was very attractive too." Jenne was like a bulldog with a pork chop as she grinned, probing his obvious discomfort.

"Yes, I thought she was too. Very much." Sorry, I had to throw a pitch too.

"Um … yeah, I guess she was. She even offered to terminate the winemaker, but I thought it best if I handled it."

It was clear that Jason was, if not smitten, then seriously interested in one Michelle Browne in more ways than as an employee of his winery. Rather than watch him fend off any further interrogation by my wife, I chimed in. "You *did* fire Davis, then?"

"After your report and listening to Michelle, there was no other option. He was casting a pall over the winery. He was terrible with clients, annoying to his peers, and disrespectful to those who reported to him. The guy was a jerk."

I could think of other words more descriptive of Uva's former winemaker, but instead I asked, "Do you think it'll be difficult to replace him? After all, he has that platinum thing around his neck."

"I don't think so. He does have the award, but it's more the winery's than the winemaker's. Those in the industry know how perfect the soil is in that valley, so it's common knowledge that Uva Cellars is one of the gems in an already up-and-coming wine region."

"How will you find someone?"

"Michelle has already put out the word to the Walla Walla and Columbia Valley AVAs. She thinks it's best to hire someone familiar with Washington State viticulture. There are always plenty of candidates from California, but she wants to try locally first."

"And you agree?"

"Hey, if she wants to go in that direction, I'm all for it. She seems to know what she's doing."

Jason noticed as I smiled with a quick nod to my wife.

"What?"

Jenne took the lead. "It seems, Jason, that you're fond of Michelle—you know, like you *like* her."

"Well, sure—she's great, a great employee."

"Jason …"

He withered under my wife's affectionate badgering, "Yeah, I kinda do, I guess."

"What about her?" It was best to give Jenne all the rope she wanted at times like this. I just sat there and watched her peel away his defenses.

"I'm not sure. Maybe. It's not like we had a date or anything. We just worked on stuff."

"Did she smile a lot when she was with you? Did she think you were funny?"

"I'm not sure, but she did smile a lot, and her eyes crinkled too."

"She likes you too, you dope." She then turned to me. "Why are men such idiots? It's a wonder the human race continues to exist when the opposite sex is clueless."

I could have begun to explain some of the inconsistencies in her postulation, but I dared not go there. At times like this, I've learned through much trial and error that it's best to nod and look at the other person at the table.

Jason shrugged, at a loss for words, and muttered, "I don't know, maybe …"

I knew this repartee could continue indefinitely, so I, being the adult in the room for once, thought it prudent to redirect the conversation. "Other than just putting the word out, how will she find someone?"

Jason looked relieved to be back on safer ground. "She knows the head of the Viticulture and Enology program at WSU and has already spoken with him about what we're looking for. They've had the program for about twenty years, and they stay in touch with most of their alumni, so there's a good chance we can find someone through them."

"Sounds like Michelle and her *boyfriend* here have things under control, don'tcha think, Jenne?"

This earned a guffaw from my wife and a red-faced headshake and hands-in-the-air surrender from Jason. "I give up, you two. I'll admit I like her, and yes, she seems to be interested as well, but I'm hesitant to get involved with employees."

"*Employees?* How about thinking of her more as a partner—maybe even making her one? Would that work?" God, my wife was a pushy one.

Once again, I tried to end the assault. "Jenne, our friend here is an adult, and he's an astute businessman. How about we let him run his own life? Remember, we're here to help, not to annoy." I said this quietly so as not to poke the hornet's nest.

Looking mildly chastised, if only for effect, Jenne replied, "Okay, okay, call me a romantic. Sorry for suggesting such a thing, Jason, but we like you and want you to be happy."

It was Jason's turn to be gracious. "I know, and I appreciate it. But Kevin's right. I'll figure things out eventually. I like her very much, and if she feels the same, we'll manage to get together somehow. That doesn't mean I don't welcome the tutelage on how to know when someone likes me." This last was delivered with a warm smile.

Thinking it was way past time to move the conversation along, I asked about his brother and how he was dealing with their father's death.

"I have no idea how he's doing. He hasn't spoken to Dad or me since as far back as I can remember. Once he left Stanford, it was like he had dropped off the face of the earth. As kids, we never got along for some reason, and I think when my dad stopped paying for his college, he turned against him too. We could only track him through postings from one of his college buddies."

I thought this odd, so I asked, "Are you saying he knows about Butch's death and still hasn't connected?"

"I am. He stayed in the Bay Area for a while after he left school and, from what I could gather, was a star at Google. But he quit after half a dozen years and moved to Santa Barbara. As far as I can tell, he's lived there ever since."

"How do you know?" Jenne asked.

"My dad established a living trust for all his assets so we wouldn't have to be bothered with probate. He specified which assets went to John and me. As you can imagine, there were lots of documents to sign and acknowledge for both of us. I hired a detective agency to confirm

John's current address and had the lawyers courier all the paperwork there. They were returned signed, notarized, and acknowledged to the law firm, so I know he was where they said he was."

"I assume you've tried to connect."

"Of course. I even got his cell number from the agency. I've called, texted, and left messages, but no luck. For whatever reason, I'm dead to him."

It was difficult for me to understand how a son and a brother could be so callous, especially when his father had just died. "I'm sorry, Jason. This has to be tough for you. Even with his inheritance, he's *still* not connecting?"

"Nope."

"Well, shit, I guess you've done all you can do. Bill Owens is doing his best to get to the bottom of the crash, and Jenne and I are helping where we can. It looks like you've got things under control at Uva, so you'll let us know if we can help?"

"You bet. I can't thank you enough for all you've done. Please feel free to stay at the winery whenever you'd like to on me. It's the least I can do."

"Thanks a ton. Maybe we'll take you up on that once in a while." My wife flashed a stern look my way for some reason. "What?"

"That's unnecessary. We appreciate the offer, though."

"Huh? Well, of course it's not necessary ..." I turned to my wife. "But maybe we could once in a *while*?"

They both shook their heads as if they somehow understood something beyond my reach. Maybe they did ...

We blessedly changed the subject to more mundane topics and spent the evening enjoying each other's company.

Twenty-Six

Santa Barbara

With nothing to do but watch his nest egg multiply thanks to Aedan's shrewd investing, John Carlson spent most days at the beach and most evenings in the bar at El Encanto. Once in a while, he'd see Evan Davis there, but mostly his was a solitary existence.

His antipathy towards his father and brother seemed to gain more focus rather than fading away during his long period of familial avoidance. While he eschewed any contact, he fueled his bitterness by scouring online postings of his father's and brother's successes. With little else to do, he became adept at finding snippets about his father's holdings even though little public information was available.

Jason and his company's rise in fame and fortune was well documented and provided John with ample fodder to augment an already burgeoning animus toward his brother.

On one sweltering evening for Santa Barbara, John was nursing a gin and tonic when Evan Davis pulled up a stool next to him. "Santa Annas are a bitch, eh, John?"

"Hey, Evan. Yeah, I hate it when they blow like this. How come you seem happy?"

"I'm happy because I finally landed a head winemaker position. As you know, I've been bouncing around this valley for years doing scut work for everyone and his brother. I've managed to get by, but this looks like a great gig."

"Congrats, Evan. Glad to hear it. Who will you be working for?'

"Well, that's maybe the downside. The job's in Walla Walla. Some lady's husband just died, and she needs someone to take over the production. I got a buddy to *enhance* my résumé, she gave me a call, and I interviewed over the phone. Gotta be up there in two weeks."

John knew that the small town in southeast Washington had begun to develop a reputation for Bordeaux-style wines that some critics insisted rivaled those from Napa Valley. He was surprised that Davis's next stop would be in his home state.

"From what I hear, they're in the news lately. What's the name of the winery?"

"Kind of a funny name; it's Uva Cellars. She says they only do a couple thousand cases but have more land to plant if we want to."

"Never heard of it, but if it's that small, I'm not surprised."

"The owner sent me a couple of bottles of their cabernet, which was very good. I think I can do something with the fruit they have there."

"I wish you luck, Evan. I'll think of you while you're freezing your ass off up there and I'm on the beach."

"Hah, thanks. Look me up if you ever get up that way. We can share a glass or two."

"I'll do that; I will."

John spent the next several years doing nothing but watching his money grow and continuing to add layer upon layer of loathing for the remaining two members of his family. His only socializing was occasionally with Aedan Boyle, and that was about it.

The hours he spent continually seeking out internet stories and postings about his father and brother seemed to do nothing but feed his hostility. He never considered Davis a close friend, but he sometimes checked out stories and articles about Uva Cellars.

They were much as Davis had described them, although it seemed that since his not-so-close friend had started working there, their wines had begun to get noticed by both critics and publications. *Maybe Davis is as good as he thinks he is.*

When he came across an article in the *Wine Spectator* about up-and-coming boutique wineries in Washington State, he saw that a portfolio manager from an East Coast hedge fund had purchased them.

With a few more searches, he discovered what he had suspected; his father had purchased Uva Cellars, the winery where Evan Davis was now working. *What are the odds?*

Although he had known Davis casually for several years, he'd never had a conversation of sufficient depth to mention his family. Other than his irrational loathing for his father and brother, they were dead to him anyway. Still, it wouldn't hurt to have someone inside the ropes to gather more intel to stack upon his list of grievances.

—Hey, long time no talk! I hear the place where you're working just got sold.

He felt sure his text was vague enough that Davis would get back to him. It had been over two years since any communication with the winemaker, but he was sure he knew him well enough to expect a response. He wasn't mistaken.

It was less than an hour before his phone buzzed. "John, I got your text. How have you been?"

"No complaints, still living the dream. I get the *Wine Spectator* and saw a story about your place being sold. That true?"

"It is. Some rich dude from up in the Seattle area bought it. Name's Carlson … *whoa*, dude, any relation?"

"Yeah. He's my old man."

"No shit? You didn't tell me you came from money."

"I haven't spoken to my father in fifteen years. The guy's an asshole."

There was no immediate response, and John could imagine Davis trying to absorb what he'd just heard.

A more subdued voice replied, "How do you mean?"

"He withheld money from me and forced me to leave school. The only person he gives a shit about is my younger brother, and he's a dickhead too."

"Can you give me any information on him—you know, how to handle him?"

"I don't know anything about him except for the stuff I see online. From what I remember, he likes to keep a low profile and rarely gets involved in the day-to-day operations of anything. Most of his holdings are passive investments, so I can't say for sure."

"Why did you text me?"

It was John's turn to hesitate. "I'm not sure. I saw the article and was certain my father bought Uva, and I guess I wanted to tell you who it was. And, um, also if you could check in with me once in a while, you know, and let me know how the fucker is doing."

"Well, sure, I guess so. I gotta tell you, though, you're not giving me the warm fuzzies."

"I don't think he's likely to upset any ongoing profitable business, so you'll be fine. Just consider this a heads-up and keep me posted on things."

"Sure, sure … I will." Davis, sounding more than a little distracted, ended the call.

Twenty-Seven

Santa Barbara

The following two years proved to be painful for John Carlson. His loathing for his family became so toxic that even his good friend Aedan gave up getting together with him.

Of course, this development was met by an overreaction on John's part, and he promptly transferred his entire fortune to an individually managed online trading account. Mistakenly, he was confident that whatever Aedan had done to multiply his wealth hadn't been too complicated, and he was sure he could do the same.

He'd become a regular at the bar at El Encanto—so much so that the servers and bartenders did their best to avoid any interaction with him. As such, he spent his time there either reading from his phone or perusing whatever newspapers or magazines had been cast aside by previous patrons.

On a Thursday evening during the last week in March, he noticed a *Guns and Ammo* magazine on the stool beside him. John could never see the sense of guns; he'd never hunted, never served in the armed forces, and thought people who liked guns were either nuts or terrorists. This cover showed an attractive young lady fondling a rifle while posing with a dead elk.

He picked it up, curious how such a beautiful woman had shot the giant animal. While leafing through the magazine, he noticed ads for pistols, rifles, and all kinds of ammo. He shook his head at the stupidity of people and tossed the thing back onto the stool. It slid to the floor, so he bent to pick it up and noticed it had opened to a display ad for a local shooting range in Goleta. *Figures*, he thought. *Wasn't that where that woman killed all those people at the post office back in 2006?* He threw the magazine in the trash and thought nothing more of it.

At first, he cautiously traded with small amounts of money based on tips from Jim Cramer's *Mad Money* show on CNBC. His early success buoyed his confidence, and he continued to invest larger and larger amounts. Sometimes he'd lose, but mostly he was successful, and his faith in his abilities multiplied. He failed to realize that the economy was expanding rapidly and even a complete moron would have had difficulty producing negative returns.

Never particularly conservative regarding money, John placed all of it in several tech start-ups that he was sure would lead to even greater returns. Alas, he was sadly mistaken. In one terrible week, he lost half of his fortune. When he finally accepted defeat, he sold the securities only to find that they bounced back four days after he sold.

He jumped back in, since the prognosis for the companies was now even more promising than ever. Two weeks later, the basis of the technology was deemed faulty; it infringed on a patent that had been registered twenty years prior. The stock cratered, and John was left with only a few hundred thousand when the dust settled.

So deep was his depression that the manager at El Encanto suggested he find another place to hang out. He could no longer afford his home on the hill above the famous Santa Barbara Mission and moved up the coast to Goleta, where rents were cheaper.

When moving into his new digs, an 800-square-foot duplex, he passed a warehouse structure with a vaguely familiar sign: "Campo de Tiro." As he picked up his keys from the leasing agent, his curiosity got the best of him, and he asked about the building.

"Oh, that's Spanish for 'shooting range.' Since that shooting, the suckers have sprung up like weeds." She walked away, shaking her head at the idiocy of it all.

John was bored to tears with very little disposable income, no means or desire for employment, and no regular tavern or friends. He was tired of the beach and petrified about investing any remaining dollars. After several days of futilely attempting to make his new place habitable, he walked through the neighborhood. When he reached the warehouse, he figured *what the hell* and walked in.

A large Hispanic-looking gentleman, copiously tattooed, stood behind a Formica counter. The *pop-pop* of gunfire was constant as the man looked up at the new arrival. "Help you?"

The wall behind the attendant was covered with pistols, rifles, and other instruments of killing, and John was unsure what to say.

"Ever shot a gun before?" It appeared this person had seen similar reactions before.

"Ahh … no, I don't think I …"

"C'm 'ere, sir. Put these on and come with me to the range." He handed John what looked like headphones and led him by the elbow.

"I don't think …" Now that his escort was wearing ear protection, he couldn't be heard. He put his earmuffs on and was surprised at their effectiveness. As the man led him to a partition near the end of the range, they passed a half-dozen shooters of all ages and genders. John was surprised that even women were shooting.

When they arrived at a vacant station, the gentleman stuck a target on a clamp, turned the pulley so the target reached the back wall, and picked up the rifle on the counter. He loaded the gun with bullets and wrapped the sling expertly over his forearm. He fired three times quickly, placed the rifle on the counter, and wheeled the target back to their stand. There were three tiny holes in the center.

He attached a fresh target, wheeled it back out, loaded the rifle again, and handed it to John. Looking at him, he mouthed the words *now you*. He helped John with the sling, and when he was ready, the man tapped him on the head.

The first shot drove his thumb into his cheek, and he was surprised at the force hitting his shoulder. His instructor chuckled and showed him how to keep the rifle tight to his shoulder and his thumb tight to his cheek. The second shot didn't hurt much, nor did the third.

With another tap on his head, they wheeled the target back and saw only one hole, and it was in the far-right corner. The man chuckled, clasped his shoulder, and motioned for him to follow. They both took off their ear protectors when they arrived at the front counter.

"My name is Hector. How was that?"

"It was … interesting, I guess."

"Most people don't understand why many folks like to shoot. Did you think it was fun?"

"Yeah, I guess I did."

"And *that's* why people do it, mostly."

"Mostly?"

"Well, there's always the gun nuts. They come here occasionally, but I do my best to discourage them. We're more of a family place. Some folks have competitions and leagues, and some like to be alone and see how much they can improve."

John was a little surprised at how he had almost enjoyed the diversion. "Thanks, Hector. Maybe I'll be back."

Twenty-Eight

Bellevue

As Butch Carlson's close friends were all mostly our close friends, our dinner the following night was like old times, although sadly minus Butch. We chatted about golf, families, work, retirement, and finally about our good friend.

Unfortunately, like us, no one knew of anyone who wished Butch any harm. We said our goodbyes and returned to the Archer, happy to have been with friends but a bit discouraged about the lack of progress.

"It was great seeing everyone, but Butch's absence left a big hole in the group."

Jenne said precisely what I was thinking, and she was right on the money. Butch had always been the life of the party. It would take time to fill the void he'd left.

"Yeah, I agree. I guess the best we can do is live our lives to the fullest, and while we're at it, maybe we'll find something, anything, that will help Bill solve this thing."

"You didn't hear anything from that woman at the Towers, did you?"

"No, and really I didn't expect to. It was a long shot anyway."

"So what? We throw in the towel and head back to Whidbey?"

"Let's get some sleep and see what tomorrow brings. If there's no news, then we pick up Emma and head back. Sound good?"

Jenne turned to me with a look that made me think I was the luckiest guy on the planet and said, "Kev, I love you very much. I don't know what I'd ever do without you."

Whether it was the suddenness of Butch's death or the dinner with our friends, or maybe everything altogether, whatever, my eyes began to water. I reached over to squeeze her hand and brought it to my mouth to kiss it. "Me too, honey. Me too."

We checked out the following day and were on our way to pick up Emma when my phone buzzed. It was an unknown number, so I let it go to voicemail; the number of spam calls seemed to increase daily. If it was something important, they could leave a message.

We picked up our dog and headed to the ferry terminal at Mukilteo, where we missed the noon boat. Since they ran every half hour, we settled down to do what everyone else in the holding lot was doing, which was staring at our phones as if they somehow held the keys to the universe. Hell, maybe they did.

I first checked the headlines and then the MLB app to see how the Mariners' spring training was progressing. Would this be the year they made a statement in the playoffs? Unlikely. I finally looked at my visual voicemail and was surprised to see a call from Penny Kirkland, who asked me to return her call. I interrupted Jenne in the middle of texting someone to show her the message.

"Well, call her, then."

I knew better than to say what I was thinking, which was "Of course I'll call her; I'm just showing you this because I think it might *be* something, sheesh!" I'm not an idiot. So I called Penny.

"Facilities, Kirkland." The snappy answer gave the impression of a woman under constant pressure yet always in control.

"Hi, Penny. This is Kevin O'Malley. You left me a message."

"I did, yes. I did as you asked and went over the list again. As I told you when you were here, most folks leave for better-paying jobs and are above reproach."

"Okay?"

"We very seldom let anyone go. If we do, it's because they don't show up or are in some other way not dependable."

"Yes?" She seemed to be waffling a bit for a person short on time.

"Well, we had one employee, an IT guy ... he was late half the time and always had some silly excuse. I finally let him go. There are too many good candidates to keep a bad one."

"Would he have known the security password?"

"Of course. He was in IT."

"Have you changed it since?"

She was quiet for a moment before she said, "Well, we changed it after the detective came by."

Well, duh, no shit. I took a deep breath and asked for the former employee's name and last-known address.

"I'll have to get it from HR. I'll go down there now and text it to you. And, Kevin, I hope this helps."

I thanked her for taking the time to take another look and told her I'd let her know if anything came of it.

By the time we were on the boat, I had received the text from Penny.

"Guy's name is Steve Pennell, and he lives in Stanwood." I read the text while showing it to Jenne.

"Well, no wonder he was late half the time if he lives in Stanwood." She had a point; Stanwood is a semi-rural community about fifty miles north of Bellevue. With the ever-increasing traffic slog south on the 405, the commute into Bellevue was always unpredictable. "Now that you've got a lead, Sherlock, what will you do?"

Before I answered, I considered my options. I could hand it over to Bill Owens, who might turn it over to the Stanwood cops, since that would be protocol. Or … I could check with the person myself, and if there was anything there, *then* I could get it to Bill. The latter seemed a better option, so I told Jenne what I was thinking.

She answered, "You know, of course, he will be upset when he finds out you did this without telling him."

"I'm aware."

"You still going to?"

"I think so. Yes, I am. If it's a dead end, then no harm, no foul. If I get anywhere, then I'll tell him. He *will* be upset, but at least he'll have a lead."

"You mean *we* will, right?"

"Um, yes, that's what I meant." If I excluded my Doc Watson, she'd make me pay for it in ways better left unsaid—something entirely undesirable.

"Good."

Twenty-Nine

Stanwood

We both agreed that it made more sense to visit Pennell personally than to attempt anything over the phone. The next day, rainy as usual, we took the ten-thirty and made our way up the I-5 to Stanwood, the now-bedroom community of Seattle/Bellevue.

Originally a blue-collar city, home to several food processing plants, the town now offered far less expensive housing than the Seattle metropolitan area. The trade-off was a commute that required a minimum of three hours on the road daily.

The address Penny had provided led us through East Stanwood and took us several miles from town on WA 532. From there, we proceeded south to the tiny community of Sunday Lake. It was there, about half a mile down a gravel road, that we came upon a tidy double-wide manufactured home, complete with a fenced chicken coop and a half-dozen raised planters topped with compost, waiting for the spring planting.

The white home with black shutters was in the center of a large clearing surrounded by towering Doug firs. When we opened the doors of our vehicle and stepped onto the gravel courtyard, the stillness of the misty rain was shattered by fierce barking from inside the house. Off to the right, a ten-year-old Jeep was only partially covered by a blue tarp.

We looked at each other, shrugged, and proceeded to the small landing at the front door. As we arrived, a thirty-something gentleman in a red plaid shirt, sporting a scraggly beard, opened the door to even louder barking. He stepped out and closed it behind him.

"Sorry about that. The girls always let me know when I have visitors. What can I do for you?"

Jenne took the lead, because we both knew she presented a much more pleasant attitude. "We were looking for Steve Pennell. Is that you?"

The man had to be at least 6'4", so we found ourselves looking up at him. His slight frame suggested an intense workout regimen or, more likely, a less than optimal diet. With a suspicious look, he answered, "It is, and who are you?"

Before we got off on the wrong foot, I thought a more direct approach was needed. "I'm Kevin O'Malley, and this is my wife, Jenne. We got your name from the folks at Bellevue Towers, and we had a couple of questions about something we're working on."

With a deep sigh, he half turned to the door. "C'mon inside, out of the rain, and we can talk. The girls will raise hell for a few seconds, but they're harmless."

While he led the way, I looked at Jenne, whose eyebrows were as raised as mine. Two red cattle dogs, barking furiously, shot toward us as soon as we entered the house.

"Enough!" As soon as the word left Pennell's mouth, the two canines retreated to a large dog bed nestled near the black iron stove, radiating a blessed amount of warmth into the room.

"Sorry about that. I've never figured out how to stop 'em. Living out here, though, I'm not certain I want to." He offered this with a self-deprecating smile, then waved a hand toward a well-worn sofa, suggesting we take a seat.

The room had surprisingly high ceilings, a nicely appointed kitchen at one end, and a large living/family/whatever room at the other. A desk-height counter spanned the wall opposite the kitchen, sporting at least a half-dozen computers in various stages of repair.

"You said you have some questions?"

Penny Kirkland's description didn't quite match this fellow sitting across from us. I wasn't sure how to begin without putting him on the defensive, so I did what any intelligent man would; I let my wife take the lead.

I looked over at Jenne, who gave the slightest shake of her head, no doubt preparing me for a scolding when we left.

"Steve, a friend of ours was killed recently. He had a penthouse in Bellevue Towers, where you were recently employed." See how much better she was at this than me.

"Okay, sorry about that, but what does that have to do with me?"

"Shortly before he was killed, someone broke into his unit and was able to do so by turning off all the security cameras. We're trying to figure out how that could have happened. Your boss told us you were let go recently, and because you worked in IT, we thought you might know something about how it could have been done." After the softer approach by Jenne, I thought I'd lay it all out for Pennell.

Rather than a quick denial on his part, Pennell paused for a beat, seemingly lost in thought.

"Steve?" After an uncomfortable silence, Jenne tried to get his attention.

"Sorry. I was just trying to recall a few things that might be helpful to you." Once again, this person didn't come across as a ne'er-do-well.

He continued. "First of all, you are correct; I *was* fired. I moved here from Portland two years ago and started an IT business. It went great guns for a year, and then my biggest client went bankrupt. I'm divorced and pay child support, so I needed to ensure I could keep doing that. I took the job at the Towers to fill the void while I tried to rebuild my business. I only worked there for about six months and, yes, I *was* late frequently. Damn traffic is a bitch, plus I can't leave the girls alone too long. Their names are Heidi and Penny, by the way."

"Penny?" I just couldn't let *that* go.

He chuckled. "Yeah, what are the odds? My boss and my dog have the same name. I gotta tell you, there were times on the job that I had to bite my cheek to keep from telling her.

"Anyway, after I was fired, I picked up a few more clients, smaller but likely more dependable, and I'm back here working from home."

"What about the security cameras?" Jenny tried to get back to our concerns.

"Here's where this gets interesting and why I tried so hard to remember stuff. Firstly, anyone who had the password—and almost everyone working there knew it—could access the LAN, and if they knew what they were doing, they could shut down the cameras.

"The day I was fired, I was a little upset, so I stopped at Purple, the lobby bar, to have a glass of wine and think about things. After a while, this guy sits next to me, and we start talking about the tech industry. Turns out he used to work for Google, and we knew a few of the same people.

"We were telling each other silly things companies do, and I told him the place that just fired me was still using *BT1234* as their password for the entire building's LAN. We both got a big laugh at the time. When I think about it, he could have passed it on to anyone or everyone. I guess this doesn't help much, but it's all I can think of."

"Do you remember his name?"

"It was something simple, short, like Bob or Jim, maybe John. I don't know. Can't really remember. Never got the last name."

I thought Penny Kirkland should have been fired for never changing their password, and even if Pennell had passed along the code to some stranger in a bar, so what? By the time of the break-in, a hundred thousand people could have known it.

"Have you seen him since, or could you describe him?"

"I haven't been back there at all, and it was dark, so I don't think so. I remember he was a little taller than me, maybe six feet, and he looked like one of those SoCal dudes that hang out at the beach all day. He was very tanned, so I guess he couldn't be from here."

Except for Heidi's and Penny's panting, the room was quiet, all of us likely picturing a different scenario. I broke the mood by standing up and offering my hand to Pennell. "Thanks, Steve. You've been very helpful. If you think of anything else, would you give us a call?"

"Of course. I hope you can get to the bottom of this, and I'll get in touch if something comes up."

We said our goodbyes to Penny and Heidi, who now considered us, if not close friends, at least visitors they wouldn't mind seeing again.

Once we got back in our car, it was mere seconds before my wife spoke up. "Very smooth in there, champ, letting me take the point."

"If it's a choice between you putting someone at ease or me pissing them off, then I'm guilty. I feel reasonably sure that Steve Pennell had nothing to do with the break-in, at least not intentionally."

"I suppose the surfer dude might have had something to do with it, but there's no way to locate him. By the way, do we still tell Bill Owens about this?"

I knew we'd have to address this, but I hoped to delay it indefinitely. "I hate to say it, but I guess we've got to tell him."

"Think he'll be pissed?"

"Nope. He'll be fucking furious."

THIRTY

Walla Walla

As he walked to his truck to leave Uva Cellars for the final time, Evan Davis reflected upon his tenure there. When Helen Hurly had owned the place, it was a sweet deal for him. He could do as he pleased, and as long as that Browne bitch kept out of his way, he was happy.

Once Carlson bought the winery, things began to change. Browne was given more responsibility; over time, she even acted like his boss. The platinum award gave him a suitable period of fame, but that wasn't enough; eventually it was back to business as usual, and he was treated as just an employee.

Sure, John Carlson from Santa Barbara had given him a heads-up, but he still hadn't been prepared for the rapidity of his downfall. The only silver lining had been his association with John. Whatever had caused the hostility between him and his father was curious but certainly not his problem. If their conflict could somehow make his life easier, then all the better.

His contact with Butch Carlson was intermittent, usually only during those few times when the new owner visited the property. For some reason, John wanted to know everything about those visits and quizzed Davis relentlessly over the phone.

He had been surprised when John had called five weeks ago; he was in town and wondered if they could get together. They met at a small coffee shop in downtown Walla Walla, where Davis, not a particularly sensitive person, noticed a conspicuous change in Carlson since their time in Santa Barbara.

The tanned individual sitting across from him was no longer the laid-back, mellow beach bum he'd known in Southern California. This person was intense, fidgety, and always seemed to be looking for something.

Davis began cautiously. "So, hey, John, what are you doing in Walla Walla? You know how bad the weather is here, at least compared to Santa Barbara."

"Yeah, well … I needed to get back here to Washington to take care of some things."

"Does it have to do with your father?"

"That's none of your business. I've just got shit to do."

"Okay, man, sorry. What did you want to talk about?"

"I was wondering how often he visits the winery. Do you know when he's coming? Like, does he have a schedule?"

So it is about his father. Davis thought it best to answer the questions and return to work. "He always lets Michelle know when he's coming, but not me. She doesn't know shit, and he treats her like she's God's gift to the wine industry. She told me he's in Arizona playing golf, and he's gonna stop by on his way back to Bellevue. She wants me to have everything looking pretty when he comes by. Bitch."

"So he'll be here when?"

"I guess maybe tomorrow or the next day."

"And how long does he stay?"

Davis felt as though he was being interrogated but supplied the answer anyway. "I'm not sure, but it's usually two or three days at most."

"When he gets here, will you know how long he'll stay?"

What the fuck's the difference? he thought, but he said, "Shit, I don't know. Maybe … probably … how come?"

"Look, I have to leave today. I've got some things to do in Bellevue, but when you find out his schedule, make sure to call and let me know. Got it?"

Just what I need, someone else telling me what to do. "Yeah, sure, I'll let you know."

Carlson stood, mumbled quickly, "Thanks, Evan. Good to see you," and left the shop without paying a nickel. After Davis had paid the tab, he went outside into the cold but sunny day and caught a glimpse of his friend behind the wheel of a black pickup, condensation spewing from the dual exhausts as it drove out of town.

The winemaker did as he was told. When he met with Butch the next day, he found out that he would be there for three days and promptly left a message for John. A week later, he was as stunned as everyone else when he heard about the fatal mishap on the west side of Snoqualmie Pass. It took him far less time, though, to assemble a series of random facts into a scenario that seemed more than probable.

Now Jason, Butch's other son, had just fired him. Evan thought John was right about their father being an asshole, but "dickhead" didn't even begin to describe the sonofabitch who had just ruined his life.

THIRTY-ONE

Bellevue

Detective Bill Owens's temper was legendary—at least as far as I was concerned. Mostly he'd yell, say what an asshole I'd been, and tell me to stay out of police business.

This time, when I told him about our interview with Steve Pennell, there was no screaming, no loud voices. It was worse; he didn't say anything, just looked at me, shook his head, and left the room.

I stopped by his office after dropping Jenne off at Shelly's place. We had driven south to Bellevue immediately after visiting Pennell, my thinking being that we needed to let Bill know right away. This might have been an error.

I was alone in a small conference room just off the lobby at Bellevue Police Headquarters. I wasn't sure whether I should leave or wait my friend out. Maybe the temper tantrum would pass and he'd return.

He did. And then the yelling began.

"For fuck's sake, Kevin, what were you thinking? You interviewed a possible accessory to a crime without a detective present."

"When I heard back from the facilities lady at Bellevue Towers, I didn't think anything would come of it. Some IT guy was fired months ago, and she said he possibly could have something to do with it, but he didn't."

"You told me he might have passed it on to the burglar."

"No, I said he had a conversation with some guy in a bar who *could* have been the thief, but he also might have passed it on to someone else, who also could have passed it on."

Now that we were talking, Bill's temper seemed to have abated slightly, so I reminded him of our agreement. "Remember when you said I could help, and if I found anything, I should keep you in the loop?"

"Ahh, shit … I knew I'd regret this."

"Well, this is me doing that. Send someone to talk to this Pennell if you want, but I'm pretty sure it's a dead end."

"He wouldn't recognize this person again?"

"He said it was dark, and the only thing he knew for certain was that the fellow had a deep tan and he wasn't short."

Bill, standing over me, finally pulled up a chair. "It's a stretch to think the break-in had anything to do with Butch's death, but it is a bizarre coincidence. You're sure he couldn't give a description?"

"It's what he said, but maybe you or Julie could get something more from him. He doesn't seem like a bad guy. I think he'd at least try to help."

"I'll have Houser interview him. Promise me if you even *think* you have a lead, you'll tell me *before* you do any investigating."

"Okay, okay, I promise. Hey, by the way, I have some information on the foot."

"Huh?"

"The foot, remember? The one in the boat. It seems like years ago, around 2007, a number of feet washed up on Vancouver Island and some of the Gulf Islands. They all had tennis shoes on and the remains of the foot inside, just like the one in the boat."

"I heard about that but thought it was just some urban legend."

"Nope, it's true. There were more than fifteen feet found." I thought I'd drag it out some to let the last vestiges of his temper trickle away.

"So?"

"It seems when someone drowns, they usually end up sinking to the bottom, where crabs and other crustaceans feed on the body. They can't munch through bones, but I guess the ankle is mostly soft tissue, and the little buggers chew up the ligaments and stuff and end up separating the foot."

Bill looked at me like I was from another planet. "Kevin, do I need to know this shit?"

"Of course. It's forensic stuff."

"Then why does the foot float when it gets separated?"

"See, interesting, isn't it? Anyway, sometime, again around 2007, the sneaker manufacturers started putting lots more air in the soles for cushioning, and voilà, floating feet in sneakers. Pretty cool, eh?"

"Seriously?"

"Yup. Some UDub doc even published a paper on it. So if this boat was derelict and floating about in shitty weather, which it was, then a decent-sized wave could easily have picked it up and tossed it inside. I guess whoever owned it drowned a long time ago."

"Well, geez, Kev, that's just terrific. Did you tell Wenzal about this research? And do you think maybe I can return to work and focus on crimes I can do something about?"

"Not yet. I wanted my good buddy to know first, but I will. By all means, please go back to what you were doing, and glad I could help out." His friendly snarl led me to believe I was back in his good graces, so I headed back to my ride to find my wife and return to Whidbey Island.

THIRTY-TWO

Bellevue

After he had met with Davis, John Carlson pointed his pickup northwest; he had things to find out and knew exactly where to go. Now that he knew his father would be at the winery for at least a few days, he felt better about his chances of success.

John had had nothing to do with his old man since the day he'd cut off his college tuition, but he remembered what a planner he was and how meticulous he was regarding record keeping. He'd grown used to his life of leisure, and the recent loss of his fortune had done little to quench his taste for the good life. He knew his dad was worth many millions; he just needed to find a way to get his hands on it.

Without much of a plan, his arrival in Bellevue shocked him. He remembered the city as a sleepy suburb of Seattle, with Lake Washington serving as a deterrent against overpopulation. Now the former town was more like a teeming metropolis. Young people scurried to and fro, phones pressed against their ears, and traffic was a virtual gridlock. Instead of one or two high-rise buildings, there had to be thirty. His father's address, noted from a past unacknowledged birthday card, was in the city center in one of the tallest structures.

With no street parking to be found anywhere, he pulled into the subterranean visitors' lot of the towers, appalled at the $20-per-hour parking fee. He managed to find the elevator that took him directly into the residential lobby of the almost 300-foot-tall building.

The reception desk, an ultra-modern structure of steel, glass, and stone almost fifteen feet wide, was staffed by two very young, very attractive women.

"May I help you, sir?"

"Um, yes … I'm here to see a friend. Is there a directory of the residents somewhere?" Carlson knew the building address, just not the unit number or the floor on which his father lived.

"I'm sorry, sir, we can't give out that information. If you give me the name, I can call them and have them come down."

The last thing he needed was to have someone remember he was there. "Thanks, that's okay. I'll just give him a call and have him meet me somewhere."

He exited the skyscraper onto 106th Avenue and turned into the first bar he saw. Knowing that his father would not return for at least a couple of days allowed him a little time to figure something out. Finding a copy of his will was all that mattered now.

Although it was only early afternoon, there was only one vacant seat at the bar. Purple was well known for offering over forty wines by the glass. The back bar was stacked fifteen feet high with blends and vintages from around the world. He wondered how so many people could afford twenty or thirty bucks for a glass of wine.

Nursing a local IPA on tap, he mulled over the possibilities of getting into his father's penthouse.

"Busy place, huh?" Dressed in jeans and a flannel shirt, the patron on the stool next to him was staring into the burgundy-colored liquid in his long-stemmed glass.

Not wanting to stand out, John nodded and grunted, "For sure."

"I just got fired."

His neighbor blurted it out so suddenly that he was unsure how to respond. He briefly thought back to Evan Davis telling him something similar at a bar in Santa Barbara.

Finally, thinking he had to acknowledge the confession, he said, "Geez, sorry to hear that. What did you do for work?"

One thing led to another. First Steve Pennell talking about his job and why he was fired, then John talking about Google, his coworkers there, and even Billy Tomlin, the kid with the eidetic memory. As time passed, they shared stories about how naïve and stupid the average citizen was regarding passwords and computer security. It was then that Pennell revealed how incompetent his boss at Bellevue Towers was, since she was still using the original setup password, *BT1234*. Carlson laughed and agreed just as he committed to memory the sophomoric key to the entire LAN for Bellevue Towers.

Still not believing he was the beneficiary of such good luck, he said his goodbyes and returned to retrieve his truck. He ended up paying forty dollars to exit the damn building and was surprised to find a curbside spot in front of the main entrance to the Towers.

Using the browser on his cell phone, he could see the wireless network called Bellevue Towers. There was a screen for the tenants' internet services, which he immediately bypassed. Under a tab called *utilities*, he found a login box for the facilities department, which he opened. He immediately plugged in the password and held his breath to see if it worked. It did.

Not only was he able to find a roster of all the tenants and their unit numbers, but he also had access to their credit cards on file for incidental purchases.

He found the HVAC and electrical plans and entry points, as well as those for the security cameras. To access these files required an additional password, although *as lazy as these folks are*, he thought, *they probably used the same one*. And they did.

Next, he pulled up the elevator schematics, where he found an override code allowing access to all the residential floors in the building. Satisfied that he was now equipped with all he needed, he headed north on 106th to find a place to stay for a night or two.

He waited until late afternoon the following day, when the lobby was buzzing with residents, visitors, and delivery people. Dressed in jeans, sneakers, and Levi's trucker jacket, he could have been a service man, visitor, or even one of the many employees. Without a key card, however, no one could gain entrance to the upper floors. Unless, that is, someone had a code to override the system.

There were only four units on the penthouse level, and the entry to Butch Carlson's home was just to the right of the elevator. John had already deactivated the security cameras and entered the code supplied by the secure roster on the keypad to the left of the door.

Pausing for a moment after he entered and quickly closed the door, he felt oddly calm at what he was about to do. Butch had never remarried; however, his home reflected stylish design complemented by expensive furnishings. *Fucker probably paid some designer a mint to do this*, John mused. Being in his father's space was enough to reignite his loathing of the man. He would have loved to trash everything in the penthouse, but instead, he did what he had come to do.

Because his father was so organized, he only had to rifle through a couple of filing cabinets before finding a folder labeled "Last will and testament." As expected, his will called for his sons to split his estate 50/50 but gave the winery to Jason and made him the executor.

He couldn't have cared less about the goddamn winery, and he was glad his asshole brother was the executor. Now that he knew he would inherit far more than he'd squandered away, he needed to proceed to the next stage of his scheme.

As he replaced the folder and closed most of the drawers, he couldn't help himself and swiped some of his father's memorabilia from the shelves. It would have been silly to steal anything; he didn't want any of his old man's shit, and he was sure he'd be coming into some money soon. On his way to the door, he noticed a *Decanter* platinum award hanging in the hallway. *Fuck it*, he thought, *I'll take that for Evan. He never stops talking about the damn thing.*

Thirty-Three

Whidbey Island

When detective Tom Wenzal finally returned my call, he seemed as distracted as usual. "Yeah, O'Malley, what can I do for you?"

"You remember that day you were here—you know, when somebody shot at me, right?"

"I do."

"Well … did you find anything out?"

"Not yet. Still got it on my desk. One thing, though; when I sent a deputy up to the top of the bluff, he found where the shooter was positioned."

"I guess that's something."

"Yeah. He found some shell casings and we got a partial print off a couple of them. We'll catalog them in case we ever get a match."

I was close to positive this investigation was going nowhere, so I thought I'd make his day with the foot story. "I found out about the foot."

"Good to know. So did I. Some UDub prof came up with a theory about sneaker soles and crabs and shit. Anything else?"

Deflated, I quietly said no and goodbye and hung up. Jenne had witnessed the phone conversation from across the room and offered her method of cheering me up.

"What's wrong, Kev? Wait, don't tell me; Wenzal knew all about the foot thingy, right?"

"He did," I replied quietly with only the slightest pout.

"And you were looking forward to making his day, yes?"

"I was."

"Too bad, so sad, baby. Let's take Emma down to the beach. Maybe we can find another foot."

While more mature folks might take offense to my wife's dark humor, not me. That's one of the reasons we're married; no one gets me like Jenne does, and I thank my lucky stars every day.

"Are you making fun of me?"

"Of course, you dope. You're such an easy target. Grab the leash and the dog and let's get going."

The tide was out, and the beach was empty save for the three of us. Overcast skies and temperatures in the mid-forties tend to have that effect.

The *Island Hunter* was still where it had washed ashore, so I guessed the Sheriff's Department had failed to get the wreck towed to Everett. Over the past several weeks, the high tides had managed to tilt the boat onto its side, the yellow crime scene tape still attached to the railing.

"That boat gives me the creeps."

I was thinking the same thing but attempted a more rational approach. "I guess me too, but it helps to know that there's no serial foot cutter-offer out there, doesn't it?"

The subtle tongue sticking out from my wife led me to believe I might have been mistaken.

"Can't we get this thing taken somewhere?"

I thought the same thing, but its condition was in such a state that it could no longer float. "Let's check with the coast guard or maybe DNR and see if anything can be done. In the meantime, how about we head in the other direction?"

We spent the rest of our walk talking about Butch's death, Jason's challenges at Uva Cellars, and the lack of progress on almost everything until it became too dark; then we headed back up the hill to our home. Emma was happy, and Jenne and I were tired enough to camp out on the sofa and watch reruns of Frasier.

With little in the way of leads to follow, we had nothing on our plates for the next few days.

THIRTY-FOUR

It was the day after he found out what was in his father's will that he heard from Evan. "Your dad is going to be here until tomorrow morning, and I heard him tell Michelle he was going to leave at eight to try and get ahead of the weather over the pass."

"You're certain?"

"I'm sure that's what he said."

"Okay, thanks, bye."

John was never a violent person, but then he'd never been broken before either. His father had ceased to exist for him years ago, and he was in his sixties now anyway. *That's plenty old enough, isn't it?*

He tried to think of some way to get rid of him without any messiness. Hiring someone would be risky; he'd have to live his life looking over his shoulder. No, that wouldn't do.

His frequent visits to Hector's shooting range had transformed him into a serviceable, if not expert, marksman, but any opportunity to kill his father from a distance and get away with it seemed remote.

As he considered other methods and means, he noticed a weather bulletin scrolling across the muted TV. The forecast was for snow in the morning, becoming heavier as the day progressed. It was suggested that any traffic needing to negotiate Snoqualmie Pass do so earlier in the day.

Although the chance of success seemed remote at best, it was an opportunity to do the job without a great deal of risk and with almost no chance of being recognized.

As he thought about the best way to intercept his father, he recalled trips they'd made as a family and how they'd always needed to make a pit stop at Thorp Fruit and Antique Mall. The landmark offered everything from gas to fruit to antiques, and, more importantly, it was located just off I-90 between Ellensburg and Cle Elum. From Walla Walla, it was about a three-hour drive and was the best place for a rest stop before the climb through the pass.

He'd bet his last nickel that his father's driving habits were still the same and immediately got back on the phone with Evan. "What is he driving?"

"Huh? Is this John?"

"Yes, it's me. What's my father driving? What kind of car?"

"Who cares?"

"Just tell me, dammit."

"It's a Tesla, a blue one, okay?"

"A blue Tesla. Great, thanks. And he's leaving at eight?"

"Yes. That's what I told you."

"Good. Bye."

If he left Bellevue at nine the following day, he could easily be at Thorp's before his father's arrival.

By the time he arrived at Thorp's, it was a little after ten. It had already started snowing when he came through the pass, but there had been little accumulation. His four-wheel-drive Denali pickup made for little difficulty anyway when driving in the snow.

Even though his father had no idea what he was driving, he took the added precaution of parking between two other pickups. He backed in to give himself a good view of any vehicles entering the sizeable parking lot.

As it approached the top of the hour, the snow intensified, and it was necessary to use the wipers intermittently to observe the traffic. Shortly after eleven, a blue Tesla pulled up to the charging station and plugged in.

Looks like he's going to be there for a little while. The man exiting the car looked substantially older than John remembered, but there was no doubt that it was Butch Carlson; John watched as his father entered the vast barn-like structure that housed the fruit and antique enterprise.

Thirty minutes later, his father returned with a grocery bag under his arm. As he unplugged and left the parking area, his son followed close behind. The snow was falling heavily, and the traffic had slowed from seventy mph to ten miles per hour slower. The climb up the east side of the pass took over an hour, and at the summit, the snow was at least ten inches deep.

Snowplows were doing their best to keep up, and the flashing overhead signs warned that soon the pass would be closing. The steep downhill on the west slope made for difficult driving, and several vehicles had pulled into the breakdown lanes to chain up.

It was easy to follow the Tesla, especially when he had no concern about being seen. His father seemed content to drive in the right-hand lane and let the more adventurous drivers proceed.

As traffic speed increased due to the severe slope, John pulled into the passing lane. Snow was flying everywhere as the cars ahead picked up chunks of it and sprayed his windshield. The wipers could barely keep up. As he passed the Tesla, he looked over at his father, who was concentrating heavily on keeping his car in his lane. *Too bad, old man,* he thought as he jerked the steering wheel into the left quarter of the car, felt a shudder, then turned back into his lane.

As he looked in the rearview mirror, he saw the blue car fishtail, slam into the guardrail, then careen over the side. The traffic behind only slowed because of the difficult driving conditions, and John Carlson continued west on I-90.

Once he made it to I-5, the snow had turned to rain, and he turned south. He'd spend the night in San Francisco and then head for Santa Barbara. Maybe he'd even head over to El Encanto for a drink; he'd be coming into some money soon, after all.

THIRTY-FIVE

Santa Barbara/Whidbey Island

"I need a favor."

"Who is this? Evan?"

"It is."

"Why are you calling me, and why do I need to help you?"

"The new owner sent some dipshit and his wife here to see how we're doing."

"So?"

"So I've got a bad feeling he's gonna try to get me fired."

"So?"

"So I need you to put the fear of god into him."

"And I should help you why?"

"Because I know that you killed your old man."

John didn't say a word for twenty seconds. *How the fuck could Evan know?*

Finally, he asked quietly, "What are you talking about?"

"I know it was you. That's why you wanted to know exactly when he was leaving here, and I know you drive a black Denali. That's what the news said they're looking for."

He'd thought he was in the clear and now this asshat winemaker was squeezing him. He needed time to think this through and said, "What's the favor?"

"Go scare this clown."

"I'm in Santa Barbara; he's up in Seattle."

"No, he's actually on an island in Puget Sound."

"You do it."

"Sorry, John, I need you to do it, and I don't care how. You've already killed your father; how hard can this be?"

"I didn't kill him. It was an accident."

"Yeah, I'm sure it was. Do this and I won't bug you anymore. You don't even have to kill him. Just scare him."

Fuck, just what I want to be—a contract hit man. "When?"

"As soon as possible, but you'd better not drive your rig up here; they're still looking for it."

Carlson landed at Paine Field on a Wednesday afternoon. The small airport in Everett, Washington, was a far better choice than using SeaTac Airport, which was developing a reputation for congestion that rivaled some of the much busier airports in the country.

He picked up a Subaru Outback at the rental counter and headed for Bart's Gunshop. The regular trips to the gun range in his hometown had made him a fan of the Ruger .22 long target rifle. Hector had suggested he use one to begin with, and he had never used anything else.

Although it wasn't a common request, the gunsmith at the shop was able to fit the used rifle with a silencer. He would rather have used his gun, but air travel frowned upon such items.

Even though he'd grown up in the northwest, he had never visited any of the islands in Puget Sound, of which there were many. Whidbey Island was the fourth-longest and fourth-largest island in the contiguous United States. An interesting fact, but all John Carlson cared about was getting his job done and getting out of town.

He spent the night at a cheap motel in Everett and took the Mukilteo Ferry to Whidbey at daylight the next morning. Still trying to figure out what he was about to do, he drove to the address Davis had provided. Since the only objective was to frighten O'Malley, he could manage that by shooting up a few windows or maybe killing the dog Davis had told him about.

Not prepared for the rural nature of the island, he was startled when he came upon his target's house suddenly after emerging from a heavily forested section of the road. As he did so, a sixty-something man and a sheriff's deputy walked down the driveway to a cruiser.

He continued, just another islander searching for an address. Driving slowly, he watched in his rearview mirror as the police car turned abruptly and headed down a twisty road that appeared to turn towards the water. After ten minutes, he turned around and followed them down the hill.

After multiple twists and turns, Carlson found himself in a clearing where the cruiser was parked; it was empty. It appeared the occupants had gone down a path to the beach, but since the cop was with O'Malley, there wasn't much he could do. He backtracked up the hill to see if there was another opportunity.

Little Dirt Road ran parallel to the beach below, but it was impossible to see anything on the beach without coming close to the bluff's edge, because it was two hundred feet higher. There were only a few houses on the road, and forested sections separated most. He pulled onto a gravel path, parked, and negotiated the undergrowth to make his way to the cliff's edge.

Through the sparse growth on the face of the bluff, he caught sight of a derelict boat below where O'Malley and the cop stood talking. The weather was clear and cold, but the distance was so great, he could hear nothing. He watched for a moment until he saw the deputy head back toward his parked vehicle, then he bolted back to his rental to get the rifle.

He was pissed that Davis had coerced him into this fool's errand, and he couldn't see the sense in it. Still, he couldn't risk the winemaker upsetting his plans. He hurried back to the bluff's edge but could no longer see his quarry.

Using the scope on the Ruger, it still took a few minutes to locate O'Malley, who was perched on one of the hundreds of logs and stumps scattered along the shore. He fired half of the ten-round magazine as close as he dared and watched as the old guy finally realized someone was shooting at him. Then he emptied the rest of the magazine as his target scurried to better cover. Although the shots were audible, he was confident the silencer had muffled them sufficiently to limit the distance they could be heard.

He hurried to his Outback, tossed the rifle into the back seat, and motored down Little Dirt Road before the cop could make it back up from the beach. The forested sections of the island were so thick that disposing of the rifle would be simple. Soon he'd be on the ferry and then on his flight back to the warmth and sun of Santa Barbara.

Thirty-Six

Bellevue

March turned into April and then May. The search for any further clues to help locate the perpetrator of Butch Carlson's life-ending crash had proven fruitless, and other crimes had moved to the top of the priority list. My good friend Bill Owens did his best to keep the investigation on the front burner, but even he had to admit there was little to work with.

Jenne and I were constantly looking for the black Denali pickup, although the ones we saw were hardly of the suspicious variety. The little old ladies, young families, and hardworking men and women who owned the trucks appeared to have other priorities than running our friend off the road.

Little by little, the alleged wrongdoing began to fade into the miasma that seemed to engulf more than its fair share of crimes. Some had even started to doubt the story Cora Montgomery and her friend had reported, although the two remained steadfast in their allegations.

Thirty-Seven

Walla Walla

Jason had taken to Uva Cellars like a kid to a new puppy. Whether it was the allure of crafting fine wines or, more likely, the attraction he felt for its general manager, his dedication was admirable. One month after his first meeting with Michelle Browne, he turned in his resignation to his company in Boulder, much to the disappointment of his associates.

Reinforcing his commitment to his winery, he enrolled in one of the extension courses in viticulture offered by Washington State University. He began to understand how those in the industry were passionate about the business, regardless of any fame or fortune that might ensue.

His enthusiasm for the winery seemed to have overtaken any distraction caused by the unsolved car crash. Through several industry publications, Michelle posted the opening for a winemaker at Uva Cellars and was gratified by the number of applicants she received.

Jason, now spending more time in Walla Walla than in the Seattle area, sat down with Michelle to cull the résumés gathered over the previous two months. They agreed that taking their time during the hiring process would bear fruit during their decision-making.

"How many did we get, Michelle?"

"There are about a dozen, but some are looking for their first gig. I think it's best to go with a proven talent—agree?"

"Yes. We can afford to pay what we need, so that won't be an obstacle. For the next few years, I want to build a first-class team here regardless of profitability. I'm confident that will take care of itself."

Michelle looked down for a few seconds, unsure how to ask. "Jason, how do you see my role here?"

"Well, geez, Michelle, you're the boss. I'm the owner, yes, but nothing will happen here unless you okay it. I plan on being active in a management role, but you know much more about the operation than I do. If you think I'm overstepping or I should back off, please tell me. I mean it."

Blushing but looking directly at him, she said, "Thanks for the vote of confidence. I appreciate it."

"I think we'll be working closely on some issues, so let me know if you have concerns. That's the only way this can work. My background is in IT, so naturally, I think I can be of use in our digital efforts. Does that make sense?"

"Perfectly. Now let's see what we have here."

They narrowed their selection down to three candidates and planned to interview them the following week. This gave them ample time to check references and gather further information from Michelle's contacts within the industry.

Most of the vines had already started blooming, and Oscar and Benny had their hands full working the vineyards, with Jason and Michelle chipping in whenever possible. It was clear that the entire team was eagerly looking forward to getting a new winemaker on board.

Even before the day of the interviews finally arrived, a clear front-runner had emerged from the three candidates. Ten years out from the program at WSU, Don Pettigrew had developed a name among the growers in the state as bright, knowledgeable, forward-thinking, and willing to try new ideas. His previous employers and instructors had all sung his praises, but more importantly, all had emphasized what a team player he was.

When they were finished with the interviews, they were exhausted. "Whew, I forgot how much work hiring someone for a key position can be. I'm glad we're done. What are you thinking?" Jason looked at Michelle for her opinion.

With a knowing look, she wrinkled her nose and said, "I think we have a new winemaker, and his name is Don."

"What about me? I'm the owner; don't I get a say?"

"Not according to what you told me. I like the guy, and I want him."

Jason chuckled and had to admit he was on the same page. The other two candidates were excellent, but Pettigrew was far and away his choice. "I'm glad we agree. I think we have a real winner here. Will you let him know tomorrow? Offer whatever you need to for a compensation package, and make sure you leave room for some incentive based on our showings at the competitions."

"Sir, yes, sir," she replied with a mock salute.

Jason raised his hands in surrender. "I'm sorry. I'm used to calling the shots, and sometimes I forget who I'm talking to. If I take you to dinner, will you forgive me?"

"Hah, no worries. Of course. Just sticking the needle in a little. I know you're no stranger to that. Someplace nice, I hope?"

"I know a cute little place in town. Will Bottles be okay?"

"You bet. Let me freshen up, and we can leave in an hour or so."

Jason returned to the barn where he stayed when at the winery. He showered and shaved and thought about the turn his life had taken. He had worked side by side with Michelle for the last couple of months and loved every minute. His previous company was a distant memory.

Now that they were bringing a new winemaker on board, he would be free to delve into the digital world, where reputations and perceptions were formulated in today's commerce. Tonight, though, would be a celebration of moving on from an enigmatic associate who eschewed being a team player to one who would hopefully propel them to greater success.

The night was clear and calm, and both were quiet during the ride into town. They were still learning the nuances of each other's personalities, and the two of them were comfortable with the silence. It seemed that the speed with which change was happening was beyond their control yet exciting because of it.

The dinner was excellent, as usual, and they celebrated with a bottle of the cabernet that had won the platinum award.

"Here's to the future of Uva Cellars and to the woman who will take us there." Jason offered his glass.

"And here's to the new owner. His dad was wonderful, but I suspect his son will inspire us all to achieve greater accomplishments. I'm happy you're here, Jason."

They glanced into each other's eyes for a split second, oblivious to the muted conversations and tinkling plates and silverware around them. Then Jason spoke. "I'm glad too, Michelle; very much so."

They clinked glasses and sipped. The temperature seemed much warmer to Jason than just a few minutes ago.

The return drive was even quieter. It was as if a threshold had been crossed and each was considering where it would take them.

Michelle pulled up to the barn to drop Jason off before going to the farmhouse. He opened the door and turned to say good night. At the same time, she looked at him. Without conscious thought, he touched her shoulder, leaned over, and kissed her briefly but tenderly. She eased back slightly, looked into his eyes, and kissed him back. When they parted, he gently took her hand, squeezed it, and said, "Thanks for the best evening of my life."

With a smile that melted his heart, she replied, "You mean *so far*, don't you?"

Thirty-Eight

Santa Barbara

John Carlson was back to his old haunts; with the inheritance from his father, money was no longer a concern. Learning from his past failures, he placed the bulk of his funds into short-term CDs. The interest was low, but the security was high, and twenty million dollars at two percent was still $400,000 a year. Yes, life was good.

It was a few months after his trip to Whidbey Island, and he hadn't heard a peep from his buddy Evan. However, he had seen a blurb in the *Wine Spectator* about a rising star named Don Pettigrew taking over the winemaking duties at Uva Cellars. *I guess scaring that putz on that island didn't help much. They ended up firing Davis anyway*, he mused.

When he first returned to Santa Barbara, he kept a low profile, fearing, perhaps irrationally, that his actions in the Pacific Northwest might be revealed. To further distance himself from any possibility of discovery, he located a long-term self-storage facility where he stashed his Denali with the dented passenger rear quarter panel. Telling the attendant that he'd be traveling indefinitely, he prepaid the rental for three years and proceeded to purchase a new ride.

He figured that after a few years, he would get the Denali repaired and ditch it. Besides, his new Jeep Rubicon pickup was a perfect look for the beach-bum persona he hoped to display.

Although his adventures in the Seattle area had been fraught with anxiety, he missed the rush he got from them. He became restless with nothing to do but piss away twenty-four hours a day. His resentment of his father was slowly replaced by an even more intense dislike of his younger sibling. Yes, they had split his father's fortune equally, but based on tidbits from the internet, Jason was viewed as an up-and-comer in the Washington wine community.

Another online posting mentioned that Uva had hired the highly regarded Pettigrew. It was rare that any wine publication failed at least to mention the promise of the coming Uva vintages. *The pissant always got the attention when he was young, and now he's getting it because of the winery he inherited.*

Unable to be content with his ill-gotten riches, John Carlson began fantasizing about tragic events that could befall his brother.

It was near the end of May, and John was sitting at a small table in the bar at El Encanto. Since his return, and with a new bartender pushing the drinks, he'd once again become a regular. Leafing through the latest Wine Spectator, he was startled when his phone buzzed; almost nobody had his new number.

"Yeah?"

"Hey, old buddy, guess who?"

Although the voice was slightly slurred, he knew the caller. "Evan? Is that you?"

"Yup. How's life?"

"Can't complain. What's new with you?" He knew Evan was no longer at Uva and was uncertain about how much he should ask.

"Your dickhead brother fired me, but you probably know that." The nastiness that always bubbled beneath the surface didn't take long to appear.

"I saw they hired some new guy. I told you my brother was a piece of shit."

"Yeah, well, you were right. I've been living off my severance, but I'm gonna get even with the fucker. They've ruined my reputation, and even with my award, I can't find a job anywhere."

"Sorry about that. If you get stuck and need a few bucks, I can send you some." John didn't want a full-fledged dependent, but he did have lots of money, and Davis knew a few things.

After a loud slurp, he heard, "Maybe I'll take you up on that. But that's not why I'm calling."

"Then how come?"

"I'm working on something that will fuck up that winery for a long time. I'm wondering if you'd like to help me with it."

John was conflicted. Davis was a piece of work—not someone he wanted to be best buddies with. On the other hand, he hated his brother, and if there was any way to fuck him over and get away with it, he was interested. Adding the possibility of Davis knowing too much about his father's "accident" into the equation, it was a no-brainer. "What did you have in mind?"

Thirty-Nine

Whidbey Island

With spring on full display in the Puget Sound region, the question of who was responsible for the death of Butch Carlson had all but faded. Other more heinous crimes had taken over top billing, and the event slowly faded from the memories of all but his closest friends and family.

The shooting on the beach was chalked up to random mischief-makers, although I was not convinced.

We kept in touch with Jason Carlson and were excited to see his steps to improve things at Uva Cellars. Jenne wasn't the only one to notice that every conversation we had with him started with "Michelle and I" or "You should see what Michelle did."

On today's call, she finally asked him, "Jason, am I mistaken, or are you and Michelle more than just co-workers?"

"Um, yeah, I guess you could say that. We've gotten pretty close over the last few months."

"How close?" The woman's persistence was a marvel.

"Okay, okay, very close. We're living in the farmhouse together now."

This time when she spoke, her grin was ear to ear. "That's wonderful. I knew you two would get along. We're thrilled for you."

"I've never met anyone like her. There's nothing she can't do. We went out to dinner a couple of months ago and got close. Ever since, we've been together."

With her phone on speaker, I was privy to all this, so I naturally felt obliged to put my two cents in. "I hope this new living arrangement isn't hurting the wine production. We *are* club members, you know."

"Hah, hey, Kev, no worries. We're on top of things here, and Don, the new winemaker, is a perfect fit."

He told us the weather had been cooperative and Pettigrew was a consummate team player. His relationships with the vineyard workers were first class—so much so that many of the workers in the valley were applying for positions at Uva.

We missed Butch, but getting to know Jason and the rest of the crew at Uva Cellars was a blessing.

"Hey, you two, we're throwing a party for all the club members after the crush. Will you be able to make it?"

"We wouldn't miss it," we said together.

"That's terrific. Are you and Jenne busy these days?"

"If you call playing golf, hiking, and enjoying life busy, then we're swamped," Jenne replied.

"How would you two like to come down and give us a hand during harvest? We could use the help, and I'd like to pick your brains on how to design the winery for our big event. You can have the barn, and I'll pay you for your efforts."

"Let's not go there, Jason. Food and lodging are more than enough payment. When should we come?"

"We think the merlot and cab will be ready the first week of October, and we're going to hold the event on the Saturday of the last weekend of the month. If you two can come down, we'd really appreciate it. Make sure to bring Emma too."

"Consider it done. We'll look forward to seeing you."

We chatted more, said our goodbyes, and smiled at each other like proud parents.

"I had a feeling those two would hit it off." I thought it best to chirp up first.

"Oh, you did, did you? You don't remember me telling you this is exactly what would happen?"

"Um … I'm not sure. Maybe." I could tell this wasn't precisely the response she was looking for when her ball cap sailed over my head.

"No, wait—yes, yes, I remember that now. You were one hundred percent correct, dear. I thank my lucky stars every day I'm married to you." Her eyeroll told me I was on safer ground again.

"On a more serious note, Kev, do you think we'll ever find out who ran Butch off the road?"

The event that had initially seemed like an accident but then an eyewitness swore was intentional was looking more and more like another carcass on the country's heap of unsolved crimes. It was unfortunate, but it was the reality we faced.

"It doesn't seem like that's going to happen, hon. The further out we get, the less likely it appears. I wish the witness was mistaken and it was just an accident, but I don't think so. It will probably always be an unsolved case."

She nodded resignedly, appearing to share similar thoughts.

FORTY

Santa Barbara

A week after the call from Evan Davis, John Carlson found himself picking up the ex-winemaker at the Santa Barbara Municipal Airport.

The building's recently refurbished Spanish Colonial Revival architecture was the quintessential representation of the Southern California lifestyle. Since the area was blessed with almost perfect weather, the structure was able to blur the lines between indoor and outdoor spaces. While still adhering to the required security and safety measures, the informality of the airport was what every visitor remembered.

Carlson had positioned himself on the front lawn where he could easily view the planes approaching any of the four gates of the main terminal. He watched as a distinctly older-looking Davis descended the stairs from the plane and walked through the terminal.

"Thanks for coming, Evan," he said, offering his hand.

"Hey, thanks for paying for the flight. God, I sure have missed the climate here. They grow some good grapes in Walla Walla, but compared to this, the weather sucks."

"No argument here. How about we head to El Encanto? We can have a drink, then dinner, and you can tell me what's on your mind."

They walked over to John's Rubicon, hopped in, and negotiated the twenty-minute drive to the hotel.

The El Encanto, originally built in the 1920s, was a favorite watering hole for the movie stars and politicians of that era. Newly refurbished, its Spanish Colonial and California Craftsman construction was perfectly sited in the lush rolling hills on the city's east side. A central building housed the bar, restaurant, and reception areas, while ninety-two suites and bungalows were scattered throughout the property. Hundred-year-old birds of paradise trees, palm trees, and other native foliage gave an exclusive feel to the property, reinforced by their pricey room rates.

As they pulled up to the valet at the main entrance, Davis said, "I never get tired of this spot. If I could afford to live here, I would."

"Yeah, I know what you mean. I *can* afford it, but I prefer living in my place without new neighbors moving in every other day. Even so, I'm more comfortable here than in any other hotel I've ever been to. Let's grab a table."

After more talk about the weather, wine, and other inane topics, Carlson finally asked, "What's on your mind, and why did you have to come here to tell me about it?"

Davis played with his utensils before looking up and speaking. "I wanted to discuss this in person, because it's a little complicated."

"Go on."

"Let's agree on a few things first. We both despise your brother—me for him firing me and ruining my life, and you for … whatever. Every time I think of Uva Cellars or see their name in a magazine or on a wine bottle, I want to puke. They cost me my livelihood and ruined my ability to find a decent position, and I think you have a hard-on for them too."

"Okay, let's agree on those things. So what?"

"What if there was a way to ruin Uva Cellars for the foreseeable future? It would devastate your brother, ruin that bitch Michelle's life, and we'd never have to see their name again."

Even though John couldn't fathom where this was going, he was intrigued by the thought. Still, he wasn't entirely sure of Davis's angle.

"I understand your need for revenge, but how does this help you in the long run? How do you earn a living?"

Seemingly reluctant to answer, Davis plowed ahead. "I, uh … I was thinking that since you're flush with dough now, you could maybe pay me for coming up with the idea."

"Why would I do that?"

"Because without me, you couldn't pull it off. You wouldn't know what you were doing. Also I'd have an incentive to keep my mouth shut about the things that happened in Washington."

And there it was, thought John, blackmail. He wondered if, when this chapter was over, Davis would keep coming back to the well. *I'll hear him out, then decide after I know the plan.*

"And how much would I pay you for this plan—this activity?"

"I thought a million bucks would take care of me for the future."

"That's all? Only a million?"

Davis's expression inferred he hadn't missed the sarcasm in John's tone. "Look, let me lay out the plan. If you think I'm full of shit, then we say goodbye—we're done. If it makes sense, then we can discuss finances."

With a sigh of acquiescence, John nodded. "Show me what you've got."

FORTY-ONE

Whidbey Island

Spring turned to summer, when all but the most pessimistic inhabitants of the northwest forgot entirely the dark, damp, overcast atmosphere that served as winter in this part of the country.

To those uninformed about the climate in the top left corner of the country, it's simple. There are only two seasons. Winter, or *the darkness*, as the locals call it, occurs from November through April. It's characterized by perpetually overcast skies, with darkness at its peak lasting sixteen hours. Temperatures are relatively mild, with average lows in the upper thirties and highs in the upper forties and low fifties.

The other season is summer. It rarely rains at this time of year, and daylight lasts sixteen hours at times. Average lows are in the upper fifties, and highs are mid-seventies. There are rarely thunderstorms and only a few air-conditioning days; mosquitoes are scarce. If there were a perfect climate anywhere, it would be summer in the northwest, and *that's* why we live here.

Whidbey Island has cooler summer temperatures and slightly warmer winter ones. There's never a need for cooling in the summer, and because of its northern latitude, it's slightly darker than Seattle in the winter but even lighter for longer in the summer.

We spent most of our days going for long walks on the beach with Emma, playing golf, and visiting neighbors and friends. With so much daylight, we often spent the evening hours on the deck overlooking Saratoga Passage and lamenting the state of politics in the country, although we swore daily it was the last time.

The Butch Carlson investigation was officially relegated to the cold case files. There was no other thread to follow save for the Denali, which proved to be a non-starter. The same held for the break-in at Bellevue Towers. Other than the wine award, no other items were missing, so that was a dead end too.

We got together with Bill and Shelly often. Now that my help solving the case was no longer needed, our friendship was without rancor. I frequently inquired whether I might be of assistance on some of his other investigations, but alas, he declined. I knew it was only a matter of time until he came crawling back for some O'Malley sleuthing.

As the length of the days began to diminish, we were looking forward to the Uva Cellars fall affair. Jason told us to extend the invitation to the Owenses, and we did, although Bill declined to get his hands dirty during the harvest. Something about rampant crime needed his attention, so we said we'd see him and Shelly after the crush. There were rumblings that the event might coincide with the owner tying the knot with his general manager, possibly floated by Jenne, but all who knew them welcomed the idea.

FORTY-TWO

Santa Barbara

Whatever John thought about Evan Davis now belonged on the back burner. As far as his plan for revenge against Uva Cellars was concerned, it was brilliant. He had given the scheme much thought—so much that it had been challenging to poke holes in.

Although he was tech-savvy and had above-average intelligence, his knowledge of chemistry was limited. He tried once more to get his arms around the concept.

"Tell me again, Evan, about this glyphosate stuff."

"It's the active ingredient in Roundup, remember?"

"The weed killer, right?"

"Correct. It's been used by the tons over the years on crops to eradicate weeds and unwanted plants."

"Do people use it for vineyards?"

"Sometimes we do, but it's touchy. You don't want to get any on the vines accidentally."

While John considered this, Evan continued, "It's one of the few herbicides that's systemic."

"And that means …?"

"Once it hits the plant, it travels through its vascular system, and that's why it kills weeds down to the roots."

"But if we aim for the fall, how does it get to the leaves?"

"All we need to do is spray the vines. The chemical will move through the rootstock and destroy the plant in the right concentration."

"You're sure?"

"This is what I do, John. I'm sure."

As convinced as he could be, John accepted his associate's words.

It wouldn't be cheap, but it was a bargain in the grand scheme of things. Even if he had to pony up the million Davis wanted, he would still be wealthy. There was little risk, almost no chance of being caught, and, if executed properly, it would seriously damage Uva Cellars' reputation for the foreseeable future.

There *was* a learning curve, but they would be in good shape for the fall implementation if they started now. The only downside was the time they had to stay in Fresno in the summer.

After spending two more days discussing the pros and cons of the operation, they committed to moving ahead with the plan. John made arrangements with the supplier of the equipment they needed and confirmed that the thirty grand he was forking over did indeed include the three-day training course.

Fresno

It was mid-September, and the temperature was in the high nineties. On the final day of their training, they would field test all phases of their plan. They were located just west of Piedra, a small rural community twenty miles east of Fresno.

The rolling hills and scattered crop fields were perfect for the rehearsal. They planned an early morning trial when the wind would be minimal and most people would be asleep. The equipment wasn't thunderously loud, but it would be hard to miss if anyone was awake.

Davis's job was to ensure the chemicals were correctly mixed and the dosage was sufficient to kill the vines entirely. Carlson had spent his time familiarizing himself with the drone software and its capabilities.

Once the mapping of the designated area was programmed in, the drone would automatically take off, apply the pesticide to the vineyard, then return to its starting location. The recovery of the drone wasn't even considered, since the two conspirators would be long gone by the time the job was complete.

The Agri4000 was only a year old and had been used sparingly. The used farm implement dealer had assured them that its state-of-the-art technology was the most advanced in the industry and even offered an extended warranty for an additional five hundred bucks. John declined, certain that this machine was a single-use product.

At five feet square and weighing a little over fifty pounds, the machine was easily transported by a pickup. Once the chemicals were in the tank and the battery attached, it weighed considerably more, but they didn't care.

For this test, the tank was filled with water; there was no need for the dealer to know their intentions. Evan stood a safe distance from the drone while John managed the remote alongside the dealer's rep.

The mechanical voice declared that the aircraft was about to take off and that humans should stand at least thirty feet away. The four propellers began spinning, reaching speeds of 140 revolutions per second. Up close, the noise was similar to that of a commercial leaf blower, so the instructor had advised ear protection.

Evan had retained the layout of the plantings at Uva, and John made sure to input the selected six target acres into the flight plan software. The drone lifted gently to about sixty feet, proceeded across a small valley, then lowered itself to twenty-five feet and began making uniform spraying passes across a fallow field. When the tank was empty, the drone rose to sixty feet again, then returned to its liftoff point.

As John removed his ear protection, the dealer's representative spoke. "Looks like you're a pro at this, sir. Any questions?"

"I think we're good, thanks. We'll take it from here."

Evan joined John, and the two of them collapsed the drone's arms and lifted it into the back of the repaired Denali pickup. He wasn't keen on using the truck, but his Rubicon's slightly smaller bed wouldn't accommodate their new toy. He had made sure the body shop that had done the work repainted the truck as well; the former onyx black was now metallic pearl beige.

FORTY-THREE

Walla Walla

We had ten days before the fall field day for the wine club members at Uva Cellars, and the harvest was well underway.

Because of the intensity of the work, the crew had doubled in size. Since each winery in the valley had its own unique microclimate, the peak time for harvesting the grapes varied from vineyard to vineyard. Many overlapped, of course, but still, there was enough variability that workers from one producer often assisted their neighboring wineries with the harvest.

As we arrived on the outskirts of town, the smell of fermenting grapes was unmissable. It seemed every other vehicle on the road was a trailer filled to the brim with grapes being towed by a tractor. The streets had turned purple from the juice seeping out of the trailers.

Pulling up to the tasting room, we noticed a sign on the door that said, "Sorry, closed for the day, picking grapes." We had started to take our things to the barn when a field hand turned the corner and bumped into us. We thought it strange that Emma nuzzled right up to him without barking.

"Oops, sorry … Jenne, Kevin, hey, great to see you. It's me, Michelle."

The person standing before us was barely recognizable. Dressed in a plaid flannel shirt under bib overalls, wearing wellies and a Carhartt vest, every square inch of fabric and face was stained with purple. With her hair tucked under an Uva ball cap, she smelled like a distillery. Once she smiled, though, we knew for sure it was her.

"Michelle, you look wonderful." Jenne attempted a hug, but Michelle held up her hands.

"Whoa, careful. This stuff stains until you throw your clothes away, and yes, I'm sure I do."

"I think what Jenne means is you look incredibly happy."

"I am. I've never had this much fun in my life." As she moved to flick a piece of grape skin from her cheek, something shiny caught the sun.

"Michelle …?"

"Yes?" Looking at Jenne, she moved her hand from her face and glanced at the ring on her finger.

"Is that what I think it is?" Once she got her teeth into something, my wife never let go.

I wasn't sure if it was even possible, but I thought I detected a slight blushing through the grape juice stains on Michelle's face.

"Yes, it is. We were going to tell you tonight. Neither of us wanted to make a big thing out of it. Jason asked me to marry him a couple of months ago, and we talked about waiting but then just said why?

"Last week we went to the northeast section, where the best cab grapes are, and had the ceremony. Perry's brother is a JP, and he performed it. Perry and Don were there, and that was about it. It was perfect."

"Congratulations," we both said together. Then the three of us— four, counting Emma—hugged regardless of the death sentence our clothes were about to receive.

"Why don't the three of you get settled in the barn, and then you can meet me in the warehouse space behind the tasting room? Make sure you wear something you're not terribly attached to."

"Sure thing. What are you doing right now?"

"We're punching down the tanks from the other day."

"Huh? Punching?"

"Just put some trashy clothes on and meet me out back. I'll explain then. I put a dog bed in your quarters for Emma. She'll probably be more comfortable there than with all the activity."

After putting our things away and getting Emma settled, we made our way to the production area. When we arrived at the two-story structure, we were struck by the beehive of activity. On our previous trips, we'd seen tanks, pumps, and things, but they'd always been sitting idle. Now I couldn't see a single piece of equipment not in use.

"Up here."

We looked up to see where Michelle's voice was coming from. She was standing on a narrow catwalk positioned over a line of eight stainless steel tanks, each filled to the brim with a solid mass of grapes and grape mush. In her hand was a long stainless pole with a flat disc on the bottom and T handles at the top and midpoint.

"I'll be down in a minute. I just need to punch one more." She stood over the last tank in the line and repeatedly plunged the cap of grape solids down to the bottom of the tank. When she had finished, she was breathing heavily and had a sheen of sweat over her smudged face.

She put her tool aside and climbed down the ladder to the main floor. "Whew, glad I don't have to do that again for another ten hours."

I had been around wine and wineries for some time but had not seen that particular process before. "What were you doing?"

"Let's get some coffee in the tasting room. It's closed for the next few days because it's all hands on deck for the harvest."

While we found stools at the tasting counter, Michelle poured us steaming cups of coffee. Jenne was as curious as I was. "So tell us, what is punching?"

"When we bring the grapes in after destemming, we put them in those fermentation tanks you saw. As the grapes ferment, the solids and the sheer weight of the grapes liquify a good portion of the mix. Carbon dioxide causes the grape solids to rise to the top of the tank, forming an almost solid cap on the tank. We need to punch down that cap a few times a day to make sure the liquid stays in contact with the skins. It's how we can produce such well-crafted wines with the intense flavor we're famous for."

"Do all wineries do this?"

"It's usually just the smaller ones. It's very labor intensive, but it makes a noticeable difference to the end product."

If making wine was this much work, I was much better off just drinking it. I was afraid to ask, but I did anyway. "What can we do to help?"

"We don't want you two overdoing it, but Jason and Don could use a hand bringing in the last of the merlot from the south vineyard. You can bring in the bins that we've loaded on small trolleys. Can you drive an ATV?"

"Are you kidding? I was born to ride those things." Judging by the look from my wife, she was less confident in my skills.

Michelle caught the doubt from my wife and came up with another plan. "How about the two of you get on that Honda four-wheeler over there and go see Jason? He'll get you started. Just drive slowly, capisce?"

"Got it. Adios."

FORTY-FOUR

Snoqualmie Pass

As we drove through Snoqualmie Pass and down the west side of the Cascades, we couldn't help but think of Butch Carlson.

"Hard to believe it's been almost a year since Butch's death, huh?" Jenne seemed to read my mind.

"Yeah. Every time we drive this way, I think about it. From the looks of things, I guess it'll go unsolved."

She thought about this for a moment, then nodded reluctantly. "At least we've made some new friends. Just think about it. Jason and Michelle might never have gotten together if none of this had happened."

"You're right, and I would never have had to bust my ass for a week working in the vineyards." I didn't think my comment was that egregious, but it did earn me a punch in the shoulder. "Hey, I'm driving here."

"If you call ferrying food back and forth to Don, Jason, and the crew busting your ass, I feel sorry for you. Those guys did the back-breaking work, and you even got to spend all day on that ATV."

In hindsight, she was right; it was actually a kick driving that thing all over the place. I played the role of delivery man while Michelle—and Jenne, when she wasn't punching—hunkered together, developing plans and decorations for the big event.

At the end of each day, the entire crew and the owners got together and shared a feast prepared by Perry and Chad, who had closed the restaurant during the crush to be available for Uva. It was a significant expense for Jason, but he could think of no better way to build morale among the team at the winery.

"I think Jason and Michelle are doing a remarkable job. The new winemaker is perfect, and his crew seems to do anything they can to please him. Those evening dinners were exceptional." Jenne was peering out the window, likely picturing our times at the banqueting table.

"I'm with you on that. It's amazing the change in the place from our first visit until now. I'm sure Butch was a good owner, but there's no substitute for one who lives on site. If they don't get winery of the year, I'll be shocked."

"What did Don say about the upcoming vintage?"

I'd had the chance to speak with him during breaks in my DoorDash service and had an inkling of his thinking. "He says it's as good as he's ever seen. The yield was high, and the weather conditions were optimal for the harvest. He even said the yield from the new acreage was much better than expected. He seemed especially excited about that."

"Don't you feel guilty about them letting us stay at the barn for free?"

Somehow I'd known this might come up, so I'd done my best to formulate an answer ahead of time, but I had to tread lightly here; no telling how I could screw this up.

"I can understand why you're asking me that." *See, this is the first step in not pissing your wife off—you agree.* "Here's how I look at it. We get to use their wonderful accommodation sometimes, right?"

"I know this; I *asked* if you feel like we're taking advantage of the situation."

I need to get to the point in a hurry. "What I think is, we helped them out by visiting the place and telling them what we thought, right?"

"Yes, but that was a long time ago."

"Also, we toiled in the vineyards for them, and you helped do the decorations for the field day, and we got them together, and geez, I really like it there."

"You sound like a two-year-old."

I do, even to myself. I need to change course here. "How about this:

when we stay there for the wine club thing, we'll tell them how you—er, we—feel—you know, the guilty thing. We'll say we'll only stay there when we visit if they let us pay and let them decide. Remember, we don't want to insult their hospitality." *I'm sure that sounds better.*

"I don't know, Kevin. I'm not sure I'm comfortable with that."

"Okay, let's do this. We'll think about it and decide how to approach it when we drive back for the event."

"You're gonna kick the can down the road?"

"Just for a week. C'mon, I'll end up doing whatever you want anyway." *And there it is. Do I know my wife or what?*

FORTY-FIVE

Boise

With less than a week before their planned assault on Uva Cellars, Evan Davis and John Carlson had spent more time together than either wanted. Evan had assured his partner that the harvest would be over and most of the foliage would be gone by the end of the month.

Returning to Santa Barbara was a waste of time, so they decided to head north and hunker down outside Boise for a few days. They planned to use the drone early on Sunday morning to avoid any contact with possible witnesses.

Staying at one of the many poorly staffed roadside hotels for three nights wasn't ideal. Still, John's desire to exact revenge on his brother overrode any inconvenience that might arise from this stupid "buddy" trip. He made sure his room was at the opposite end of the floor to lessen any chance of inadvertent contact with his road companion. The time the two of them were together in the truck was plenty as far as John was concerned. The guy was beginning to get on his nerves.

It was as if the years of bouncing from job to job had finally caught up with Davis. Even though his abrasive personality had consistently outshone his technical and agronomic skills, it was far easier to blame his downfall on those who had chosen only to better their teams while ridding themselves of malcontents.

Jason Carlson had fired him, yet it seemed he placed most of the blame on Michelle Browne and those old fuckers the O'Malleys.

If John's dedication to payback for imagined transgressions was an exercise in paranoia, then Davis's singleminded focus on vengeance was genuinely psychotic. If he ran into Davis at mealtime, their only conversation revolved around the satisfaction he'd get from his revenge. He began to worry that the winemaker's psyche had suffered so much that there was no chance of a return to normalcy. Once they had completed their mission, he would pay the man, drop him off somewhere, then hope never to see him again.

Afraid of prying eyes, John had purchased a bed cover before picking up the drone. Even though it was lockable, he felt better knowing the pickup was parked just outside the window of his first-floor room. He'd be glad when this was over and he could return to his life of leisure in Santa Barbara.

John arrived at a nearby tavern on their final night in Boise only to run into Davis, sitting by himself, munching nachos and slurping beer. John had been looking forward to catching up on news of the Walla Walla harvest from the *Wine Spectator*, but now he was forced to sit with his companion and listen to his griping.

As Davis looked up, John pulled out a chair and sat. "Hey, Evan, last night in beautiful Boise, eh?"

"Yeah. Can't wait to get up to Walla Walla and destroy those fuckers."

Afraid of further setting off his dining companion, John ordered a beer, nodded at Davis, and opened his magazine, hoping it would deter any conversation. A few days more and he wouldn't have to see Davis again.

As he stared absently at a page, he noticed a calendar of fall events for many of the Washington wineries. His focus narrowed when he saw the name Uva Cellars. "Evan, hold on a sec …"

"What? Didn't you hear me?"

"Shh … I did. Wait, dammit!"

After a few seconds, he continued. "Listen—it says here that Uva is having a fall celebration for all the wine club members. And guess when it is?"

"Tell me."

"It's this weekend. They're having a goddamn party this coming Saturday, and we're shooting for Sunday morning."

"Okay … so?"

"Give me a minute to think about this. Just shut up for a minute."

John ran through the possibilities in his mind while his associate, sitting across from him, drummed his fingers on the table and took deep breaths. Finally, he said, "Maybe this isn't a bad thing. There'll be so much activity that no one will notice another vehicle in town."

"Great, so nothing to worry about, right?" Davis looked for reassurance.

"I don't think so. I might even stop by the big event."

"Why? You're crazy. What if someone notices you?"

"The only person there who knows me is Jason, and I haven't seen him for over fifteen years. With this beard and my darker skin, there's no way he could recognize me."

"Why take the chance?"

"Because I want to see the faces of the people we're going after. Jason was always the favorite, and now, finally, I'll get to hurt something he cares about."

"What about me? What'll I do?"

"We'll find a place outside of town but near the winery. You can drop me off at the big event Saturday afternoon, and I'll call you when you can pick me up."

"So I'm supposed to hang around and cool my heels until I hear from you?"

"Evan, I'm giving you a million bucks to get on with your life. Suck it up, will you? We'll be done with this in a few days." As John got up to head back to the hotel, he noticed Davis gripping the table's edge tightly, as if he needed the distraction to control his emotions. *This guy's losing it. I'd ditch him now if I didn't need him to deal with the chemicals.*

Forty-Six

Eastern Washington

I had successfully deferred any further conversation about compensating our hosts until we were headed back to Walla Walla, and now we were. The good news was we had three hours to discuss it, but that was also the bad news. Three hours. Shit.

If I had had any doubts about Jenne remembering our discussion about doing away with free lodging, they vanished as soon as we crested Snoqualmie Pass.

"So, Kev, we're gonna pay them, right?"

"Let's say you're right about this. What—we make up a number and leave a bunch of cash on the counter? I'm not sure that's a good idea."

"So far that's the *only* thing you've said that makes any sense."

"So far? Hell, I'm just getting started." *Oops, maybe too much …*

"*Kev*-in …"

"Sorry. I think this whole discussion is silly, though. We did some stuff for them and they feel obligated to give us free lodging. So what? I know, I know, you feel guilty. Suppose we compensate the housekeeping gals, then pay for our food and wine. Would you feel less guilty about that?"

She paused for a moment, considering my proposal. "Less, I guess, but not completely."

"Let me do this. I'll get Jason aside when there's an opportunity and tell him our concerns. He's smart and practical; I'm certain he'll come up with something. Will that be okay?"

"You promise to make sure he knows how I feel?"

"Promise."

"Okay, I'm holding you to that. By the way, when did Bill say they're going to arrive?"

"He said they'd get there tomorrow morning."

"That's Saturday."

"Yes, it is. I guess it's all the time he could take. He said he was going back Sunday morning but if we were staying longer and Shelly wanted to, she could come back with us."

"Great. I figure there'll be lots of cleaning up after the event. Maybe we can work off some of our lodging …"

I knew I had gone to the well once too often when another punch landed.

"Ow!"

"Serves you right. Tell me again where Bill and Shelly are staying?"

"There's an empty suite in the farmhouse that Michelle said they could use because, you know, they're friends of ours."

"Are they paying?"

Yikes, this thing won't die … "Geez, hon, I don't know. I'll check with Bill when he gets there. Say, how about those M's?"

Finally, the response I was looking for; she shook her head, gave me a sort of half-smile, and looked out the window, where what was left of the fall colors whizzed by.

Walla Walla

We got to Uva shortly after noon and let ourselves into the barn with the key Michelle had given us the previous week.

On the way up the drive, we passed several workers putting the finishing touches on the decorations for the field day. There were strings of lights over the entire lawn from the farmhouse on the hill down to the tasting room. The walkway to the cave beyond the barn was also illuminated by landscape lighting a foot or two off the ground. The plan was to test everything out this evening to make sure all was in order for the next day's festivities.

Scattered across the lawn were several kiosks, which would be staffed by hospitality groups, caterers, resort communities, wedding planners, and other vendors seeking to land customers from some of the many well-to-do wine club members. Because Uva was a boutique winery famous for wines that commanded high prices, their clientele was coveted by others searching for those with plenty of discretionary income.

In addition to the outside vendors, there were several food booths where the attendees could satisfy their cravings with gastronomic delights prepared by Perry and Chad. A dozen or so smaller stands serving various wines—from Uva Cellars, of course—were sprinkled throughout the grounds.

Michelle had thoughtfully put a dog bed in the corner for Emma. We got her settled and put our things away before we went to find our hosts to see how we could lend a hand.

"Hey, Jenne, Kevin, happy you made it. Where's Emma?" Michelle was leveling off one of the tables at a wine stand.

"We thought it best to keep her out of all the activity for the moment. What can we do to help?" Jenne was always ready to pitch in.

"We've got things in pretty good shape already. Jason was making sure all the equipment was put away for when we do the tours. How about giving him a hand in the production area?"

"Got it. See you later." I could also be accommodating.

We made our way through the tasting room to the back warehouse that housed the winemaking equipment, where Jason was moving stainless steel canisters and hoses into a back closet. The room was humid with the smell of fermenting grapes.

His red hair sticking from the sides of his ball cap, he looked up as we entered. A broad smile creased his face, making me feel like a proud uncle or something.

"Glad you made it."

"We wouldn't miss it. Michelle sent Jenne and me here to help. What can we do?"

"I think we're all good, as much as we can be. We've got that last harvest of cab fermenting over there, so we'll need to keep that area off limits. One of us still has to do the punch downs every so often."

"Is that why it feels so humid in here?" Jenne asked.

"Yup. We have the ceiling vents open to help the CO2 dissipate, as well as those exhaust fans up in the corners, but there's still plenty in the air."

A lot of effort was being put into an event for a winery with a waiting list for folks to buy their stuff, and I said as much.

Jason said, "I know it seems like we could save the money, but here's how we look at it. We charge a lot for our wine because it's unique. There's only one place on earth where this combination of soil, temperature, amount of daylight, breezes, and humidity exists, and that's right here in this microclimate. I'm not saying we're the best in the world. That's for others to decide. I am saying that people like what we produce so much that it's become a cult wine.

"We're incredibly lucky to have this natural resource, and we feel it's a duty to share it with our customers. We charge high prices and try our best to make our customers feel like part of our family. If we have to spend a little money to put this on, that's okay with us."

I was at a loss for a comeback after hearing the passion in Jason's voice. Clearly, his dedication to the success of Uva Cellars and to the lifestyle it provided had become paramount in his life.

"While I'm doing the final punch down for the day, why don't the two of you take a quick look in the cave to make sure it looks presentable? We'll be doing tours through there tomorrow—the subscribers always like to see where the barrels are kept. Oh, and we're having a team get-together tonight in the tasting room. Just hors d'oeuvres and wine, but it'll give us a chance to get everyone on the same page for tomorrow. See you there, and if Emma's with you, bring her."

"Got it," I answered as he mounted the catwalk above the open tanks. We left immediately to check out the cave.

With dusk approaching, the landscape lighting illuminated the paver walkway curving past the barn and around the hillside. One of the heavy barn doors had been pushed aside, saving us the energy needed to open it.

"Wow, looks great now that all the construction gear is gone. It's so much bigger." Jenne's comments mirrored my thoughts. Half of the space was taken up with racks loaded with oak barrels, with the balance of the area having only the racks. The tasting table and glassware shelving had been moved to the enlarged section, closer to the newly installed second set of doors.

The interior was dimly lit by shaded sconces spaced equally around the perimeter walls. An iron chandelier hung over the farmhouse table, highlighting its rough-sawn teak. The overhead lighting was recessed and turned down to give the cave a medieval feeling.

I walked to the panel beside the doors and turned up the rheostat switch controlling the ceiling lights. They had been at the lowest setting, and now, turned up, the cave resembled more of a barrel warehouse than a dark, mysterious underground bunker.

"I liked it better when you could only see the barrels," Jenne said as she meandered through the cave.

"Me too, but I guess they need to see what they're doing when moving things around and doing the barrel tastings. Both sets of doors should make things easier for the tours tomorrow."

"For sure. Do you see anything that looks out of place or needs cleaning up?"

"Looks like the electrician left his cutters and strippers on the table. We can stuff them in one of those drawers in the sideboard. Everything else looks shipshape."

We closed the twelve-foot door with some effort, then headed back to the barn to get Emma.

FORTY-SEVEN

Pendleton

The three-and-a-half-hour drive from Boise had proved uneventful. Since Davis's mood had turned darker, John Carlson did his best not to say or do anything that would set him off. The silence was better than listening to his companion bitching about Michelle Browne, the O'Malleys, and Uva Cellars.

He had initially thought of the operation as payback for his brother's reaping all of his parents' affections, which was still his primary objective. Additionally, though, he was enjoying the thrill of the adventure and the challenge of covertly managing the drone strike. He would have enjoyed it more if he hadn't had to put up with Evan Davis. *The guy is indeed a putz.*

The plan was to spend the night in Pendleton, then make the hour-long trip to Walla Walla the following morning. Davis had told him it was stupid to go to the event at Uva, but John wasn't deterred. Even though he held considerable animus for his brother, he was mildly curious about what his last surviving family member was up to. Additionally, it would allow him to scout possible staging areas for Sunday morning's flight.

Once again, they had chosen a low-budget national chain hotel. When he got to his room, the relief he felt at no longer being in the presence of his psychotic accomplice was palpable. Davis had mumbled something about getting some takeout at a nearby restaurant and eating it in his room, and John had done nothing to dissuade him.

He had only been through Pendleton via I-90 on his way to someplace else, so he was surprised at its charm when he drove through the quaint western downtown area. He knew that Pendleton Mills was famous for its textiles, but that was about it. He was also vaguely aware that this town hosted one of the biggest Western roundups in the country, and the many signs advertising the September event reflected its importance to this community. He was glad it had happened the previous month and the 20,000 cowboy invaders had returned home.

The staffer at the hotel front desk had mentioned Hamley's if he went into town, so that was where he headed. The establishment looked like an old Western saloon and, according to the signs, had been there since 1883. There was a large general store and saddlery attached to the place, but at this time of the evening, it appeared the entire town was in the restaurant.

With the only vacant seat available at the bar, he slid onto the stool. It was as if he were on the set of *Gunsmoke* or *Bonanza*. The Western theme permeated the bar, with giant Victorian framed mirrors over the back bar reflecting stepped lighted shelves of every libation imaginable.

Ordering one of the local brews, he selected the ribeye from the menu and relaxed in the absence of Evan Davis. Oblivious to the cacophony surrounding him, he absently perused the wine list offered by the bartender and noticed many of the selections were from nearby Walla Walla. Several of the higher-priced ones were from Uva Cellars.

"If you don't mind spending a few bucks, give that Uva juice a try." The voice came from the twenty-something man wearing tortoiseshell glasses and a Seahawks ball cap and sporting a wispy beard who was seated next to him.

"Beg your pardon?"

"Didn't mean to bother you, but I saw you looking at the Walla Walla wines on the list. We're club members at Uva Cellars, and we're going to their field day at the winery tomorrow. We've only been members for a year, but everything we've purchased has been lights-out."

At first, Carlson was annoyed at being interrupted, not to mention once again being reminded of how *special* his brother's wines were. But it passed as he sensed an opportunity.

"I've heard their wines are excellent, but I've never tried them."

"My wife and I are drinking their cabernet right now. I'm Terry, by the way, and this is Cora." He leaned back, indicating the attractive blonde sitting on his other side.

John considered his situation and quickly improvised. "Nice to meet you. My name's Bob Mason. It sounds like you'll be enjoying yourselves tomorrow."

"You bet. Hey, try some; you'll see what we're talking about." Terry took an empty wineglass from the bartender, poured an inch, and then handed it to John.

John wasn't a big wine drinker, but he had to admit that whatever this was, it was delicious. The explosion of flavors in his mouth was unlike any wine he had tasted before, and, if anything, it fueled his resentment at his brother's success even more.

"You're right. This stuff is great. I wish I were joining you tomorrow."

Terry turned to his wife and said, "Hey, Cora, didn't they say we could bring a guest?"

Although much more interested in watching the Seahawks playing a rare Friday night game on the TV over the bar, Cora nodded and mumbled something that sounded like "Think so, yeah."

"If you'd like, Bob, you can be our guest. We're planning on being there around one-thirty, so show up if you want and we'll get you in."

Carlson couldn't believe his good fortune and enthusiastically agreed. "Geez, that would be great. Thanks a million."

"Do you have a wife or partner? I think that's okay too."

John was thankful the answer to both was no and said, "It's just me. I'll meet you there tomorrow."

Forty-Eight

Walla Walla

The tasting room was as full as we'd ever seen it. Jason and Michelle were there, as were Oscar, Benny, Don Pettigrew, Perry, his brother Chad, and at least another half-dozen vineyard workers and part-timers helping with the event.

We'd brought Emma along, who was slightly apprehensive of all the activity; even without a leash, she stayed within touching distance of my left leg. In our experience, she would settle down after a suitable acclimation period.

We made the rounds, introducing ourselves to those we didn't know and greeting again those we did. The food was, of course, excellent, as was the wine. When the noise abated somewhat, Jason tapped his glass to get the attention of the room.

"Folks, if I could get your attention for a minute ..." The crowd respectfully quieted down.

"If you haven't already met them, those people with that beautiful dog are our good friends the O'Malleys. I wouldn't be here without their help, so please make them welcome.

"All of you have put tremendous work into making this year's field day the best ever. Michelle and I want to thank each of you, and those who work here will find a little something more in next week's paycheck." A loud cheer arose from those who did the difficult work in the vineyards.

"A couple of reminders for tomorrow: remember, the people attending the event are our customers and we are still in business because of them. Also, do your best to be polite, even if one or two might drink too much. Remember, the last thing we need is to have a customer over-served and then get behind the wheel. If it looks like that might happen, contact me, Michelle, or Don. We'll handle things.

"Again, great thanks, and see you all tomorrow."

As the happy workers returned to eating and drinking, the three of us walked over to our hosts, and Jenne said, "That was very kind of you, Jason, but our role was a small one."

I agreed. "Yes, what she said."

"We don't think so. You were my eyes on this place when I wasn't sure what was happening. It was largely your recommendation, along with Michelle's, that convinced me to get rid of Davis. Ever since Don's been here, everyone's been happier. The crew is a real team."

"Jason's right," Michelle chimed in. "We're naming the barn 'Emma's Place.' It's yours whenever you want to visit—no arguments."

I couldn't help but sneak a look at my wife that said something like *Told ya*. I think she got my drift, because I felt the slightest pinch in my side—the one opposite the Carlsons.

Jenne smiled and said, "I don't know what to say. That's unbelievably kind of you." I had to hand it to her, she was a consummate team player.

FORTY-NINE

Walla Walla

John Carlson drove while Davis pouted in the passenger seat. They left Pendleton just after ten a.m., and he was still slightly hung over from being entertained by his new friend, Terry. After he had gone through two glasses of the cabernet, his host had insisted he try the sangiovese/ cabernet blend, which was also exceptional.

Not wanting to offend his ticket to the Uva field day, he finally managed to escape just before eleven. He was glad it was only a short drive to the hotel.

Davis had very little to say during the hour's drive to Walla Walla, and John was thankful for it. The plan was to find a place to stay for the night, then have Davis drop him off at Uva Cellars, but finding a hotel proved to be more of a challenge than anticipated. Evidently Uva Cellars wasn't the only winery having a fall celebration.

"What do you want me to do? I've tried three different places, and they're all full." Just hearing the whininess in Davis's voice turned his stomach.

"Just google 'lodging' and go down the list while I'm driving. There's gotta be something open."

"It's Saturday fucking night, you know. Maybe you shoulda thought about that before you decided to go to the goddamn fair."

"It's not a fair, asshole. Just make some calls so I know where to go."

It took five more calls before they located a vacancy at a place called the Merlot Motel.

"You're shitting me, right? Who names a place the Merlot Motel?"

"Don't blame me. You're the guy who just *had* to go to the fair."

Rather than risk another annoying conversation with his accomplice, John shut up and followed the directions of the android-like voice of *the* Google.

At first, he thought they couldn't possibly be going the right way. They were on a single-lane, rutted, gravel-packed road that wound through a heavily forested area about ten miles southwest of Walla Walla. Then they saw a small directional sign on the right, informing them they had two more miles to go.

The closer they got to their lodging, the deeper the potholes. "Why does anyone ever stay here?" Davis asked as they almost bottomed out in a particularly deep one.

Carlson began to think they were the only ones who did as he struggled to keep his truck on the road. The hole jerked the steering wheel to the right, and as he pulled out of it, he brushed up against a lethal-looking thicket of blackberry canes. He winced as he heard them scrape across his fender.

Finally, they entered a little clearing where three small buildings were clustered. The surrounding growth of Ponderosa pine and Douglas fir had seen to it that a thick covering of moss coated every available surface. It appeared the structures had been painted yellow at one time, but now the color resembled more of a chartreuse.

Hanging from a post on the short porch that projected from the largest building was a sign identifying it as "Merlot Motel Reception." Carlson almost snickered at the ridiculousness of it all. "I think I can see why this place was available. I'll check us in."

He exited the truck, stepped up onto the wooden floor of the porch, and tried the door. It was locked. He peeked through one of the tiny windows, knocked, and waited. Before long, a frail-looking octogenarian shuffled to the door and opened it.

"Welcome to the Merlot Motel, young man. How long will you be with us?"

"Just the one night. We want two rooms, please."

"I'm sorry, sir, we only have one available. The other cabin is undergoing renovations."

"Seriously? You call yourself a motel and you only have two cabins?"

If Carlson thought badgering the old woman would solve anything, he found out otherwise.

"Let's cut the shit, young man. I know the only reason you're here is that you couldn't find another hotel. We have one cabin with two twin beds and an indoor bathroom. We charge two hundred a night for this exquisite lodging, in advance. Would you like it, or would you like to find somewhere else?"

Afraid that any comment he made would jack up the rate exponentially, he nodded, paid the requested amount, and took the key.

As he turned to exit the "reception," he heard her say to his back, "Have a pleasant stay, now, sir." As he shut the door, he could have sworn he heard a slight chuckle.

The cabin's interior was claustrophobic but clean. Twin beds were positioned on opposite walls, each with a minuscule nightstand. A closed door near the back of the room was likely the bathroom.

"Isn't this just peachy?" Davis's revulsion at spending the night in the same room was clear, but John let it go.

Since tonight was the last night he'd ever see the man again, he bit his cheek and hung his few clothes on the hooks on the wall at the foot of the bed. The place *looked* clean, but the smell of mold and mildew was pervasive.

"When are you going to pay me?" It was the fifth time Davis had asked over the last several days, and John was sick of him.

"Do you have an account you can access online?"

Davis, sitting on his bed, looked up at him in anticipation. "Of course I do."

"Give me your account information and I'll transfer it over. Maybe then you'll leave me the fuck alone."

Once the deed was done, it would put a muzzle on Evan Davis. If John had only known, he would have done it sooner, although he could imagine his associate taking off without cooperating in the drone attack if he had.

FIFTY

Uva Cellars

Davis and Carlson left their cabin in plenty of time to get to Uva at one-thirty. Driving through quaint downtown Walla Walla on their way to the winery was challenging. Hundreds of tourists strode along the sidewalks, most stopping at wine-tasting kiosks on almost every corner. Most of the 120 local wineries were represented in town, attracting tourists from the northwest and around the country every fall.

When they arrived at Uva Cellars, they found various-sized groups of people meandering around the grounds of the picturesque property. The air was clear and crisp, with the temperature hovering around sixty degrees—a perfect day for the festivities. Cars were parked along the main road and halfway up the drive.

Rather than risk anyone recognizing Davis, John made sure he was dropped off at the long drive to the winery. He ambled up the gentle hill just in time to spot his old pal from the previous night.

"Hi, Terry. Thanks for asking me to be your guest. After tasting the wine last night, seeing this place will be fun."

"Hey, Bob. I wasn't sure you'd make it. I think I might have overdone it a little."

"No worries, I feel fine. It seems you and Cora are old hands at this, so if you don't mind, I'll take in some of the tours."

"Of course. Sounds great. We'll catch up with you a little later, but first, let's make sure we get stamped."

"Stamped?"

"Yes, we need to go through the checkpoint at their sign over there. They'll put a stamp on your hand so they know you're part of the club or a guest of someone. All the tastings are comped, so they do their best to make sure there aren't any freeloaders. Come on. It'll only take a sec."

Looking at the woman checking the guests against a printout, John—or *Bob*—saw a strikingly attractive woman with deep, penetrating brown eyes looking directly at him as he approached. She wore a plaid Pendleton shirt and stylish jeans, and her dark brown ponytail was pulled through the back of her Uva Cellars ball cap.

She greeted the three with a warm, hospitable smile. "Welcome to our fall field day. My name is Michelle Carlson, and my husband and I own the winery. Your name, please?"

Terry spoke up with their names and told Michelle that Bob Mason was their guest.

"We're thrilled that you and Cora could join us, Terry," she said, then turned to John. "And we're delighted to have you as a guest, Bob." As she said this, she grasped his hand and gave it a sincere shake, and then she proceeded to stamp each of their hands.

John Carlson was gobsmacked. First because this stunning woman had made such an impression on him, and second because his brother, once again, seemed to have gotten the better end of things. It reinforced his commitment to destroying the crucial part of what made this winery famous.

The wine club members had been arriving since noon, and Jenne and I pitched in wherever possible to help the Uva Cellars crew. We thought it best for Emma to sit this out, thinking the old girl would tire of all the activity.

We even offered to help check the attendees in, but Michelle and Jason were adamant that they personally greet the people who spent their hard-earned dollars on the wine they produced.

Oscar and Benny led the tours of the vineyards while Don Pettigrew escorted folks through the production areas and the winemaking process. A little later, when all the guests were checked in, Jason and Michelle would station themselves in the cave to show off the new section, and a special tasting of some of their best vintages for a few of their charter members would be available.

We watched as Michelle continued to greet each invitee with the skill of a seasoned politician. She had a gift for making each person she met feel special. We watched as a young couple shook her hand while their guest, a deeply tanned man with a dark beard, seemed mesmerized by her.

"Looks like Michelle has a way with people," I said.

"She's perfect for the job, that's for sure. I'm so happy for her and Jason, especially after all they've been through."

"Me too, Jenne, me too. Well, lookie here, guess who finally showed up …" We both watched as the stern-faced, physically imposing chief of detectives for the Bellevue Police Department made his way up the hill toward Michelle. He was accompanied by his much smaller yet even more strong-willed wife, Shelly, who leaned into him, no doubt suggesting he put on his happy face.

They had yet to see us, and it gave me great pleasure to see my good friend being handled by his wife. We watched as Michelle, who had yet to meet the Owenses in person, gave both of them a hug, no doubt after finding out who they were. She turned to direct them to us, and we waved them over.

"Glad you could finally make it. We go to all this trouble to get you VIP status here and you're late to the party." If there was an opportunity for needling the man, I never passed it up.

"The big chief here felt it necessary to go to work this morning—something about crime never takes a holiday," Shelly explained as she patted him playfully on the back.

"Come on, Shelly, let's leave these two jokers alone and check out some of these resort booths. Who knows what we might be able to find?" Jenne steered her away.

The two women had left before either Bill or I could warn them of the dangers of booking expensive holidays without their husbands.

"I thought I'd take one last look at the Carlson files before we hit the road—you know, in case Jason had any questions."

"If it's any consolation, I think Jason and even Michelle have accepted that the case will go unsolved. They seem to have moved on with life. They're very much in love and have committed to making this winery the best they can."

"I'm glad to hear it, Kev. It still pisses me off that we were never able to close the case, though."

Rather than dwell on regrets, I changed the subject. "You've never been here before, have you?"

"No, of course not. I didn't know Butch owned it until you told me. That, plus the damn stuff is a little pricey for us."

Bill may have been a public servant, compensated by the requisite low wage structure, but his wife was a multimillionaire. Even though this was low-hanging fruit, I showed maturity by ignoring his absurd excuse.

"Well, now that you're here, prepare to be impressed. I know you've had some of their wine before, because I brought it over, but what you don't know is that it wasn't even their best stuff. We'll get to taste that later."

"Really?"

"Yes. Remember you're the guest of the celebrity O'Malleys."

"Put a cork in it, will you?"

"Good one, Bill. Glad you're getting with the program. Come with me, and we'll take a stroll through the vineyards."

FIFTY-ONE

Uva Cellars

Meeting Jason's wife had unsettled John. It could have been the proximity to his brother or someone he loved, or it might have just been the look of selflessness from the wife.

In any case, the feeling was gone, and he was now focused on his mission. As he started to follow the signs to the vineyard tours, he noticed a tall red-headed man striding down the hill to the initial check-in for the attendees. It was his brother, Jason.

Although he had retained his youthful features, the decade-and-a-half interval had considerably changed his appearance. Far from his pimply-faced, skinny, pain-in-the-ass brother, this person seemed much taller and more muscular than he remembered. He also moved with the kind of self-assurance that only folks who have experienced failure *and* success seemed to possess.

Instead of being proud of his brother or happy about his success, he was envious. Sure, he had money, and with it the freedom to do anything he desired. Unfortunately, his singular focus was on taking away.

He watched as Jason hugged his wife and then took over her duties. *You'll be singing a different tune tomorrow, brother*, he thought.

He walked toward the vineyards on the eastern perimeter of the property where the tours were being directed. According to Davis, this was where the best-quality grapes were from, and these half-dozen acres were programmed into the drone software. They were also visible from the farmhouse, so finding another staging area for when they used the drone the following morning was necessary.

Lagging behind those following Benny and Oscar, he noticed a significant drop-off on the northern end of the vineyard. He made his way through the dozen or so oenophiles and raised his hand.

"Yes? You have a question?" Benny asked.

"I was just wondering why the vines stop here and don't continue over that lower section beyond this hill."

"That's easy. Down there, it's too dark for good grapes. We use that section as a fill area. We dump the trimmings and dead vines there, then chip and compost them to use in plantings around the winery. Much of the produce and most of the herbs Perry uses are grown with the mulch used as an additive to the soil."

"I see. How do you get it down there?"

"Oh, an access road splits off the main drive down by the entrance. Anything else?"

"No, no … just wondering, that's all."

Bill and I caught up with the tour group just as Benny was explaining something about where they dumped all the pruning waste.

I thought it odd that we were standing on some of the most cherished grape-producing land in the country and this guy was asking about where they dumped the waste from pruning the vines.

I remembered the fellow because of his deep tan and his startled look when he met Michelle. I chalked the question up to some people feeling they *had* to ask something.

We strolled through several rows of vines as our two guides extolled the virtues of the soil, the sun, and the expertise of Don, the winemaker. As we made the loop back to the tasting room, I noticed the guy with the inane question was no longer with the group. *Just as well*, I thought.

Because Bill had never gone through the wine production, we headed there just as Don Pettigrew took a group into the fermentation area. The grapes needed to ferment for at least another week, so he went through the "punch-down" process.

My buddy seemed mesmerized by the operation and raised his hand.

"Yes—Bill, right?"

He looked startled that Don knew his name but recovered quickly. "Yes, right. Where on the property did those grapes come from? We were just over on the eastern side. Was it there?"

I hadn't thought about it, and now I was curious too.

"These grapes are from our newest planting on the south side of the property. It's the first year we've been able to harvest enough for wine production from that section, so we're anxious to see what we've got. So far, it looks terrific."

As he continued punching down the caps in the tanks, Bill asked, "How did he know my name?"

"I told you we were celebrities. If you hang with me, you might get there too."

"You're such a putz."

"Thank you."

"How?"

"I'm sure Michelle told him you'd be with us and that we were friends."

"It's no wonder you have so few …"

"That hurts, Bill … let's go find our wives."

"Anything to get you to be quiet, but let's see the end of this first."

That was why I loved the man—no pretending and never any excuses; my kinda guy.

FIFTY-TWO

Walla Walla

Evan Davis was sick of Carlson ordering him around, and now he'd been paid, he couldn't care less about the arrogant asshole. He'd follow through with the drone attack on Uva's prized vineyard, though, because—well, they deserved it.

While the dad owned the winery, he was fine. Evan didn't like the man, but at least he left him alone. Now that he thought about it, it was really John's fault that he was without a job, because he'd killed his old man. But at least he'd got paid by him.

No, the real cause of all this was Michelle Browne; she'd never liked him. Then when the other son had taken over and sent those O'Malley assholes to look things over, the shit had hit the fan. He was positive he and his snotty wife had said everything they could to make him look bad.

Once Browne had started screwing the new owner, he was fucked. The million bucks he'd got from Carlson would help, and the drone attack would royally screw them for years, but that bitch wouldn't get what was coming to her unless he did something about it.

After tomorrow he was certain Carlson would cut him loose, which was okay with him. As soon as he'd dropped him off at the goddamn field day at fucking Uva, he made some calls.

While employed at Uva, he lived just outside town and rarely mixed with the locals. He had a favorite watering hole, but he kept to himself even there. If he wanted to get laid, he'd go up to Yakima or Wenatchee. He could always hook up with someone on Tinder or, if necessary, he'd pay for it. Keeping his sexual escapades far from his place of employment had always served him well, so he continued the practice.

Before his trip to Santa Barbara, he'd sold his truck. Once he was no longer paid an allowance from Uva Cellars, he couldn't afford it. Now, however, things were different.

His first call was to the local Ford dealer where he used to have his truck serviced. He told the first salesperson he talked to that he needed a low-mileage used F-150 and would pay cash for it. He figured he had a few hours before picking up Carlson, so he drove directly to the dealership.

"Is that the rig you're trading in?" the effusive young woman asked.

"No, no, this is a friend's."

"Tell him he scratched the shit out of his front fender." Slightly surprised at her use of the colloquial term, he nodded.

"How much for this?"

"Don't you want to test drive it?"

"Miss, the truck's only two years old and has twenty thousand miles on it. How bad can it be?"

A little taken aback, she recovered quickly. "Of course, sir. Sticker on this is thirty-seven thousand, but I think we can knock a grand off."

"Tell you what, I'll write a check for thirty-five thousand right now. You can verify with my bank if you like. Will that work?"

"I need to check with my manager."

"You do that. I'm giving you the check, though, and then I'm leaving. I'll assume the deal will work. If not, you can tear the check up. I want all the paperwork ready tomorrow at ten, when I'll come in, sign it, and leave. If it takes longer than fifteen minutes, the deal is off. Got it?"

"Sir, yes, sir."

"Good. I'm leaving now. Make sure the rig is spotless."

Now that he had taken care of his transportation needs, he headed to the nearby agricultural supply warehouse to pick up the glypho-sate for the next day. He could have gone to Home Depot, but their formulation wasn't concentrated. Even at the higher percentage of the active ingredient, they would have to make at least two trips.

Since the drone took up most of the bed, he was forced to put the five-gallon containers on the rear floor of the crew cab. Just as he loaded the last of it, he received a text telling him to pick up Carlson at the end of the drive. On his way back to the winery, he scheduled an Uber pickup for the following day; he was leaving nothing to chance.

FIFTY-THREE

Uva Cellars

It had been a long afternoon, but judging from the final remarks of the departing guests, all had had a good time.

It was approaching eight p.m., and except us, the Owenses, and Jason and Michelle, the balance of the staff had gone home. Most of the heavy cleanup would be done with the knockdown of the kiosks on Monday morning. Tomorrow was a scheduled sleep-in day per order of the owners of Uva Cellars.

Perry and Chad had been kind enough to leave a tray of sandwiches, which we gladly consumed, along with what remained of the vintage wines tasted by the charter club members.

Our only quality time with Emma had been during the two trips we made to the barn for necessary watering and walking, but at least now she was with us.

"Thanks to all of you for helping out. Michelle and I couldn't have done it without you. We're serving breakfast at the farmhouse at ten, so please join us."

I was never one to turn down a free meal, but even I felt slightly guilty about how we were being treated. "That's not necessary, Jason. Why don't we go into town and have brunch somewhere? My treat."

"No can do. It's Sunday morning, and most places are closed. Besides, I never get to cook, and if I screw anything up, how can you possibly complain?"

I looked around at Bill and Shelly, shrugged, and gave up. "The man makes an excellent point. He's hard to argue with."

Leaving the glassware on the table, we exchanged hugs all around, and we departed for the barn while the other two couples climbed the gentle slope up to the farmhouse. My guess was there would be no early risers in the morning.

Fifty-Four

Uva Cellars

I was wrong.

Whether the cause was the amount of wine consumed or the constant grazing, I woke up at 6:30. I stared at the ceiling for half an hour, listening to the rhythmic breathing of my wife, then decided I would take Emma for a walk.

Although the skies were clear, the sun had yet to make its appearance. I donned my jeans, sweatshirt, and fleece vest to ward off the promised morning frost and headed to the east vineyard.

The eastern sky was brightening as we began the uphill climb. The silence was eerie, broken only by my Hokas crunching the frost crystals on the soil's surface and Emma's rapid breathing. I frequently paused to fully appreciate the absolute lack of any ambient noise.

Just as the sun broke the horizon line, I stopped to snap a photo, attempting to juxtapose the naked vines against the developing crimson tint of the early sunrise. As I did so, Emma barked a warning seconds before I heard the faint crunch of someone walking much the same route I'd taken. I waited, wondering who could be up at this hour in this vineyard.

Her barking suddenly stopped as she recognized the scent of a friend.

"Couldn't sleep either, eh?"

It was the sound of my good buddy's deep baritone voice invading the silence of the moment.

"Bill, hey ... beautiful out here, isn't it?"

"Unbelievable. I can see why folks, at least rich ones, do this for a living. Thank you for inviting us and Shelly for making me come. I never dreamed it would be as interesting, and it's given me a new appreciation for what it takes to make the good stuff."

This was a side of Bill that I knew but seldom saw. He was one of the finest people I knew, although he did his damnedest to hide it. He was kind and considerate, but it was his fanatical determination that made him excel at his job. I was grateful he was my friend.

"I'm glad you enjoyed it. How are the accommodations, by the way?"

"You're kidding, right? Have you not stayed in the farmhouse?"

"Um, no; never been up there, actually."

He snickered at this, thrilled that he knew something I didn't.

"It's better than any hotel I've ever been in. Bedding is phenomenal, bathroom is like a spa. Even Shelly was impressed. Now she wants to redo hers."

"That's great. The barn where we are is equally nice."

"And here's the kicker—I tried to pay Jason last night, and he refused and said he'd kick me out if I left any money."

I raised my eyebrows but couldn't resist a jab. "Told you if you hung with the famous O'Malleys, you'd be taken care of."

"Shut up."

"What, you can't handle it?"

"No, shut up. Listen."

At first I thought he was making things up, but then I heard the faint crunching of tires on gravel, then more barking from Emma.

"Emma, shh. Maybe someone from one of the neighboring properties?" I offered.

"Yeah, maybe. The sound probably travels out here. I think it's stopped, anyway."

We walked silently for a few minutes before I asked him, "When are you heading back?"

"We thought around noonish. Shelly wants to meet up with her mother later today, and I have some reports to get off my desk. How about you?"

"We thought we'd spend the night, then see if we can help with the Monday morning thing."

"I sorta feel guilty about the free room and food situation."

"Don't go there. I've been over it with Jenne more times than you can imagine. Look, Jason is a great guy and extremely generous. He's grateful for whatever we've done, which wasn't all that much, between you and me. If we even suggest paying him, he slams the door. I think the only thing we can do is accept his kindness and be thankful for it."

"Makes sense to me. Do you think you can come and explain that to Shelly?"

"No thanks, pal. You'll have to handle that yourself."

Fifty-Five

Uva Cellars

When Evan Davis and John Carlson got into the Denali cab, the thing smelled like a chemical factory.

"Did you *have* to put those chemicals in here?"

"No choice. The only way to put them in the bed was to uncover the drone. Didn't think you would want that."

They were leaving the Merlot Motel just after sunrise and had ten minutes to reach the staging location.

"You sure the place we're going will work?"

John, thinking more about the execution of their plan and its lasting effect on his brother's winery's reputation, ignored the question.

"I said, is this spot we're going to gonna *work*?"

"I heard you, and yes. I walked down there yesterday before you picked me up. It's perfect. There's a gravel access road off the main road and one off the driveway to Uva Cellars. You can't see anything down there from the winery buildings.

"Once the drone is in the air, someone might see it, but I doubt it. The profile is too small to be seen from either the farmhouse or the winery. We'll be done in less than half an hour anyway."

Davis was mercifully quiet the rest of the way, right up until they turned onto the access road. "This place is a dump."

"Of course it is, you moron. It's where they put all the stuff from the pruning and the leaf collection."

"It smells like mold."

"Right again, dipshit—the material is one big compost pit. Now, let's get this over with."

They parked behind a huge pile of twigs and leaves and unloaded the drone in the small clearing beside it.

Next they unloaded the five-gallon glyphosate containers and several quart containers of something else.

"What's in the small bottles?" John asked.

"It's a wetting agent I add to ensure the spray doesn't waft into the air. There's almost no breeze this morning, so we should be okay, but no sense in taking any chances. I think the downdraft from the drone might be a concern too."

"You don't know?"

Davis replied, "I'm an agronomist, not a drone pilot. I've never done this before, but the chemistry makes sense."

He took his time filling the drone's reservoir while John attached a fully charged battery. They'd purchased two with the drone, so the downtime for the second pass would only be to refill the chemical reservoir.

When their tasks were completed and they both stood admiring their handiwork, John asked Davis, "You're sure we've got the correct rows programmed in here, right?"

"I told you, it's the exact copy of the plantings from the GPS map."

"Okay, let's get this show on the road. Stand back a little."

As John flipped the power switch on, the four rotors began to spin while the mechanical voice warned them to stand clear. The flight path navigation program called for the drone to rise fifty feet to clear the hill's crest and then level off twenty-five feet above the ground, which, according to their instructor, was optimum for spraying crops.

As he engaged the active flight toggle, the speed of the rotors increased dramatically, along with the sound of a million bees. The Agri4000 lifted off the ground and rose over the hill to perform its assigned task of murdering hundreds of the most famous grape vines in the country.

Fifty-Six

The East Slope

We made it out to the fence on the east perimeter of the east slope of Uva's property and then turned around to make our way back to the farmhouse. It was approaching eight o'clock, and the cool morning walk had awakened our taste for coffee.

I planned to leave Bill at the farmhouse, then go down to the barn and see if Jenne was up and about. "See you around ten, buddy."

"Sounds good. We can— What's that?"

"What's what?"

"That sound. Can you hear it?"

"Not from here. Hold on." I reversed the few steps I had taken down the slope and stood perfectly still. It was faint, but it was there—a high-pitched buzz, barely audible above the light breeze that had sprung up.

"Yeah, I hear it now. What do you think?"

"I don't know. Could be anything. Sounds like one of those toy gas airplanes we used to fly in a circle when I was a kid."

The sound seemed to get louder and then recede, as if it were moving. "Is it coming from over on the east slope?"

"Somewhere over there. Come on, let's take a look."

I tied off Emma's leash, much to her dismay, then Bill and I headed back the way we'd come, but with a much brisker stride.

The east slope was actually a big hill, with the crest being the center of the vineyard. The far east side was below the top of the hill, as was the section closest to the farmhouse. The sound was coming from the easternmost section, but we needed to be at the top of the hill to see the cause.

It took us another ten minutes, but what we saw was alarming.

"Can you reach Jason? Maybe he's scheduled something—maybe fertilizer or something."

I tried his number but failed. "He's still in bed or in the shower, or somewhere he can't reach his phone."

"How about Michelle? Maybe she'll know."

I was met with the same result when I tried her. "Maybe they're involved … you know."

Bill ignored my suggestion while his cop's instincts seemed to take over. "Let's go. We need to climb down there and see what's going on."

"I don't think so. When we were on the tour I remember how steep the hill is. I think we'll need to drive around."

"All right, then. We need to get back to the farmhouse and talk to Jason or Michelle. Let's go."

Bill took off at a jog, but the guy was ten years younger than me and in great shape, so I let him go at his own pace. I'd get there eventually.

Five minutes later, when I arrived, Bill and Jason—looking like he'd just gotten out of bed—were standing in the doorway.

"It's not us, Kevin. We've got nothing going on over there. Somebody is fucking with us."

Michelle, holding on to Emma, and Shelly were watching from the kitchen, both with serious looks on their faces.

"Let's get over there. We'll take my truck." Jason ran to his pickup while Bill hopped into the back seat, and I rode up front with Emma. I called Jenne to let her know where I was and suggested she get up to the farmhouse, where Michelle could fill her in.

Jason tore down the driveway and turned onto the access road. We were only minutes away.

Fifty-Seven

The East Slope

The first pass went off without a hitch, and the drone returned to the exact spot from which it had left. Davis immediately refilled the pesticide reservoir, and John attached a fully charged battery.

As soon as his part was done, Davis stood to the side and watched as the drone operator completed the second liftoff. While John was occupied with the camera relay on the controller, Davis hurriedly walked back down the access drive to the main road, where a red Toyota Prius was parked on the shoulder.

He opened the door and sat in the rear seat. "Glad you made it on time."

"I wasn't sure about the coordinates you gave me, but here I am. You're going to the Ford dealer in town, right?"

"Yup. Let's go."

As they took off, Davis saw a pickup whiz by with Jason at the wheel and O'Malley riding shotgun.

He waited the twenty minutes it took to get to the dealer before he texted the phone number he still kept in his phone.

Tell whoever picks up the guy flying the drone to check out his ID and his truck. Tell him thanks for the money too. Evan.

The second pass, too, was flawless. When he looked up from the controller to congratulate Davis, it was the first time John Carlson noticed his absence. He couldn't figure out where he'd gone, but he didn't care either. Screw him, he thought. I'm done and would rather never see the asshole again.

He left the drone where it was and dropped the controller on top of it. The entire operation had only taken forty minutes, but he wasn't keen on spending more time than necessary here.

As he backed up to turn around, another pickup blocked him and three men jumped out. When he saw who it was, he knew he was fucked, but he also knew better than to say anything.

FIFTY-EIGHT

The East Slope

As Jason slammed on the brakes, we piled out, Emma leading the way and barking furiously. The man driving the truck had nowhere to go. I never know quite where he hides it, but Bill Owens always seems to have his gun with him, and this was one time I was glad of it.

With his gun in one hand and his shield in the other, he approached the driver and demanded he raise his hands and get out of his vehicle. It was the same man who had asked the stupid question of Benny the previous day. Now I knew why.

With an arrogant stare at Jason and a fearful look at Emma, the man complied with the order deliberately, without so much as a word.

Rather than ask *What the fuck are you doing here?* Bill treated the situation professionally. "Your license?"

"It's in my pocket. Is that dog dangerous?"

"Only if you give her a reason. Which one?"

"Back left."

"Get it, Jason, will you?"

Jason retrieved a worn wallet with only a few credit cards and a California driver's license, which he glanced at before handing it to Bill. As he did so, he reached out to the truck's door for support.

"John? You're my brother John? What are you doing here, and why haven't I heard from you?"

John said nothing and looked back at Bill, who asked him, "Is that true? Are you his brother?"

No answer.

"What are you doing here?" Bill continued.

No answer, but this time Emma growled.

During this time, Jason stared at his brother, looking like he'd seen a ghost.

"Jason, will you look at those cans and that drone and see what they were doing?" I thought that he might have been able to figure things out with all he'd learned since his father had died.

"You're under arrest for trespassing for now. Hands behind your back." Bill somehow found a sturdy zip-tie and used it to bind John's hands.

"Is that necessary?" Jason, finally accepting that the man before him was his brother, was now concerned for him.

"Let's be cautious for now. Something seems off about this." *Bill Owens, the cop.*

Jason inspected the cans and the drone, then darted to the three of us.

"Tell me you didn't!" he shouted, spittle flying from his mouth. He grabbed at his handcuffed brother. *"Tell me you didn't!"*

I did my best to pull him away as John stared at him with a malevolent grin and finally said something. "I did, little brother, and your little fairytale life is over."

Bill and I looked at each other, neither grasping the situation.

"What is it, Jason? What has he done?" I asked.

"This sonofabitch has sprayed our most valuable vines with glyphosate, and he's killed them."

"He only just did it. Can't we do something?" Bill was as much in the dark as I was.

"Nope. Maybe if there was a way to hose them off with water, but the irrigation is done with drip lines, so it isn't possible."

Just then, Jason's phone buzzed, and he looked at it. "It's Michelle. Yeah, honey?" There was a pause while he listened. "She says she got a text from Evan Davis. He says to check someone's ID and truck, whatever that means."

At the mention of his truck, John Carlson looked worriedly towards it.

"She also said he thanks him for the money, whatever that means."

John's agitated look now turned calculating; it was clear there was some serious conflict in play.

With the report from Michelle still sifting through my gray matter, I looked inside John's truck through the open driver's door. Nothing stood out besides fast food wrappers and the expected detritus of a long road trip.

With me looking through the Denali and Jason still fuming at his brother, Bill took charge. "Jason, put your brother in the back seat of your truck while I look around."

He walked the few steps to the open door while I went around with Emma to the other side to check the glove box.

"Not much to see here, Kevin. Anything in there?"

I shuffled through a few insurance cards and registration slips showing a Santa Barbara address, but nothing noteworthy appeared. "Nope. Why would Michelle get a text from Davis?"

"I'm not sure, but if he knows about Jason's brother, then he must have had something to do with this operation."

"So he's ratting him out?"

"Looks like it. Still, what could he mean by 'check out the truck?'"

I had no answers, so I closed the glove box, then the door, and walked around the front of the truck, Emma following.

"Hey, Bill, maybe he meant to say Carlson was a shitty driver."

"What are you talking about?"

"This side looks like he drove through barbed wire. Take a look."

"I don't care if he drove blindfolded. Let's get him off to the locals— they have jurisdiction on this anyway."

Looking more closely at the scratches, I saw the black paint beneath the beige. Something clicked, causing me to step back and look at the entire vehicle, not just the scratched fender.

"Hey, Bill, come over here and take a look."

Something in my voice caught his attention, and he walked rapidly to where I stood without any protest.

What?"

"Look at the scratches."

"So what? The guy's a shitty driver."

"Bill, *look*. Look at the color *under* the scratches."

He bent over to get a better look and became very quiet. Then he too stepped back until the entire truck was in his view.

Then, almost whispering, he spoke. "It's a Denali … it's beige, but it used to be black. It's got California tags too, meaning it was so far away, it would never have been reported."

I had already reached the same conclusion and had taken the next step. "How do we determine if this truck was in Washington when Butch was killed?"

"That might be a challenge, but barring a confession from him, which I doubt, there are a couple of avenues we can take."

"And they are?"

"We'll get his cell and have the carrier do a locate on its position during the dates involved. It won't prove he did it, but it'll tell us if he was there. If this Evan Davis has first-hand knowledge, we may get something from him."

"Will it be enough to hold him for a while?"

"I hope so. We'll need to search the body shops and dealers where he lived to get records of what they did. If they replaced the fender and we can find it and trace the paint, that would be a big help."

"Sounds like a stretch."

"It is, but we'll take it a step at a time. These cases are tough, especially when so much time has passed. Much of the evidence has either degraded or disappeared."

"Maybe you'll get lucky."

"Hope so. Let's get this asshole booked on something at the local constabulary. They can keep him for at least a few days, with any luck. Do you think you can tell Jason what we suspect without him losing it? I'd rather not let his brother know we might be on to him."

"He's a levelheaded guy. I think so."

"Do it."

When Bill was in cop mode, his orders were to be followed with no questions. I called Jason over and filled him in. He was shocked but seemingly held things together.

Then the three of us and Emma left the Denali where it was, joined our prisoner in Jason's truck, and headed to the sheriff's office. Since the wine industry was the backbone of the economy in the southwestern corner of the state, the local police took a dim view of anyone seeking to disrupt the tax base … a very dim view.

Fifty-Nine

Uva Cellars

Michelle, Jenne, and Shelly sat in silence at the massive butcher-block island in the center of the kitchen in the farmhouse.

They had finished listening to the report from Jason several minutes ago. The gravity of the situation had finally registered with Michelle and, to a lesser extent, Jenne and Shelly.

"Michelle, I'm so sorry for this whole mess. I know those vines were the backbone of the winery." Jenne was the first to break the stillness.

After a few seconds, Michelle spoke. "That's a punch in the gut, for sure. I think the thing that upsets Jason the most, though, is that his brother is the one who did it. Wait … I'm getting a text from Jason … oh my god …"

Michelle's face suddenly turned ashen, causing Jenne to ask, "What is it?"

"There's a good chance that John's truck is the one used to run Butch off the road. He says Bill has the situation under control, and they'll probably be at the sheriff's office for a while."

"Jesus, this is awful. How could his own son do that?"

"We'll have to wait until they get back to fill us in on the details, but rather than sit around, I'd like to do something. Would you two mind helping me take down the booths?"

Both Jenne and Shelly were all too happy to do anything to move on from the bizarre turn of events.

After an hour of knocking down the temporary kiosks, the women were exhausted. Just as Michelle voiced her concern that they hadn't heard from anyone, Shelly's phone trilled.

"Bill, what's happening? Okay, okay, sure. I'll tell them. See you in a little bit.

"He says they've booked Jason's brother on something else but need to get the exact details separately from Kevin and Jason. He says it'll take an hour or two."

"What about Bill?" Jenne asked.

"Since he's a cop, he'll be able to put everything in a report and get it back to them. The station is a few miles north, so instead of waiting for the locals to finish, he told me to take our car and pick him up. He wants to get back and work on the Butch Carlson connection."

"Go ahead, Shelly. Jenne and I can manage the rest here. I think we'd rather Bill get going on this as well."

Shelly hugged both of them and retrieved her things before getting on the road to pick up her husband.

Sixty

Uva Cellars

His paperwork at the Ford dealer went off without a hitch, and his new ride felt great.

As he headed back to Uva Cellars, he fleetingly considered ditching his plans and hitting the road for parts unknown. But just as he was picturing himself on a beach in SoCal, the vision of Michelle Browne intruded.

None of his ill-fated employment experiences had ever been his fault. The cumulative effect of his constant temper tantrums and firings had possibly reached tipping point. Now, his reputation sullied throughout the entire wine community, he could no longer participate in the only thing he had ever cared about—and it was her doing.

As he covered the last mile to the winery, a late-model SUV driven by a cute pixie-like woman passed the opposite way, traveling considerably over the speed limit. Other than wineries and a few farms, there was little traffic on this road except during the tasting hours, and he considered that she might have been coming from Uva.

He stopped and waited when he got to the end of the drive up to the winery. He saw two women, one of them Browne, hauling tarps and metal frames back and forth, presumably returning them to storage. He recalled that several smaller outbuildings behind the barn were used for such purposes.

There were only two vehicles in the parking area. One he recalled was the O'Malleys', and he assumed the other was Browne's. The winery pickup was gone, so he figured both men were still involved with his buddy John.

He'd devised a plan for Browne, but the other person was a complication he would have to deal with.

He waited until they had their arms full and were headed back to the storage shed, then quickly drove up the hill and parked. Rather than go around the building, he entered the tasting area and went to the section that housed the fermentation tanks.

Off to the side were several large storage lockers where Benny and the other field hands stored their tools and boots. He found what he was looking for, grabbed the items, and turned to exit through the rear door.

"Coffee?"

"Sounds great, Michelle. In the tasting room?"

"Sure, it'll only take a few minutes. I'm looking forward to Jason getting home. The damage that's been caused will take a while to assess, but I'm afraid it will put a big dent in our reputation."

"You have a dedicated following and a long waiting list. If anybody can weather this storm, it's you and Jason. Maybe the damage won't be as serious as you think."

"I hope you're right."

They entered through the rear door of the fermentation room and proceeded to the tasting section up front.

He heard the door open and ducked back into the cubby that housed the lockers. Initially, his plan had only been aimed at making Browne pay for what she'd done, but now that the O'Malley woman was here, he could kill two birds with one stone. Literally.

The Ranshou grape scissors he grasped were razor sharp, precision pointed, and featured a three-inch carbon steel blade. When closed, they resembled a stiletto more than a tool used in the vineyard.

He waited until O'Malley passed by, then, as Browne followed, he grabbed her by the neck from behind.

Her scream caused Jenne to turn.

"Not a word." Holding the point of the scissors against the side of Michelle's neck with enough pressure to have already drawn blood, he addressed Jenne. "Any more noise and my old associate here gets what she deserves."

Michelle's face had turned bloodless, and the symptoms of shock were already noticeable.

"What are you doing, Evan? Please let us go."

"Sorry, sweetie, no can do. I've had six months to think about getting even with this bitch, and nothing's stopping me now. Grab those two folding chairs over there and bring them here." He was standing between two of the four-foot-diameter fermentation tanks, one hand holding the scissors, the other grasping a roll of tape with his arm wrapped around Michelle's neck.

Jenne did as directed, carrying two of the chairs used during the tours to the tanks.

Blood was dripping freely down Michelle's neck. Davis, still standing behind her, dropped the duct tape roll and kicked it over to Jenne.

"Unfold those chairs, then tear off a piece of tape and put it over your mouth. I'd like some quiet while I prepare things."

Both women looked frightened at what Davis might have in mind. Jenne did as directed and stood there silently.

"Now, this part's a little tricky, but I'm sure we can get it done if we work together. You, O'Malley, sit down and put your hands behind you."

She did as directed, then Davis said, "Now, Michelle, we're going to walk over to your friend, and you're gonna pick up the tape and wrap it around her hands. Got it?"

She nodded, and the two of them shuffled to where Jenne sat. Awkwardly they bent together, the scissors still poking through Michelle's skin, and she picked up the roll. Her hands shaking, she wound the tape around her friend until Davis told her to stop.

"Now your turn. Stick some tape over your mouth so I don't have to listen to you, then sit down and put your hands behind you." Michelle complied, and as soon as she was seated, Davis pulled the scissors away and immediately wrapped her hands with several turns of the sticky tape.

Next, he wrapped multiple turns of tape around Michelle's body, effectively binding her to the chair, before doing the same to Jenne.

When he had finished, he stood back, admiring his handiwork. "You two look great—like a couple of gray mummies. If you don't mind, I'm gonna drag you over a little closer to the tanks, you know, so you won't miss any fun."

Sixty-One

Uva Cellars

Michelle was frightened beyond anything she had ever experienced, but at least the scissors were no longer sticking into her throat. It had hurt like hell, but they hadn't gone too deep, so she was okay, other than a bloody sweatshirt.

She felt she had gone somewhere for a minute, but now she was trying to piece together what Davis was up to. She watched as he pulled Jenne's chair over to the space between two tanks, then did the same with hers.

When she'd put the tape over her mouth, she'd been careful not to apply too much pressure, and one of the corners was now loosening up some.

She watched Davis go to the wall and turn off the venting fans that constantly ran during fermentation. Then he mounted the catwalk and picked up the plunger used to punch the caps.

Suddenly it dawned on her. *He's going to kill us, and I know how.* Once he began punching down the caps on each tank, the carbon dioxide in the air would increase exponentially. Since CO2 is heavier than air, it would be forced upward after punching, then drop down and ultimately suffocate them. Since Davis had positioned them between two of the tanks, it wouldn't be long before the effects were felt.

With the ventilation off, the toxic gas levels would build up rapidly, and she could do nothing about it. She watched in horror as the ex-winemaker began with the first tank.

Michelle looked at Jenne, who was looking upward, watching Davis punching the first tank. She was sure her friend had no idea of what was to come.

After the first two tanks were done, the rise in humidity in the room was noticeable. Using her tongue and rubbing her mouth on her shoulder, Michelle was able to get the tape to the point where she could talk if necessary. She looked up at Davis, who, without the fans, was sweating profusely with the exertion of the task.

By the time he had moved on to the third, fourth, and fifth tanks, the sweat was pouring off him, and Michelle couldn't be sure, but his breathing seemed to be labored. She noticed Jenne's head had started to droop, so she banged her foot on the floor to get her attention.

Jenne, startled, looked over as if waking from a dream. Michelle tried to look stern and shook her head forcefully, and she mumbled a very quiet "No," hoping Davis wouldn't notice. Jenne's nod hopefully meant that she understood.

As he began on the sixth tank, the one they were adjacent to, it became more difficult to see their captor, since he was now directly over them. Michelle felt the plunger penetrate the cap several times, but each punch seemed less powerful. Then they stopped.

Michelle heard the clang of the plunger as it bounced first off the catwalk, then the tank, almost hitting them as it struck the floor. The two women looked wide-eyed at each other for several seconds, then Michelle heard a muted *sploosh*, followed by a tiny shower of mushed grapes and fermenting wine.

Even though she was getting drowsier by the second, she was afraid to say anything. When Jenne began nodding again, though, she said *screw it* and yelled, *"Jenne!"*

Other than Jenne sitting bolt upright, she heard nothing. She tried something. "Hey, Davis, you asshole …" No response.

"Jenne, I think the fucker fell into the tank. With the vents shut down, the CO_2 must have skyrocketed during the punch down. He must have passed out and fallen."

Jenne nodded.

Michelle spoke loudly. "We need to stay awake. I'm gonna see if I can hop over to the wall and reach the switch."

Younger than Jenne by twenty-something years and in tremendous physical shape, Michelle was able to move her chair an inch at a time by throwing herself forward and pulling with her feet. Finally at the switch, she lifted it with her forehead and heard the wonderful sound of air being sucked from the room. Thankfully, the ventilation system included openings for makeup air, and the cool breeze began to revive them.

Sixty-Two

Walla Walla

John Carlson was sitting in an interrogation room wondering if he should say anything or play dumb.

Sure, they had him for destroying the grape vines, but how bad could that be? He was sure the fine would be huge, but he had money. He supposed there could be the threat of jail time, but then again, he had no record, so he would be fine.

They hadn't said anything yet, but when they'd looked at the scratches on his truck, they'd spent too much time huddling together. He began to consider his chances of being convicted of the killing of his father. They would find a way to track down the body shop that did the work in Santa Barbara, although the possibility of finding the fender and matching the paint with his father's Tesla was remote.

They might also be able to track his movements through his cell phone activity while in Washington State, but so what? No witnesses could identify him, and he could always say someone else had been driving his truck.

Davis *could* be a problem, he thought. He had been in contact with him regarding the timing of his father's departure, and he might try to cut a deal with the cops to get out of the vineyard operation.

He considered all the ramifications and looked at the two investigators across from him. The sheriff's deputy was young and inexperienced, but the older guy, the one from Bellevue who had caught him, could be a problem. There was talk among them about him being shipped to the Seattle area to be arraigned for his father's death, but he figured they were trying to scare him into talking.

Maybe it made sense to get out in front of the vineyard thing by blaming Davis. *Isn't he the agronomist, after all? Isn't he the one who has the hard-on for Browne? Yeah, maybe that's the way to go.*

"It was Davis's idea to kill the vines."

"So you'd like to talk now?" the deputy asked, getting a look from Owens.

"I'm just saying it was his idea. The guy's a little psycho. He's convinced Browne is at the root of all his troubles. I wouldn't be surprised if he's got other plans for her. He's nuts."

Bill took the lead now on the questioning. "Why wasn't he with you if he was involved?"

"He was for most of the time. He must've snuck away while I was working the drone."

"How?"

"I don't know. Maybe he arranged something. When I turned around, the little bastard was gone."

John wasn't sure if his comments were helping his situation, but he was encouraged when the Bellevue cop got up and left the room.

Bill Owens came out of the interrogation room and walked to where we were seated, Emma underneath our chairs.

"I'm convinced your brother is Butch Carlson's killer." He looked at Jason. "But proving it will be a challenge. While the charge for the damage done to the vineyard is serious, it will be difficult to hold him for any length of time, and he can easily make bail."

"What can you do?" I jumped into the conversation.

"I can return to the office and turn over every rock I can find. If I have anything to say about it, he will not get away with this. I'll have Shelly pick me up, and then we'll hit the road."

We said our goodbyes to Bill and hung around the station for another forty minutes until the deputy came out and filled us in.

"He's not very cooperative except to tell us it's the other guy's fault. We'll be able to hold him for a day or two, but that's it. Your friend thinks he can get him on a more serious charge, so we'll see. I'll let you know if we learn anything more."

Still furious with his brother, Jason was reluctant to leave. I said, "Let's leave it for now and go back to Uva. After all that's happened, I'm sure Michelle and Jenne will be glad to see us."

"You're right. I'm sorry. I never figured out why John turned against us, and I still don't get it. He's my only brother, and this is what he does."

There wasn't much I could say, so I put my arm around his shoulders and guided him out of the station with Emma following. Once in the truck, he called Michelle to tell her we were on the way.

"No answer."

"Maybe she's out with Jenne. I'll call her." There was a pause while I did so. "Funny, no answer there either. Let me check the Life360 app. It'll show me where her phone is."

I pulled it up only to find Jenne, or at least her phone, was smack dab in the middle of Uva Cellars. "Huh, it says she's at Uva, but she's never without her phone, and if she saw it was me, she'd be sure to answer."

Jason instantly stepped on the gas as he said, "I've got a bad feeling about this, Kevin. Hold on."

SIXTY-THREE

We took the drive up the hill to the winery at a speed for which it was not designed. The truck's rear end fishtailed before it regained purchase, and we sped up to the parking area in front of the tasting room.

Emma was first out, with Jason and me close behind. Except for Emma's frenzied barking, the only other sound was the thrumming of the ventilation system at the back of the building, where we headed next.

As we got closer to the section that housed the fermentation process, we could hear Michelle shouting, "In here, Jason, in here."

He slammed the door open while Emma darted through and rushed to the fermentation tanks. Jason ran to Michelle, who was duct taped to a folding chair.

"No, Jason, get Jenne first."

I wasn't sure what she was talking about until I looked where she was nodding, over near the tanks. There I saw my wife similarly tied, her head slumped over, Emma barking and licking her face tenderly.

"Don't bother freeing her yet. Take the tape off her mouth and carry the chair outside as fast as you can." Michelle, even trussed up as she was, was shouting instructions.

Jason seemed to know what had happened. He rushed to Jenne, pushing Emma aside, picked her up, chair and all, and shouted at me, "Kevin, get the back door. Hurry!"

Fortunately, Jason's shouts startled me out of my frozen state of shock at seeing my unconscious wife. I ran to the door and opened it just before Jason arrived. Before putting her down, he instructed, "Get the tape off her mouth. Do it fast."

Afraid to hurt her but somehow knowing it was critical, I ripped it off. Her eyelids fluttering, she shook her head and looked at me. "Jesus, Kevin, that fucking hurt."

My eyes teared up and I hugged her, duct tape and all. Emma, patiently watching the proceedings, now joined the embrace.

Despite everything, Jenne had the awareness to ask about Michelle. "Where is she?"

"She's fine. I'll get her now."

As we began to unwrap both of them, Michelle filled us in on what had happened while we were gone. She also explained that because Jenne had ended up being closer to the tanks, she had received a greater concentration of CO2.

"Because I was able to get the tape away from my mouth and get the fans started, I was in better shape than Jenne."

She told her story without a pause, then stopped for breath.

"Are you telling us you think Evan Davis is in one of those tanks?" I had trouble grasping the picture.

"I'd say take a look in number six. At least, that's the one I think he fell into. I got some mush and wine splashed on me from the fall." She said this as though she were giving a newscast, with no emotion whatsoever.

Both Jason and I walked back inside and took a peek into number six. Evan Davis lay sprawled face down in the vat of fermenting grapes. Although the buoyancy caused by the CO2 had eliminated any chance of him sinking, it made little difference to the result.

Jason explained, "He was unconscious when he hit the grapes. They'll likely find he inhaled some of the slurry and drowned."

"How do you know?"

"I don't know, but I've read about accidents like this. I hate to say it, but it couldn't have happened to a more deserving person. The sono-fabitch was trying to murder Michelle and Jenne."

Jason had had a rough day, but I was inclined to agree with him.

Sixty-Four

Uva Cellars

The rest of the day was a blur. We first called Bill, who was passing through Yakima on his way back to Bellevue and was ready to turn around and come back to assist.

I suggested he'd be more productive trying to work through the Carlson case and asked him whom we should contact first.

"Where Uva is located covers several jurisdictions. Eventually this will end up with the state police, since their investigators have more resources than the county or city cops. So call them first."

While Jason made Jenne and Michelle comfortable in the tasting room, I stayed with the now wine-saturated body of Evan Davis. During my call to the state police, I couldn't help but peek over the rim of the tank, and yes, he was still there.

I was immediately transferred to a detective who assured me help was coming. Boy, was he ever right.

Within fifteen minutes, the sheriff, the state police, and the city of Walla Walla cops arrived. After a few minutes, the stateys took over, and the others just stood by. Apparently, it wasn't every day that an attempted murderer drowned in a vat of fermenting grapes.

It wasn't until early evening that the detectives, the medical examiner team, and the mental health support team departed Uva Cellars. We had taken Emma back to the barn earlier, figuring two abductions and the death of a madman were enough excitement for her for one day.

The four of us were exhausted, but Jenne and Michelle especially. It was unanimously decided that I should retrieve our guard dog and we should all spend the night in the farmhouse. Having us all in one place felt good after the staggering events of the day.

Sixty-Five

Whidbey Island

The happenings at Uva Cellars became national and international news. The tale of two women, abducted and tied up, waiting to die while their captor falls into a vat of fermenting grapes was too much for any media outlet to pass up.

Lost in the hubbub surrounding the event was the fact that lasting damage had been done to the winery's prized vines, and their loss would take years to recover. The drone attack had taken a back seat to the visual of a dead man floating in a vat of grapes.

Bill Owens took point on the investigation into John Carlson and his role in his father's death. It was almost a year since Butch had died, but Bill got lucky.

It seemed the wireless carrier stored cell phone location data for at least a year. With the appropriate warrants, he could document Carlson's travels from Santa Barbara to Walla Walla and then to Bellevue. He followed the trail to the fruit stand in Thorp on the day of Butch's death and then through Snoqualmie Pass on the same day and at the precise time of the crash. He was able to locate the body shop in Santa Barbara that had repaired the Denali and repainted it, but the damaged fender had been disposed of.

All in all, the evidence was sufficient to arraign John Carlson for reckless manslaughter. The damage to the property at Uva Cellars was not prosecuted because of the more serious charge.

There were long discussions regarding the best way to go about the prosecution, and in the end they may have been too aggressive.

The trial was big news in the northwest but not so much nationally.

It lasted three weeks and went to the jury on a Tuesday afternoon. In my conversations with Bill, he was convinced Carlson would be found guilty. He had testified to all his findings, and the defense attorney could poke no holes in the evidence.

The closing arguments were what was expected, with the prosecution summarizing all the salient facts and the defense posing absurd alternatives. The favorite one being that yes, they knew where Carlson's phone had been, but what if someone else had been in possession of it?

Carlson shrewdly refused to testify in his defense, and the jury was admonished to infer neither guilt nor innocence.

The jury deliberated for three days without a verdict. Finally, on a Friday afternoon, they reported to the judge that they could not reach a decision because of one lone holdout. It turned out that a young lady was adamant that another individual *might* have been in possession of Carlson's phone during the time of the crime.

It was a mistrial, and Bill Owens was one pissed-off civil servant.

The trial had been long and expensive, and the state was reluctant to attempt a retrial of the case. The defense had cost John Carlson a great deal of money, but then he *had* a great deal.

"What pisses me off most is that the prick gets to go home to Santa Barbara. He gets the money he inherited from the father he killed, skates on the damage he did to Uva Cellars, and gets away with it all."

We were having dinner at our place on Whidbey Island two months after the trial, and Bill was still having difficulty putting it behind him. He was here with Shelly, and so were Jason and Michelle, who happened to be in town.

The tide was out, so we strolled on the beach below the bluff in the late afternoon sun. Even with the temperature at a comfortable sixty-five degrees, we were the only souls in sight. Emma, as usual, was bounding through the water and sniffing everything in sight.

Rather than stoke the fire, I ignored my friend and addressed Jason. "What brings you two to town?"

"Two things. We're meeting with a law firm about suing John for damages."

"That sure as hell makes sense. What do they think you can get?"

"According to them, there's the actual cost of replacing the crop for three years, and there's also the harm to our reputation. They think it'll be well into the millions."

"Are they confident?"

"Very. There's tangible proof and witnesses that he did it. That, plus he got away with murder. It's our only recourse right now."

I thought the money would be helpful for them, but I felt bad about the loss they had to deal with.

"Did you say two things?" I asked.

He turned to Michelle, and they both grinned.

"What? What are you two hiding?" Jenne suspected something.

Michelle said, "We're here meeting with the *Wine Spectator*. They're doing a feature on Uva Cellars."

"About the episode with Davis?" I thought that story had been done to death, but what did I know?

"I'm sure they'll cover that aspect, but it's more about the damage done by John and the resilience of the winery."

"You mean that even though you've lost the best vines in the valley, you can replant in the same soil?"

"There's a bit about that, but the article's thrust is mostly about our new vintage cabernet. Early tastings say it's even better than the vintage that won the platinum award."

I was confused. "How can that be? You lost the east slope section, and I thought the other fruit was very good but couldn't compare."

"Well, that's what we thought too."

"Come on, Michelle, spill the beans." Leave it to Jenne to go for the throat.

"Okay, here's the deal. You remember when Davis tied us up? And you remember how he died?"

"How could I forget?"

"Well, the grapes in those tanks were the first harvest from the new acreage. It looks like the microclimate there could be even better than on the east slope."

"You're kidding!"

"Nope. Evan Davis died in a fermenting batch of what looks like one of the finest cabernets in the country."

There were high-fives all around as we congratulated Jason and Michelle.

After another ten minutes, I realized we were beneath our house, some two hundred feet below. "Hey, guess what isn't here?"

Bill answered first. "The boat, right? The boat with the foot."

"Yup. DNR took the damn thing away last month. It's great to have the beach clear again."

"Did Wenzal ever get any further on investigating who took shots at you?"

I thought back to almost a year ago when the foot in the boat was big news. I remembered how frightened Jenne had been for me too, and I was glad all of that was behind us.

"Nah. He said they found some casings, but …"

"But what?"

"Hey, Bill, when you got that location data from Verizon for Jason's brother's phone, did you check anything past the day Butch died?"

"Not really. Didn't see any sense in it, but … are you saying what I think you're saying?"

"I don't know, but it might be important if you can find out if his phone was on Whidbey Island on the day someone was taking shots at me. Wenzal told me the last time I talked to him that they got some partial prints off the casings they found on the bluff."

"And you're just telling me now?"

Shelly intervened immediately. "Knock it off, Bill. You're lucky Kevin made the connection." I loved it when she laid down the law.

Bill grumbled something I couldn't quite make out before saying, "I'm returning to your house where the service is better. I want to get Houser on this immediately."

Now that there was a possibility of getting to John Carlson again, all of us were anxious to do so.

SIXTY-SIX

Bellevue

Verizon still had the location data for Carlson's phone, which showed him traveling from Santa Barbara to Whidbey Island and back. More importantly, it showed his location on Little Dirt Road at the precise time the shots were fired. The partial prints taken from the casings were also enough for a positive match.

With this new evidence, the attorney general for the state of Washington ordered another trial of John Carlson, but now it was for attempted murder.

This time, John Carlson took the stand against the advice of his attorney. Even though the jury was advised to ignore the previous charge against Carlson, a member would have had to have come from another planet not to be aware of it.

Their already dim view of the defendant was not helped by his insistence that he was only trying to scare Kevin O'Malley and that he was only doing it because a dead man was blackmailing him.

When the prosecutor asked what he was being blackmailed about, he had no answer. The fact that his posthumous blackmailer was himself an attempted murderer was also not helpful.

The trial lasted a week, went to the jury on Friday at noon, and they returned with a guilty verdict at two.

At the sentencing hearing the following week, the judge spoke directly to Carlson. "For the attempted murder for which you were found guilty, I am sentencing you to twenty years in prison. Since it was done with premeditation and with a firearm, I am adding an additional five years. I sincerely hope you spend the time reflecting upon your crimes and making restitution for your acts."

SIXTY-SEVEN

Uva Cellars

It was October again, and we were back at Uva Cellars for their fall field day. Jenne, Emma, and I were in Emma's Place, formerly known as the barn.

Bill and Shelly were there, staying in the farmhouse, and this time they needed no convincing to attend. We had all pitched in to set things up for the following day and were now relaxing in the farmhouse's great room while Perry and Chad whipped up something that smelled otherworldly.

"Every time I think back to last year, I get the chills." Jenne shook her shoulders at the image.

"Yeah, and just think, you were sleeping during most of it …" My clever observation drew sighs and guffaws from everybody but my wife, who launched half a baguette at my head.

I managed to duck and quickly recovered. "Aw, honey, you know I'm only kidding, you do? Right?"

Her eye roll told me I was back on safe ground. She said, "I'll admit I *was* out for a bit until you ripped my lips off with that duct tape." She feigned a hurt pout and continued. "If it hadn't been for Michelle getting the vent fans back on, it would have been a different story. She's the real hero."

Michelle blushed while all agreed; even Emma barked her appreciation. She interrupted the adulation by saying, "I try not to go there anymore. I'm just thankful for how everything worked out. We got a three-million-dollar settlement from the civil suit, John's locked up until he's too old to come after us again, and we have a platinum award for the new vintage cabernet. The article in the *Spectator* created such a buzz that our waiting list is longer than ever.

"We replanted the east slope with new clones, so in a few years, maybe we'll have an even better crop than before."

After Michelle's summation, Jason took his glass and stood up. "If you don't mind, I'd like to offer a toast."

We all raised our glasses as he continued. "Here's to all present, the best friends we could ever hope to have, and here's to my dad, wherever he is. I know, looking down, he's proud of what we've accomplished, and I hope he knows it's because of him we're together and Uva Cellars is a success."

With "hear, hears" all around, we clinked our glasses and raised them to Butch.

Cast of Characters

Kevin O'Malley—Retired designer, amateur detective

Jenne O'Malley—Retired designer, Kevin's wife

Emma—O'Malleys' German Shepherd

Bill Owens—Chief of Detectives, Bellevue Police

Shelly Owens—Bill's wife, Jenne's best friend

Butch Carlson—Hedge fund manager, winery owner

John Carlson—Butch's oldest son, lives in Santa Barbara

Jason Carlson—Butch's younger son, lives in Denver

Michelle Browne—General Manager, Uva Cellars

Evan Davis—Winemaker, Uva Cellars

Aedan Boyle—College friend of John Carlson

Billy Tomlin—College friend of John Carlson

Julie Houser—Detective, Bellevue Police

Tom Wenzal—Detective, Washington State Police

Roger Wilkie—Deputy, Island County Sheriff

Chad and Perry—Walla Walla restaurant owners

Benny and Oscar—Uva Cellars vineyard workers

Penny Kirkland— Facilities Manager, Bellevue Towers

Steve Pennell—IT Manager, Bellevue Towers

Acknowledgments

This book is a work of fiction. Any similarities between the characters and real people, either alive or dead, is purely coincidental. It's possible that the physical and emotional traits of these fictional characters may be found somewhere on the planet, but again, it is unintentional.

The places, however, are real. Bucolic Whidbey Island is a gem in Puget Sound, as often described in my books. Walla Walla, home of the fictional Uva Cellars, is a mecca for some of the most sought-after wines in the country. The Snoqualmie Pass is famous for its treacherous conditions during the frequent winter storms, and the Thorp Fruit and Antique Mall is a popular rest stop for I-90 travelers.

The El Encanto Hotel in Santa Barbara is situated high on a hill overlooking the city and celebrates over a hundred years of service. It's one of the most luxurious settings anywhere in the world.

The explanation for the foot is also true. Since 2007, twenty-one detached feet have washed ashore on coasts of the Salish Sea. Dr. Karan Raj, of the National Health Service in the UK, explains the phenomenon in a TikTok video for those interested. The chances of one plopping into a passing boat, however, are remote.

Thanks to my friend Jeff, who is my source for wine-related activities and who will ceaselessly give me shit for the mistakes I've made.

Finally, thanks to my wife, Patte, who is caring enough to wade through my first drafts with patience, good humor, and kindness, and who is my favorite person in the world.

Other Works by Ted Mulcahey

Bearied Treasure

Teed Up for Terror

Little Dirt Road

Juiced

www.tedmulcahey.com

www.ingramcontent.com/pod-product-compliance
Lightning Source LLC
Chambersburg PA
CBHW051146190726
48290CB00006B/2017